DEATH AND POETRY

MCBRIDE AND TANNER
BOOK 2

RACHEL MCLEAN

DEATH AND POETRY

CHAPTER ONE

"Jeez, Helen, why did you think we'd want to climb this bloody hill?"

Helen looked round to see her friend Bal standing in the middle of a patch of gorse, hand wedged into the small of her back, face red as Helen's hair.

"You'll be fine, Bal. It's worth it, I promise."

Bal shook her head. "Nothing's worth this. It's torture."

Lisa was a few feet ahead of Helen, poking around in a hole in the hillside. "D'you reckon this is where the castle once was?" She deepened her voice and stood straighter. "'By interims and... something-or-other, we have heard the summons of the castle'."

Helen rolled her eyes. You couldn't get away from Macbeth references in these parts. "There's no castle, not really, and you know it. Just an old fort." She shook her head. "And it's further up. Almost at the top."

"We *are* almost at the top."

"Uh-huh. Once you get over that wee rise up there you'll

find there's more. The top's obvious when you get there. Big cairn, views over to Dundee."

"Why would I want to look at Dundee? I spend enough of my life looking at it from the inside."

"It's not the same." Helen smiled. "Dunsinane Hill isn't beating you too, is it?"

Lisa raised her eyebrows. "Of course not. I'd just rather be back in that tearoom we saw. The Three Witches. Great name."

"The tearoom will be our reward once we've got to the top and back down again."

"I'm stopping here!" Bal had sat down on the ground below them, having found herself a small clearing in the gorse.

Helen resisted the urge to go back and drag her up the damn hill. That would mean doing this last section of the climb twice. And she wasn't as fit as she'd been the last time she was up here. Giving birth to Roddy had made sure of that.

She sniffed and looked out towards the Cairngorms in the distance. Roddy was over there, with his bastard of a dad and evil granny. Fenella was worthy of a cauldron herself. Maybe Helen should bring them all up here and leave them for the crows.

"Right," she said. "The sooner we get up, the sooner we'll be down again. There's clouds coming in from over past Pitlochry."

"Rain, too," moaned Lisa. "All we bloody need."

"You've got sensible clothes, you'll be fine." Helen tried to inject some breeziness into her voice. When the three of them had been at Uni in Dundee, they'd regularly gone out walking. They'd even done this hill once, hungover. She was surprised Lisa didn't remember the deceptive summits and the way the hill tricked you into thinking you were at the top. She wondered if Macduff and his troops had thought the same when they'd attacked Macbeth's castle.

Not that they had. A King Macbeth had existed up here at one time, but chances were he'd never set foot on Dunsinane Hill. Or lived in the fictional castle that Shakespeare had made so famous.

"We're most of the way there," she said, and started walking, not turning to check if Lisa was keeping up. She tucked her frizzy red hair into her beanie and ignored the dampness in the air.

Ten minutes later, she could see the top. *Thank fuck for that.*

She turned to see Lisa a few paces behind and Bal nowhere in sight.

Shit.

Should she go down?

Don't be daft. Bal was a grown woman. In London, she had a responsible job as deputy director of an international charity. Of the three of them, she was the one who'd gone furthest. But all that work had affected her fitness, it seemed.

"Do we go back for her?" Lisa asked.

"You want to?" Helen replied.

"No."

She laughed. "Then we don't. We can bag the top, then it'll be no time before we're back where we last saw her."

"She's probably in the car, eating all the chocolate."

"It's fine. We've got tea and cake to look forward to, remember?"

"I hadn't forgotten. I had my eye on that Snickers, though."

"You and your Snickers." Lisa had been addicted to chocolate at Uni, and judging by the expansion of her hips in the last ten years, she still was. When Lisa had arrived at Helen's house in Perth yesterday, she'd been unable to stop her gaze flicking up and down her friend's body. She'd said nothing, but she was sure Lisa had noticed. It probably explained her foul mood.

"Right." Helen could make out a shape next to the cairn. Someone had beaten them to it. She was surprised; most people tackling this hill were experienced walkers, and would have done it much faster than her and Lisa had. But no one had overtaken them on the route up.

"Race you to the top!" Lisa passed her, her footsteps heavy on the spongy grass, her waterproof jacket making a swishing sound against her hips as she strode.

"OK." Helen picked up pace.

To Helen's surprise, Lisa made it to the top first. She bent over, the flats of her hands on her thighs, her body rising and falling with her heavy breathing. As Helen arrived, Lisa straightened up.

"What the hell?" Lisa said as she looked up.

"Huh?" Helen looked at her friend, then followed her gaze. "Whoah."

Someone had beaten them up here, alright. A man was slumped against the cairn, his jeans damp from sitting on the wet ground.

"You alright, pal?" Lisa approached the man. He didn't move.

"Is he...?" Helen said. The man's face was pale and his beanie had slipped over one eye. She felt her stomach constrict as she took in just how bad he looked.

How long had he been up here?

She pulled out her phone. "We need to get help."

Lisa turned to look at her. "There's no signal here, surely."

"There is." They were between the Cairngorms to the north, Perth to the south and Dundee to the east. It felt remote, but in reality, they weren't far from civilisation. And it seemed there was a mobile phone mast somewhere nearby. She dialled 999.

"He doesn't need help," Lisa said.

The phone was ringing out. *Come on.*

"What d'you mean?" Helen asked Lisa. "Look at him."

Lisa was crouched on the ground beside the man. She looked at him, then up at her friend. "I'm sorry, H." She bit her bottom lip. "But he's past help. He's dead."

CHAPTER TWO

Dr Petra McBride's phone rang just as she was about to kiss Aila. She paused, closing her eyes.

"Sorry, sweetheart."

"Ignore it." Aila pulled Petra towards her.

Petra shook her head. She'd been getting the calls again, the ones where she'd pick up and there'd be nothing but silence at the end of the line. She was convinced that if she picked up fast enough, eventually her stalker might give themselves away.

So far, they hadn't.

She whipped her phone up from the table of the coffee shop just off Edinburgh's Royal Mile and slammed it into her ear. She said nothing, waiting.

The line was silent.

Petra swallowed, straining to listen. There was background noise: an office?

She waited.

Nothing.

She checked her watch. Normally, after thirty seconds, the caller hung up. She'd been on the line for thirty-five.

"Why do you keep calling me?" she asked.

Nothing.

"Talk to me, dammit. Tell me who you are, you slimy little fuck."

"I'm sorry?" A woman's voice.

Petra felt her breathing slow. Aila was looking at her, her eyes wide. "Is it...?" she whispered.

Petra shrugged.

"You heard me," she said. "Leave me alone, or I'll call the police."

"Dr McBride," the voice said. It was Scottish, with a gentle Glasgow burr. "Are you OK?"

Shit.

Petra knew that voice.

"Jade?"

"Yes. Why did you call me a... a slimy little fuck?"

Petra felt her heart sink into her stiletto heels. "That wasn't you I was talking to."

"It felt like me."

"Sorry. I've been getting calls. Silent ones. I thought it was one of them." Petra paused, frowning. "You didn't speak when I picked up."

"That's coz I butt-dialled you. You should report it, if you're getting that kind of thing."

Petra knew that. But she also had an inkling she knew who the anonymous caller was. And if she was right, it wasn't something she wanted to have a nice wee chat with Police Scotland about. "I know. What do you mean, butt-dialled?"

"My phone was in my pocket and I hit your number."

"With your butt? That's quite a feat."

"You're in my stored contacts. Sorry, I'll leave you alone."

"Thanks." Petra put a hand over the microphone. "It's Jade."

Aila nodded, sipping her chai latte. She hadn't met Jade, but she'd heard all about her and Petra's work for the Complex Crimes Unit.

"Actually," Jade said. "While I've got you..."

Petra sighed. "I'm a bit busy." She looked at Aila again. Her girlfriend of four months – somewhat of a record, for Petra – had had her hair cut this morning, and it made her look even more gorgeous. "Can't it wait?"

"I just wanted to tell you," Jade said, "the unit's being disbanded."

"The CCU?"

"Fraser says it's resourcing, but between you and me, I reckon it's internal politics. Glasgow CID never liked us being here."

Petra had no idea. She'd worked for plenty of police forces and made a point of closing her ears whenever there was talk of politics.

"I'm sorry to hear that," she said. "Will there be work for me in other units, or is that the end of our beautiful friendship?"

Jade's laugh was nervous. "We only worked two cases together."

"I was being sarcastic. But I hope it doesn't mean you're losing your job."

"I'll be transferred to another unit. Not sure what'll happen to Mo, though."

DS Uddin was Jade's sidekick. Petra had worked with him in his previous posting, down south in Birmingham. "He's still in Scotland?"

"Bought a house in Stirling."

"Good for him." Petra looked at Aila, who was drumming her fingertips on the table. "Look, Jade, I really have to go. You take care, yes?"

"I will. You too, Petra." Jade hung up.

"What was all that about?" Aila asked. "And since when have you been getting silent phone calls?"

"I'll tell you about it later," Petra promised. "But right now, I'm planning to kiss you."

CHAPTER THREE

Jamie Douglas took a shallow breath and cursed Scotland's murderers.

This was the second time this week he'd been forced to climb some bloody great hill to get at a crime scene. OK, so he needed the exercise, but he'd rather get it at the gym, thank you very much. Not out managing crime scenes.

Still, it was quite a spot. Dundee lay in the distance before him, the mouth of the Tay and the North Sea beyond it. Behind him to the right was Perth, not that he could see it under a bank of low cloud. And to the north were the peaks of the Cairngorms, still snow-tipped even in April.

But the man slumped against the cairn in front of him wasn't here to admire the view. And whoever had either dragged him up here or come up here to kill him hadn't been either.

Why go to all the trouble of committing murder on the top of a hill, when there's a perfectly good and pretty secluded car park at the bottom of it?

A car park that was big enough for three, maybe four, cars, but was now overflowing with squad cars and forensic vans.

He felt for the local villagers.

"Bugger me. That was a climb and a half." His second-in-command Heather Reynolds appeared beside him, her breathing as heavy as his felt. He nodded, incapable of speech just yet. Dunsinane Hill had been deceptive, hillocks and undulations giving the impression that he was just about to reach the summit every ten minutes, then disappointing him as he reached the top of a rise and found more to come.

Bloody hill.

He was going to make damn sure he didn't have to climb it any more times than he had to.

"What gear have we got?" he asked Heather.

She gestured towards three duffel bags. The two of them had dragged one up the hill between them. The other two had been carried by two burly uniformed officers, once he'd used all his charm to persuade them.

PC Sinclair and PC Grant stood a short distance away from them, chatting quietly and admiring the view. They were from Perth station; Jamie wondered if they'd ever had cause to come up here before.

"OK," Heather said, her voice thin. "We've got a geodesic tent, one of the new ones they asked us to try out."

"Perfect," Jamie replied. "The regular tent'll be about as much use as a haggis in a snowstorm up here."

"Exactly. We've got a couple of soil analysis kits, a bag of taping, recovery and transfer equipment and as many evidence bags and tubes as you can shake a stick at."

"So we can take boot prints and soil samples."

"And analyse some samples from the body and his clothing, all without tramping back down this blasted hill."

Jamie smiled, glad he wasn't alone in hating the thing. "Heather, you're a bloody star."

She smiled. "Of course I am. So where are we going to start? The body?"

Jamie nodded. They'd been given permission to examine the body as soon as they had a comprehensive set of photos. It seemed the pathologist had no plans to come up here and was happy to rely on a post-mortem at ground level.

Lucky pathologist.

"OK," he said. "Let's start with the camera. I want to get all the shots we can of the body first, and then a set of photos of the surrounding area. I'll have a word with the two PCs. Tell them to sit tight and not cause too much damage until we've got an idea of what we're dealing with."

"Do we need to wait for the SIO?"

"He's on his way up. Didn't look like he'd make it any time soon, though." Jamie had spoken with DI Wallace from Dundee in the car park, but the man had had little to say.

"OK. Let's get started, then." Heather rummaged in a duffel bag and brought out the camera equipment.

Jamie walked over to the two PCs, careful to watch where he was treading and keeping his eyes open for footprints.

"Thanks for your help with the kit, fellas," he said.

"Aye, no worries," PC Grant, the younger of the two men, replied. "It's a hell of a climb."

"Hell of a view, too."

"You starting already?" PC Sinclair asked. He was in his forties at least, but his fast progress up the hill with a full bag of forensic kit on his back had impressed Jamie.

"The SIO's on his way," Jamie said. "We're going to examine the body first, then check the area."

"DI Wallace. We know him." PC Sinclair didn't pass any further comment. "You want us to begin a search?"

"You know what you're looking for?"

Sinclair smiled. "We've both been trained in crime scene management. We know not to go wading all over the place in our size nines, if that's what you mean."

Jamie felt himself blush. "Of course."

"And we followed your footsteps on the way up, to minimise prints."

"Good. In that case, let's take a spiral route, search for anything that might have been left behind by either killer or victim."

"It's definitely murder?" Grant asked.

Jamie nodded. "A knife wound to the chest." Heather was photographing it now, as best she could. There was little blood around the body, which meant this wasn't as straightforward as Jamie would have liked.

The lack of blood made the whole thing even more bizarre. It meant the victim was most likely dead before he'd got here.

Why take the trouble to drag someone you've already killed all the way up this hill just so you can dump them somewhere with a good view?

Hopefully, they'd find forensics that would clarify it all.

"Jamie!"

Jamie turned to see DI Wallace surfacing from below the rise nearest the top of the hill. He was quicker than Jamie had expected.

Good. Now the SIO was here, they could get on with things and get home. The clouds over Perth were thickening, spreading northwards up the Tay Valley. And in a couple of hours, it would get dark.

He tramped back towards Heather, careful to watch his footing.

"Anything helpful?" he asked her.

"Puzzling."

"How?"

"Not sure." She pointed at the man's jacket. He wore a red puffer jacket with a thin hood. Not what Jamie would have chosen for a hike up a hill, but then, this man probably hadn't been expecting to come up here.

"See his pockets," she said. "There's greenery spilling out of them."

Jamie bent over. He turned his head to one side to get a better view. "That's pine needles."

"Conifers, at least," Heather said. She stood up.

The hill at their feet was covered in spongy grass. The route up had taken in gorse and more grass.

No conifers.

"So where was he, to get his pockets filled with pine needles?" Heather asked.

Jamie felt something tug at his memory.

"What's happening?" DI Wallace asked, behind Jamie now. He was panting. Jamie turned to see him red-faced and sweating through the collar of the blue shirt he wore under a black donkey jacket.

"We've found pine needles in the victim's pockets." Jamie looked down. "They're stuffed full of them." So full that it felt deliberate.

"So maybe he went somewhere with needles before he was killed," Wallace said.

Jamie turned to look past the DI. About fifteen miles away, just on the edge of the clouds moving up from Perth, was the Tay Forest Park.

Including Birnam Wood.

He smiled, despite himself. "You bastard."

"You talking to me?" Wallace asked.

Jamie looked at him. "No." He pointed at the body. "Those needles. We're on Dunsinane Hill. I'll bet any money those are from Birnam Wood."

"Why would you do that? It's miles away."

"Ohh..." said Heather. "We're going to have to get Carla in."

Jamie nodded. Carla Moreau was a forensic ecologist. She could pinpoint a crime scene just from examining the contents of someone's tyre treads.

"Great Birnam Wood to high Dunsinane hill," he whispered.

"What are you talking about, lad?" the DI asked.

"It's a Macbeth reference. And if this is what I think it is, I reckon we need the Complex Crimes Unit."

CHAPTER FOUR

JADE SAT outside Detective Superintendent Fraser Murdo's office at the Police Crime Campus in Gartcosh, tugging at the sleeve of her fleece. If she'd known she was going to end up here this morning, she'd have worn something smarter.

She was supposed to be back in Glasgow, talking to her DS about his future in Police Scotland. She still wasn't sure if Mo Uddin planned to go back to Birmingham now the CCU was being shut down, but she hoped not. He'd be an asset to the force. But Fraser would have to offer him something better than local CID if he was going to hang onto him.

The double doors to the hallway opened, and a man stepped in. He gave her a pinched smile and checked his watch. He took a seat two along from her.

She glanced at the man, trying to remember where she'd seen him before. He wore a black donkey jacket and a blue shirt beneath it. Mud stained his sleeve.

Dressed like that, he certainly wasn't one of Fraser's colleagues at the Crime Campus. The name had always tickled her; it was like the high-ups had decided they were running the CIA now, and not Police Scotland.

Fraser's door opened. "Ah, Jade. Good to see you. And Lyle. Come on in, both of you."

Jade gave the other man a puzzled glance, then stood up and walked into Fraser's office, making sure she was ahead of the man. Was he joining her team? No, that didn't make sense; the team was disbanding. Was he a DCI in charge of another team she was being posted to?

She sighed, not liking the idea of other people taking charge of her career. There was Rory to think of, and her mum. If anything, she probably needed to take some time out before she found another posting.

"Take a seat, both of you," Fraser said. "Have you met?"

"No," Jade replied, taking the middle of the three chairs opposite Fraser. She didn't come here much; Fraser preferred to get out from behind his desk and spend time with his subordinates on their patches.

"Yes," said the man at the same time. He frowned and looked at her. "COP26 planning, two years ago. Don't you remember?"

She narrowed her eyes. Should she lie, be polite?

No.

"I'm sorry. Remind me..."

"DI Lyle Wallace, Dundee CID. I was working in Edinburgh when we met. You and I were both seconded to work on a risk mitigation team from CID."

Ah, yes.

"I remember." She smiled at him, making sure not to look down at his clothes. The Lyle Wallace she remembered had been slim, dressed in close-fitting suits and with a clean-shaven jaw. This version was quite different. "Pleased to meet you again." She turned to Fraser, anxious to know what was going on. "What do you need me for?"

"Both of you," Fraser said. "DI Wallace here is working on a case that I think your unit might be able to help with."

"My unit? But you were—"

Fraser waved a hand. "Don't worry about that for now. I'm calling Petra in. I want you to assist with a specific aspect of the case. Lyle's team will focus on the more... straightforward elements."

"With respect, Sir." Wallace was leaning forward, tugging at his collar. Jade spotted a green stain on his elbow. Did the man ever get his clothes cleaned? "My team is fully capable of conducting all aspects of the investigation. The body was found on our patch, and we can—"

"I want Petra McBride brought in," Fraser said. "And Jade has a pre-existing relationship with her."

Not much of one, Jade thought. But she wasn't about to argue, if this meant her team got a stay of execution. Stuart had already applied to Glasgow CID. She'd have to speak to him. Find out where he was up to with that.

"Why do you need Petra's input?" she asked.

Fraser turned to her. "Good question. She's one of two specialists we'll be involving. The other is Carla Moreau."

"The forensic botanist."

What kind of case brought together a forensic psychologist and a forensic botanist?

An interesting one, Jade considered. One worthy of the Complex Crimes Unit.

"This sounds just my team's sort of case," she said.

"He hasn't told you what the case is yet," Wallace muttered.

She looked at him. *So it's going to be like that?*

"I need both teams to co-ordinate," Fraser said. "Lyle, your people can work on the local angle. Jade, I want your team on the Macbeth angle. The soil and the psychology of the killer."

"I'm sorry, Sir," she said. "But I've no idea what you're talking about. What Macbeth angle?"

Fraser looked between the two DIs. "You didn't talk while you were waiting? I deliberately gave you time."

Jade wasn't about to tell him that DI Wallace had arrived fifteen minutes after she had. "We didn't get a chance."

"Great. Here's a potted summary, then. A body was found on the top of Dunsinane Hill yesterday lunchtime. White male, in his twenties. PM still has to be done, but there's a stab wound."

"On the top of Dunsinane Hill?" Jade asked.

"Ten miles from Dundee," Wallace told her.

"I know that. So that's the Macbeth angle?" She looked at Fraser. "The castle?"

"There wasn't an actual castle," Wallace said.

"There was a hill fort," she replied.

"That's not the link," Fraser told her. "It's the—"

"It's the pine needles," Wallace interrupted. "Sorry, Sir."

Fraser raised an eyebrow at him and turned back to Jade. "Pine needles stuffed in the victim's pocket. They've come from Tay Valley Park. Possibly from Birnam Wood."

"That's in Macbeth too. Isn't it?"

"'Macbeth shall never vanquished be, until great Birnam Wood to high Dunsinane Hill shall come against him'," Wallace intoned.

"You've been practising," Jade said.

He smiled. "I might have."

"Which is why you're bringing in Carla Moreau." She looked at Fraser.

"Exactly."

"And you want Petra to help us understand what would motivate someone to carry out a crime like that."

"I do, and quickly. Macbeth has plenty of action. Lots of locations. I'm worried the killer might strike again, elsewhere."

Jade breathed in, casting her mind back to a production of Macbeth she'd seen in Glasgow years before, with her late husband Dan. Inverness Castle? A moor, somewhere? She couldn't remember.

"It's a straightforward case," Wallace said. "No reason to think it's a serial killer. All we need to do is identify the body and—"

Jade turned to him. "You don't know who the victim is yet?"

"He was only discovered yesterday."

"Is he still up there?"

"No," Fraser said. "Jamie Douglas and his team have been examining the scene, and the body has now been taken to Dundee morgue."

"Good," Jade said. "Lyle, you can worry about the PM. I'll focus on the Macbeth aspect."

"Just like the Superintendent suggested," Wallace replied.

"Yes."

He shook his head. "It's unnecessary. Give us twenty-four hours and we'll have an ID and an arrest."

"That would make me very happy," Fraser said.

But it's not going to happen, Jade thought. This was no simple killing. Whoever had done this, they'd planned it. And they were motivated by something more than the urge to kill one victim.

"I'll call Petra," she told Fraser. "And I'll set up a meeting with Carla. Send my team to Birnam with her."

Fraser smiled. "I knew you wouldn't let me down."

CHAPTER FIVE

"I'm sorry, love," Catriona said. "I know you've got this meeting to get to, and the girls are holding you up."

Mo's two daughters were in his car, waiting. He turned to see the eldest, Fiona, slap her little sister. He drew in a breath.

This wasn't how he'd been expecting to start the day.

"It's fine, Cat," he said, gritting his teeth. "Jade rang to cancel. She's been called to a meeting with the boss. And your mum needs you."

"My surgery needs me. They'll revoke my partnership if I carry on like this."

He put a hand on her arm. "They'll understand."

Catriona shook her head. "She wants us to go back to Birmingham. My Aunty Moira is in Stratford, my cousin's in—"

"We've just got the girls into that school." Mo felt his stomach sink as he remembered how much money it had taken to buy a house in the catchment area. "We can't move again."

Catriona's shoulders slumped. The phone was in her hand; her mum had called at 7.30am, on the dot as usual. She waited for hours after waking, until she knew Catriona would be up. Recent widowhood had turned her into a shell of the woman she'd been, someone who dragged herself through the days and seemed half the size she used to be.

"I need to get the girls to school," Mo said. "Can we talk about this later?"

"I need to talk to the practice manager," Catriona told him. "And besides, your unit's being disbanded."

Mo swallowed. She was right. But he was confident he'd get another posting up here, and he was loving it.

"I thought you'd be happy to go back to Birmingham," she said. "Work with Zoe again."

"Zoe's moving, remember? She's got a job in Cumbria."

"Maybe she'll change her mind."

"It doesn't work like that," Mo told her. He hated himself. Catriona's mum was grieving and confused. Right now, she wanted to tuck her tail between her legs and run away from the place where she'd lived with her late husband. But how could they be sure that in a month, she wouldn't have changed her mind?

He heard a commotion behind him. Isla had opened the car window and thrown Fiona's shoe out.

Bloody hell.

"I have to go, love. They'll be late." He leaned in to kiss his wife on the cheek. "You look after yourself. You think you'll make it to work?"

A nod. "I'll go in, at least."

"Good."

He turned and sprinted for the car. It was an eight-minute drive to school, and he had six. Sometimes he wished he could bring a response vehicle home.

He picked up the shoe, threw it through the car window,

and gestured for the girls to close it. He dived into the driver's seat and buckled up.

"Seatbelts on, both of you. And not a peep till we're at school. You know your mum needs you to behave right now."

"Sorry," Isla said.

He glanced at her in the rearview mirror, his eyes crinkling. They were good kids, really. But Fiona hitting the teen years and Isla coming not far behind had changed them. He'd lost the sweet little girls who used to squeeze into his lap together, and found them replaced by two monsters whose idea of fun was to wear their school skirts too short and talk in a language as indecipherable to him as anything a Glasgow junkie could come out with.

He hit the accelerator and drove off, jerking the car and making Fiona slump against the back of his seat.

"Seatbelts on, I said!"

"I heard," she replied in a voice laden with irritation.

"You could get yourself killed. Did you know th—"

"Dad, don't. We've heard it all before."

Giggling.

At least when they were against him, they weren't trying to kill each other.

"Strapped in?"

"Yes, Dad," came an exasperated chorus.

"Good. Now sit tight and keep quiet, both of you. I'm dumping you at the school gate and then I've got to get to work. I'm late for a meeting."

CHAPTER SIX

"Morning, folks." Jade was in the meeting room at the CCU's office, a desolate space inside a light industrial estate outside Glasgow. DC Patty Henderson and DC Stuart Burns had been here when she'd arrived, and Mo had turned up moments later. Carla Moreau had driven up in her green Honda half an hour after that and Jade had spoken with her about the contents of the murder victim's pockets. Now it was time to discuss what they had and allocate roles.

"Morning," Patty said. Mo scratched his chin and yawned. Stuart grinned at the newcomer. Carla was younger than Jade had expected, with shiny black hair and wearing a slim floral dress. She hoped Stuart wouldn't try to get too friendly.

"So," she said, "we've got a fresh case. Fraser is keeping the team together for as long as it takes to solve it."

"We'd better not move too fast, then," said Patty.

"You don't mean that?"

"Of course I don't, boss." Patty chuckled.

"Good." Jade knew Patty better than to believe she did.

"First, let me introduce Dr Carla Moreau. She's a forensic ecologist, which means her job is—"

"Why don't I explain it?" Carla stepped forward from her position beside Jade. The rest of the team was arranged around the long table.

"You go ahead." Jade took a chair.

Carla smiled. "I'm like a sniffer dog, but in human form. If your victim has been somewhere where they've come into contact with natural substances, like mud, or grass, or a very specific kind of pollen you only find in a single hedgerow on a specific estate, then my job is to work out what and where that is. Likewise, if your killer walked through mud that contains seeds from a plant you only get north of Inverness, or they've brushed against dog hairs from some rare breed, I'll identify it for you. The crimes you can solve using natural materials are surprising. And it's cheaper than DNA, too."

Jade wasn't so sure about that. But she *was* sure they didn't have time for the doctor to wax lyrical about her work for too long.

"Thanks, Dr Moreau."

"Carla."

"Carla." Thank God for that. *Dr Moreau* kept making her think of Bond villains. "So Carla's role will be to help us establish whether the needles found on our victim really do come from the place Jamie Douglas thinks they come from."

Carla smiled at the group. "And I haven't been told where that is. Think of this as a kind of treasure hunt."

"Why not?" asked Stuart.

"If I know where the evidence is likely to have come from, my judgement will be compromised. I imagine there'll be a point in the investigation where I need to ask you for your working hypotheses, but to start with I'd rather go in blind.

Give me the evidence, and I'll spend some time trying to match it to locations and sources I'm already aware of."

"Not too much time, I hope," Jade said.

"That's why I might eventually ask you for your hypotheses. If I can narrow things down without knowing all of your thinking, that will help you get your conviction once you catch the killer. Provides the jury with evidence that isn't muddied by prior knowledge. But if the samples don't allow me to narrow things down enough, I will get your input. And document it all, of course."

Stuart was staring at Carla.

Calm down, thought Jade. The woman was attractive, but not *that* attractive.

"So, won't we be bringing Petra in?" Mo asked.

"We will," replied Jade, "but we won't be discussing her side of the investigation in Carla's presence. Especially for now."

"Great," said Carla. "Sounds like you know what you're doing."

"We do." Jade didn't like the insinuation that she might not. "I gather Jamie has already arranged for samples to be sent to your lab."

"He has. It's just down the road in Shawlands, so I'll let you know as soon as I have anything."

"Thanks."

Jade and the team watched in silence as Carla left the room. Jade felt some of the tension leave her as she heard the outer door open and close.

She turned to the team. "OK. Now let's run through the rest of the evidence. Or at least the evidence we'll be assigned."

"What d'you mean?" asked Patty.

"Local CID were first on the scene. They'll be working on

the site itself, and on witness interviews. Getting an ID for the body."

"Who's SIO?" asked Mo.

"DI Lyle Wallace, Dundee CID," Jade told him.

"What are *we* supposed to do, then?"

"We've got two angles. First, the pine needles Jamie and Heather found in the victim's pockets. Next, the hypothesis that this crime is influenced by the events of Macbeth."

"Macbeth by Shakespeare?" Stuart asked.

"Do you know any other Macbeths?"

"Hamish Macbeth," Patty muttered. "That was a good show."

"And the real life Macbeth," Mo added. "He was a king of Scotland, wasn't he?"

"You're right," Jade said. "We need to factor in the possibility that the killer's motives and actions might be motivated by either the fictional Macbeth, or the real one."

"Or both," suggested Patty.

"Or both."

"We really are going to need Petra," Mo said.

"We are." Jade had been trying to call Petra since leaving Fraser's office, with no luck. She hoped the psychologist wasn't screening because of this mysterious anonymous caller of hers.

"DI Wallace is running the other side of the investigation," she continued. "We'll be working closely with his team. In fact, Patty, can you find out if there are any empty offices at Dundee nick we can commandeer?"

"Dundee?" Patty asked. "You want us to go to Dundee?"

"It's not that far." Jade was used to commuting from the shores of Loch Lomond to Glasgow every day. A bit of driving didn't bother her, although it might make childcare challenging. "And not for long. But I'd like to have direct access to the other side of the investigation. And it's not as if they'll be coming here, with the murder on their doorstep."

"OK," Patty said, not sounding entirely convinced.

"Good."

"So, what do we know about the victim?" asked Mo.

"Young man in his twenties. Not wearing the kind of clothes you'd expect for a walker."

"You never know, if he's young," Patty observed.

"True. But Dundee are working on that."

"Any more information on him? Anything that might connect him to Birnam Wood, or to Macbeth?" Mo asked.

"Or Shakespeare?" added Stuart.

"Until we have an ID," Jade said, "that's gonna be tough. But I'm sure Dundee are looking through Mispers as we speak. We'll find out who he is, and that'll put us a step closer to finding his killer."

"Or a step further away from all this Macbeth nonsense," Patty said.

"You think it's nonsense?"

A shrug. "Just strikes me as a bit overcomplicated. Killers aren't normally all that bright."

"Let's reserve judgement until we have more evidence," Jade told her. "I want to go to the two sites. We should send different members of the team to each. I'll track Petra down and take her to whichever site she feels would be most helpful in establishing the psychology of the killer. Stuart, you'll be with us. Mo and Patty, I want you at the other site. Carla will need to go to Birnam."

"I can take the doctor," Stuart said.

"No. You're coming with me and Petra."

He sniffed.

"No problem," said Mo. "It's not that far from where I live, anyway."

"Of course. How's the decorating work coming along?"

He grimaced. "Almost done. Bloody torture."

"And how's Catriona? Her mum?"

"Coping. Just."

"Hopefully you working on a case closer to home will take some of the pressure off."

Mo glanced at Stuart and Patty, his expression drawn. "Maybe."

"OK. Right then, I'll call Petra and we can get things kicked off."

CHAPTER SEVEN

PETRA LEANED back against the pillows and stretched. She could hear Aila in the bathroom, humming in the shower.

She smiled. Four months was an achievement for her. Petra had a way of messing up relationships. She'd either say the wrong thing, forget to call at an important time, or get distracted by work. And then she'd be dumped.

Her last girlfriend, Ursula, a hot New Yorker, had become frustrated when Petra had been too busy investigating the death of a tech billionaire to call her. Petra had been all set to fly out to JFK after solving the case, but by then, Ursula had moved on.

This time, she was determined to do things differently. And Aila was special. There was something about her that made Petra remember all that stuff, instead of having to put reminders on her phone.

She smiled as the pipes clanged in protest at the shower shutting off. Her flat, the first she'd owned in her fifty-three years, and that only because she'd inherited it from her Aunt Lydia, was old and faded, but she was gradually dragging it into the twenty-first century. She'd thrown a vast quantity of money at the ensuite bathroom with its walk-in shower and hers-and-hers sinks, but still the elderly pipework shuddered every time she turned on a tap.

It gave the place charm, she supposed.

The door opened and Aila emerged, clad in a fluffy dressing gown and with a towel piled on her head. Aila was tall, maybe too tall for Petra, really, given that she was only four feet ten herself. But her highest stilettos and some work on her posture were helping with all that.

"You look gorgeous," she told Aila.

Aila raised an eyebrow. "I look like a wet kipper."

Petra laughed. "Never. Maybe a wet salmon."

"What, pink and shiny?"

"Intelligent. The only fish that can swim upstream."

"Stupid, more like. Why would you want to do that when there's a perfectly good sea to hang out in?"

"Fair point." Petra pulled herself up to a sitting position. She didn't have any work until next week, when she was booked to speak at a conference in Madrid. In the meantime, she was looking forward to exploring Glasgow's West End, where she lived. There was an arts festival in a cinema somewhere and she thought it might not be too dull.

Aila, on the other hand, had to go to work. She was an investment banker, a breed that Petra had previously thought only existed in films and at right-wing dinner parties. She imagined Aila was the only socialist investment banker at the dinner parties she attended, and almost certainly the only lesbian.

The door opened a crack and a small furry shape slid in. Aila's cat, Monty.

"There you are, boy." Aila scooped him up and rubbed her cheek against his back.

Petra felt her skin twitch. This was Aila's only downside: the bloody cat. She adored the thing with a ferocity that Petra feared might never be directed at her. She'd even moved it into Petra's flat for the week she was staying here.

Petra, eager to impress the woman she'd been dating longer than any other, had agreed. And regretted it.

She drew back the duvet, and the cat jumped down from Aila's embrace onto her leg. She yelped, then sneezed.

"Have you taken your antihistamine?" Aila asked.

"Not yet." Petra reached for a tissue. She'd been dosing up on every brand of antihistamine she could find, all at the same time. But still she was sneezing.

She hoped the cat would go back to Aila's sleek flat in Edinburgh soon, although hopefully not with its owner.

Petra sneezed again, causing the cat to dig its claws into her thigh. She slapped it.

"Get off, ya bloody thing!"

"Hey." Aila picked the cat up and stroked its back. "It's OK, Monty. Just keep off Auntie Petra, and it'll be OK."

Petra clenched a fist. "I'm no animal's auntie."

Aila smiled. "You know what I mean." She disappeared into the bathroom. The cat sat on the carpet for a few moments, staring at Petra with a look that seemed designed to turn her to dust.

"You can look all you want, ya wee bastard. I'm never gonna be your auntie."

It miaowed and left the room.

Petra pulled herself out of bed and shut the door just as her phone rang.

She checked the display. *It had better not be you again.*

It wasn't. It was Jade Tanner.

She picked up. "Detective Inspector Tanner, it's a delight to hear from you. What can I do for you?"

"Sorry?"

"What can I do for you?"

"No. The delight bit."

"Ignore me. I'm having a funny kind of day."

"Er... OK. Are you available for a day or two? I've got a crime scene I'd like you to see."

Petra looked at the closed bathroom door. The bloody cat was scratching at it, trying to get in. She sighed.

"I'd be more than happy to, Jade. Just tell me where and when."

CHAPTER EIGHT

"There's no way you're getting me up that hill," Petra told Jade. They were standing with Stuart at the edge of the car park below Dunsinane Hill. There was one other car and Jamie's van in the car park.

"You'll be fine," Jade said. "If someone can get up here carrying a body, then you can manage it unencumbered."

Petra eyed her. "I'd imagine our killer was over five feet tall."

"Don't make assumptions," Stuart said.

"That wasn't what I meant. And height or no height, I also imagine our killer wasn't wearing four-inch stilettos."

Jade smiled. "I thought of that. You're a size four, right?"

"I am." Petra looked suspicious.

"So's my mum. I borrowed her walking boots."

Petra's eyes widened in horror. "No offence to your mum, hen. But I'm not wearing her boots."

"She's never used them. They're box-fresh."

A laugh. "In that case, they need wearing in. They'll

bloody kill me." Petra folded her arms across her chest. "You don't want the blood of my feet on your hands, DI Tanner."

Jade sighed. "I want you to see the spot where he dumped the body. You always say that seeing the crime scene is the single fastest way to get inside the head of a killer."

"First thing, let's stop assuming it's a bloke, yes? Second thing, this is no ordinary crime scene."

"Why not?"

"It's all about context. It doesn't really matter what's up there. We all know that Macbeth never really had a castle at the top of that hill, and that there never really was a castle there at all. It's symbolic."

"And that means you don't have to see it?"

Petra squinted up the hill. "How about you make a start and I'll follow on. Walking part of the way on my own will be all I need."

"You're sure?"

"Aye." Petra wrinkled her nose. "But on reflection, you'll need to lend me those shoes. I'm not messing these up."

Petra lifted her feet from the ground. Jade looked down to see her shoes had red soles. Wasn't that some sort of designer brand? She wasn't familiar with this kind of thing. Maybe she should be, in case it was ever relevant in an investigation.

"Sounds like a plan," Jade said. "Come on, Stuart. Race you to the top."

He looked at her. "Really?"

"No. You'll trounce me. And we need our wits about us when we're up there, rather than to be exhausted wrecks."

"OK." He started walking.

Jade watched him head up the hill.

"On you go then," said Petra. "Don't wait for me." She was pulling on Jade's mum's shoes.

"OK. See you on the way back down."

"Aye."

Jade looked up to see Stuart drawing level with a clump of gorse bushes. Jamie Douglas was on the way down, approaching him. She started walking, then rested for a moment. Jamie and Stuart were in conversation.

Her phone rang: Stuart.

"Stuart. What's up?"

"Jamie says we shouldn't all go tramping up there."

"It's only you and me."

"Still. He says the ground is pretty messed up already, what with the team from Dundee having been up while he was away from the scene."

So Lyle had got a head start on her. But this wasn't a competition.

"OK," she said. She wanted to tell Stuart to go up on his own. He seemed so keen. But she was in charge of this side of the investigation. She needed to see the scene.

"Wait there. I'll go up."

She pocketed her phone and walked up to join Stuart and Jamie.

"Jamie. What's this about you restricting access to the Scottish countryside?"

"Very funny. This isn't about the right to roam. It's about messing up my crime scene."

"I thought it was already pretty messed up."

"Exactly. Heather's up there taking some reliefs, and the degradation is making it tricky. It rained earlier, which didn't help."

"OK. Will you go with me?"

"I was planning on a break. I've got a flask of tea in my van and—"

"Surely you don't want me up there unaccompanied, wrecking your crime scene?"

Truth was, Jade could see how slippery the grass was and wasn't all that keen on tackling the walk alone. She knew from living in a rural area how risky that could be.

He sighed. "Fair enough."

"Grand. Stuart, you keep the doctor happy, won't you?"

Stuart looked past her at Petra, who was poking around in a hedge near the road. "If you're sure..."

"I'm sure. Don't bother her, just listen to her. I want to know what she's thinking." She turned to Jamie. "I take it you've examined the roadside."

"We have. And there's nothing."

"So our killer didn't leave us a nice big calling card."

"Nope. Dundee CID are talking to villagers, asking if anyone saw an unusual car. But this is a public road, so they're not expecting much."

Of course. Solving a crime in a remote spot like this would never be easy.

"OK," she said. "Right, let's get walking then."

CHAPTER NINE

"Hey! DS Uddin. Not so fast."

Mo turned to see Carla Moreau behind him, still near the car. He'd parked in a lay-by on the B687, which ran past Tay Forest Park, and had headed straight for the nearest path, Patty keeping pace with him.

"Sorry," he said. "I assumed we'd be heading into the forest."

"We will be," she told him. "But first I want to take samples from the spots where he might have parked."

"We don't know it's a he," said Patty.

"Good point. Where *they* might have parked." Carla stood still, sniffing the air. She breathed out, long and slow. "Question is, was the victim brought here, or were the needles gathered and placed in his pockets?"

"That's one thing we're here to work out," Mo said.

She nodded.

"How did you pin it down to this area?" he asked.

She smiled. "You want the tutorial?"

"Not the full story. But are you sure the DI didn't tell you?"

Carla laughed. She'd changed from the dress she'd been wearing back at the office into a pair of walking trousers and a fleece. The fleece looked well-used.

"No," she said. "Nobody told me. And it isn't magic. It's just about knowing the flora and the soil composition of an area."

"OK."

She eyed him. "OK. Here's how it works. Your crime scene people gave me a sample of the needles in the victim's pockets. I was immediately able to establish the species of plant. *Pinus Sylvestris*, Scots Pine. More importantly, I found seeds in the soil that had stuck to the needles, from *Rumohra adiantiformis*, a species of fern, and other seeds from junipers. From that, the database of native Scottish species I have on file and a quick online search, I was able to narrow it down to half a dozen areas. All large tracts of forest, only two within twenty miles of Dunsinane."

"The other one being?"

"Blackcraig Forest, further north. Shall we start walking? I'm happy with what I've got from this lay-by." She'd taken a sample of the mud behind Mo's car and placed it in a rucksack, then slung the rucksack over one shoulder.

"Lead on," he told her.

"Thank you." The ecologist strode ahead, her head up, her gaze roaming around the forest. She reminded Mo of his sister-in-law's spaniel sniffing out a squirrel.

"So," Carla said as they reached the beginning of a footpath leading off the road, "the next thing I did was to look at the state of the needles. They were reasonably fresh, still green at the tips. Which meant they'd been on the tree within the last few days." She looked up, putting a finger to her lips.

Mo exchanged glances with Patty. She shrugged.

"What are we listening for?" he asked.

"You hear the wind rustling the trees?" Carla said.

"Yes."

"That's what pulls the needles off. That and contact between trees. It has to occur with a certain force, though. So I checked the recent weather." She stopped suddenly and crouched on the floor, peering down at the needles on the ground. "Here we are."

"What are you looking for?" Patty asked. The forest was silent, and her voice sounded like a megaphone to Mo.

"I need to get samples from various parts of the forest."

"You definitely think it's this forest?" Mo asked.

Carla stood up, placing another bag inside the rucksack and shouldering it. "Like I say, there's two possible forests in this neck of the woods with the right species and soil type. It wasn't just the needles in the poor guy's pockets I analysed, but the soil that had been left with them, too. Given how recently the needles were on the trees, I thought there was a better than even chance they hadn't come from far away. And then I saw the name of one of the options."

Mo smiled. "I wondered when that would come up."

Carla dug inside her fleece and brought out an Ordnance Survey map. She unfolded it, refolded it, and placed a finger on a spot that corresponded to where they were standing. "If I'm not mistaken, that wood up there is Birnam Wood."

"It is."

"Which explains why you also wanted to bring in Petra McBride. The Macbeth angle, the psychology of it."

Mo nodded. "Have the two of you worked together before?"

Carla shook her head. "You'd think we would have,

wouldn't you? But no. She does more jet-setting than me. Gets cases all over the world. I got to go to France for a project once, but it was a long way from being glamorous." She shivered.

"So what d'you do with those samples now?" Patty asked.

"I'll take more, then I'll compare them with the ones from the body." Carla looked up and over Mo's head, in the general direction of Dunsinane Hill. "Someone's playing with you."

"They might be," said Mo.

"Or it could be coincidence," added Patty. She was sitting on the trunk of a tree that looked like it had blown down in a storm.

"Get off there, Patty," Mo said. "This is a crime scene."

She stood up. "Sorry, Sarge."

Carla bent to run her fingers through the soil next to the tree. "A shame there's no sign of him being here."

"The killer?" Mo asked.

She looked up. "If he gathered these needles as recently as he must have done, he'll have left traces."

Mo felt his muscles tense. "In which case, we need to leave."

Carla sighed. "I was waiting for you to say that. It's so nice here. And your scene of crime guys are going to wreck it."

"Just doing our job."

"I don't rate your chances of finding traces of him in a spot as big as this. Let me take a few more samples first, it'll help narrow things down."

"OK," Mo said.

"You two stay here. The fewer of us there are trampling all over this place, the better."

Mo watched the ecologist walk away from them, her steps careful and her gaze on the ground. Patty was still sitting on the tree.

None of this made sense.

What made someone go to so much trouble just to make reference to a Shakespeare play? And had Wallace's team even discovered the identity of the body yet?

CHAPTER TEN

Petra was aware of DC Stuart Burns behind her, hanging around nervously and trying not to look like he was watching her.

Every time she looked round, he made a point of looking away. It reminded her of Aila's damn cat when it wanted food from her.

Next thing, he'd be miaowing and shedding fur all over the place.

She stifled a sneeze at the memory of the cat and called to him.

"You don't need to babysit me, you know."

He frowned. "I'm not."

"I told Jade I needed to be alone. You're hanging around like a nasty smell."

He looked hurt. *Jeez. Can these kids not take a bit of directness?*

"Sorry," he said. He retreated towards the car.

Thank fuck for that.

She opened the gate leading up the hill, examining it as she let it close behind her. The forensics people would have checked it for traces. Analysed it for blood. It looked like they'd done everything they needed to. So why were they still being fussy about how many people went up there?

Truth was, she'd been grateful to that Jamie lad for stopping her from going up. Petra wasn't built for hill walking, and it would take more than a fancy pair of walking shoes to change that.

What she *was* built for was imagining. Standing here in the silence pierced only by the occasional bird and a distant aeroplane somewhere behind her, she closed her eyes and put herself in the mind of the killer.

The victim had been dead a while, Jade had told her. Very little blood at the scene. Which meant he'd been brought up dead, rather than attacked at the top. If he'd been killed after heading for the top under his own steam, there'd probably have been a car down in the car park.

Petra put her arms out to the sides. Standing here on a hill with her eyes closed was making her dizzy.

She tried to imagine what it would be like carrying a body up here. Depending on how long the victim had been dead, rigor mortis might have set in and that would have made him feel even heavier than he was. And that hill...

She couldn't see it. There had to be two of them, at least. Carrying him between them on some kind of stretcher. You certainly wouldn't get a body up here by jamming him between two of you and just staggering up.

She scanned the path ahead of her for signs of disturbance. She knew that was the SOCOs' job, and that they would have thought of many more possibilities than she could, but she couldn't resist. One individual – or even two – carrying another would cause the sort of pressure that would leave footprints.

The path was mainly grassed, clearly regularly walked over, but there were no noticeably deep indentations.

Stop it, Petra.

She needed to do her job. Focus on the psychology.

Right. She stepped to one side to stand next to a low wall, make herself feel grounded. She closed her eyes and breathed in. And listened.

The plane she'd heard before had gone. She could hear birds. She wasn't sure what kind. That forensic ecologist woman would know. Not that she needed to.

She opened her eyes again and looked back towards the car park. Stuart was down there, pacing. On his phone.

She looked up. Jade and her SOCO pal had long since disappeared over a rise. There was a wood up ahead, to the left, then thick gorse.

Could the forensics people be wrong? Could the needles have come from that wood, or up in the gorse? That would explain things better. If the victim had been alive when he arrived here...

Close your eyes again. She didn't need to worry about that. She needed to imagine how it would feel to bring a body up here. Or to kill someone at the top, if that was what had happened.

The two scenarios required a different mindset. Both involved a degree of obsessiveness about Shakespeare, or Macbeth at least. The killer was clearly referencing the play and not the real Macbeth, as only the fictional king had ever set foot on Dunsinane Hill. Let alone had Birnam Wood travel to meet it.

So you're a Macbeth nut. A Shakespeare fanatic. With the strength and determination to kill a man, quite cleanly, and bring him up here for some poor bastard hill walkers to find.

The killer would have planned this. If he'd brought the victim up here to then kill him, he would have had to get the man up in the first place. If he'd brought the body here after death, he would have researched the best time to do that. He would have checked the location of local houses, been aware of potential witnesses.

You're not just some nutter, and that's for sure.

The killer was obsessed, but not to the point of being unable to function socially. And it might not just be Macbeth, or even Shakespeare, they were obsessed with. Scottish heritage? English plays? Would the next victim, if there was one, be left somewhere that pointed to Rabbie Burns, or to Chaucer?

Birnam Wood to Dunsinane. It was specific. It was from the end of the play, when Macbeth was defeated. The king had thought himself invincible, after the three witches had predicted he would remain king until the wood moved to the castle.

And then it had. Macbeth had died. And so had the poor fella they'd found up on that hill yesterday.

"Everything alright?"

Petra opened her eyes to see Stuart approaching. She sighed.

"Fine. Thanks."

"You getting a good feel for him?"

"Or her."

"You really think a woman might have been able to drag a lad in his twenties up here?"

Petra shook her head. "To be fair, I think it'd be a tall order for a man to do, on his own."

"You reckon there's more than one killer."

"Maybe a killer and an accomplice."

"Both killers, under the law."

Petra didn't need to worry about that. She just needed to understand the kind of person who would do this.

"He functions," she said.

"Sorry?"

"He holds down a job. Perhaps a good one. He's intelligent. He might have a partner, a family."

"So you still think it's a man."

Petra narrowed her eyes. A car passed below them. She sneezed.

"Bless you."

"Thanks." She pulled a tissue out of her pocket and blew her nose. *Damn cat.* She'd have to find a better brand of antihistamine, if she was going to make things work with Aila.

"I do think it's a man, yes. He's not young, but not old either."

"Sounds like a nobody man."

She looked at him. "You could have a point there."

"I was joking."

She cocked her head. "It's a man with self-esteem issues. This is an ostentatious crime. One that's designed to draw attention to itself. It might not even have been committed by a Macbeth nut. Just someone who knows that if he makes us think the whole thing's about Macbeth, it'll get our attention."

"I'd have thought that just killing someone would be enough to get the police's attention."

"Not just the police. The media. Has this been reported on the news yet?"

"Not sure, sorry." Stuart brought his phone out. "It's on the BBC Scotland website. Just the murder. No mention of Macbeth."

"That's not enough. Any old murder gets reported in the

local press. But a Macbeth-themed murder, that could hit the international news sites." She whistled. "Your guy might even be American."

"American?"

"They love this kind of thing. History. Literature. Heritage. The three of them all smushed up together in the story of Macbeth."

"So you think we're looking for an American man in, what, his forties?"

"I need to do some more work. Ignore the American thing. It's a possibility, but not a definite one. I can tell you one thing, though." She threw her head back to look up at the sky. It was clear and pale, not quite blue.

"What's that?" Stuart asked.

"Whoever he is, he's going to be following the case closely. Watching it on the news." She glanced down the hill. "Maybe watching us in person while we investigate."

CHAPTER ELEVEN

"Blimey," Jade panted. "How the hell did someone drag a body up here?"

"It's not visited that much," Jamie replied. "They could have done it under cover of darkness."

"Which means no one came up here until those women found him Tuesday lunchtime."

"Exactly."

"And whoever brought him up here, they'd have had all night to do it in." She looked to the east, where Dundee lay faint against the coastline. "Still, making this walk in the dark would have been treacherous. I still think it's more likely they found some way of getting him up alive."

"There was hardly any blood."

"And he died from a stab wound?"

"There *was* a stab wound. Post-mortem hasn't confirmed that was the cause of death."

"Maybe they got him up here, killed him some other way, then stabbed him." She considered. "Are there stabbings in Macbeth?"

Jamie laughed. "Oodles of them. 'Will this hand ne'er be clean?' 'Out, damned spot.' All thanks to murder by stabbing."

"So maybe the killer wanted us to think he – or she – stabbed the victim when in reality they killed him some other way."

Jamie nodded, pushing his curly hair back. The wind was rising now and Jade could feel her own hair being whipped about.

"That makes some sense," he said.

"I wish Petra had bloody come up here."

"We'd have been here all day."

"Don't make assumptions." She turned towards the east. "Where's Birnam Wood, from here?"

Jamie pointed. "See the forest over there? That's the Tay Valley Forest. Birnam Wood is within that."

"Is it big?"

"Not particularly, but it's big enough to make it hard to find a killer. Heather's headed over there to see what she can find."

"And my team are taking Carla Moreau over, too."

"Good," he said. "I've heard she knows her stuff."

Jade shrugged. "I've barely met the woman." She turned back to look at the cairn where the body had been left. It was about four feet tall, piled with stones. "Did the pathologist come up here?"

Jamie shook his head. "We were asked to take photos of the body, samples too. After that they send it down to Dundee for the PM."

"Pathologist didn't fancy walking up here."

"Pathologists don't always visit the scene."

No. Jade felt it hard to understand why anyone involved in a murder investigation wouldn't want to visit the crime scene. She was frustrated enough that she wasn't looking at Birnam

Wood, too. But of the two scenes, she knew this one was likely to provide more evidence.

"What about the path up?" she asked. "Did the killer or victim leave anything?"

"We've done an initial trawl, and we've had Uniform go over it in more detail. There are a few bits and bobs. A woolly hat, a water bottle, that kind of thing. Nothing you wouldn't expect to find on a walking trail. If you don't mind me saying, Jade, I think your killer was much too methodical to leave anything obvious."

"I agree." Petra had already suggested that the killer was intelligent and organised. She'd been hoping they might have left traces, but that was looking increasingly unlikely.

"I don't envy Lyle Wallace," she said.

Jamie shrugged. "He's got a team of twelve on it. If there's anything to find, they'll find it."

"You're liaising with them?"

"With DS Gail McKinnon."

"I don't know her."

"I haven't met her before, but she seems OK." He turned to look at her. "I thought you were focused on the psychology?"

"We are." Jade breathed out and clapped her hands together. "Doesn't do any harm to know what's going on, though." She had to establish a better working relationship with Lyle Wallace, and fast. "I'm wondering if the victim was taken to Birnam Wood, or if the needles were brought from there and put in his pocket." She squinted over towards the woods, one hand shielding her eyes.

"Carla will be examining the victim's clothing, as well as the pockets. If he was in the wood prior to his death—"

"Or after," Jade corrected.

"Or afterwards, there'll be evidence elsewhere on his clothing. And I'm sure Carla will report back to you."

"I'm sure she will."

Jade took one last look around. The crime scene was tranquil now, no evidence of what had happened here. "You've definitely found no blood elsewhere?"

"None. Sorry."

"In which case, it's likely he was stabbed after death."

"Let's wait till the PM."

"You're right." She was still looking towards the woods. "I need to drive that route. See if there's any CCTV cameras."

"I'd imagine Wallace's team are already doing that."

Jade screwed up her face. "Yeah. OK, thanks, Jamie. Let's get down and see what Petra's up to."

CHAPTER TWELVE

JADE'S HOTEL room had seemed spacious when she'd checked in an hour earlier, but now the whole team was in there with her, it felt like a box room.

She'd tried to find a private meeting room in the hotel, but budget hotels in Perth didn't stretch to such luxuries, it seemed. And the Dundee office still hadn't offered them a space.

No mind. This meant they were near both crime scenes, and they could talk in private.

Petra sat on the bed, stockinged feet up on the duvet cover and head resting against the pillows. She had her eyes closed and her hands folded in her lap. Carla had taken the chair next to the desk and was scrolling through her phone, while Stuart and Patty were in the two armchairs by the window. Mo had gone to fetch drinks.

There was a knock on the door. Jade, standing by the wardrobe, went to open it. Mo stood outside, a cardboard tray of coffee cups in one hand and a paper bag in the other.

"You've brought food."

"I thought we'd need something to keep us going." He put the edge of the paper bag in his mouth and handed her a cup.

"Thanks." Jade edged the lid open and peered inside: a skinny latte with an extra shot. That would perk her up.

"That was quick." Petra opened her eyes and sat forward, her legs still on the bed.

Mo shrugged. "We come up here a bit on the weekends. I'm getting to know my way around." He handed her a cup.

"Have you been to either of the crime scenes before?" Carla asked. Jade noticed Petra watching her, her gaze intent. The two doctors hadn't worked together before. Would she have to navigate professional rivalry?

Mo placed the tray of cups on the desk. "Whose is the black Americano?"

"That's me," Carla said. She took it from him and sipped, then winced. "Hot."

Stuart and Patty got up from the armchairs and grabbed their cups.

"What's in the bag?" Stuart asked.

Mo handed it over. "You can be in charge."

Stuart opened it. "Doughnuts. I approve."

"I should think so, too," Mo replied, as Stuart handed the bag round. Carla demurred, and Petra, who received the bag immediately after her, took two.

"You sure you don't want this?" the psychologist asked.

Carla waved a hand. "Be my guest."

Petra's lips curled at one side. "Kind of you. Thanks."

That was something, Jade thought. By the looks of it, the two of them wouldn't be sniping at each other, at least.

"OK," she said. "Now that's all sorted, can we get onto the real reason we're here?"

Patty snorted. "I thought you were hosting a party, boss."

"Fat chance."

"It's not the most... glamorous of venues," Petra observed as she licked sugar from her fingers. Her nails were painted an iridescent purple.

"It's not, but it's what we've got," Jade told them. "We won't be staying up here for long, but I'd prefer to be nearby."

"D'you want us staying over, too?" Patty asked, exchanging glances with Stuart.

"Can you?"

"I can," Stuart said.

"I might struggle," said Patty. "It's my mum."

Jade nodded. "We'll need someone working on the system. You head back to Glasgow after this, and base yourself in the office from tomorrow morning."

"No problem, boss. Thanks."

"I can stay with a friend in Dundee," Petra said.

"Good." Jade looked at Carla.

"Don't worry about me. You won't need me onsite for long."

"I'd like to know what you found at Birnam Wood today."

Carla put down her cup. "First, I'd like to know what the structure of this investigation is. Are you SIO?"

Jade lowered her cup. "DI Lyle Wallace from Dundee CID is SIO. I've been put in charge of expert liaison, given my existing work with Petra."

"You haven't worked with me before."

"No. But I think Lyle appreciates the extra resource."

"Will I be needing to talk to both of you?"

"Definitely not. You give your findings to me, or to Jamie Douglas. We'll work on them, along with Petra's findings, and pass them along to the rest of the team as necessary."

"It all sounds very odd to me."

And to me, Jade thought, but said nothing. Was this Fraser's way of trying to protect her team? Or was it a genuine need for her experience with Petra?

Petra could be prickly, but not so bad that Lyle wouldn't be able to work with her.

It didn't matter. For now, they had a case to solve.

"It's not for us to question staffing decisions taken at a higher level," she said. "Let's just focus on gathering evidence. Carla, do you need access to the Dunsinane Hill site?"

"Not as far as I can see, no. I've spoken to the pathologist and I'll be sent samples from the man's pockets and clothing. I've got samples from Birnam Wood. That will be enough for me to identify a match, if there is one. Once we've got that, the rest is up to you."

Jade nodded. "Thanks. Petra, what were your observations at the Dunsinane scene?"

Petra cleared her throat and placed her cup on the bedside table. "Well, I think you're looking at one of two psychological types."

"That sounds like a start."

"I wouldn't be so sure."

"Tell me the types."

Petra counted on her fingers. "First, there's the Macbeth nut. Someone so obsessed with the play that they'll commit a Macbeth-themed murder just for kicks."

"They went to a lot of trouble," Mo said.

"They did. It can't have been easy getting that poor fella up the hill. In fact, I'd bet my girlfriend's cat that the victim wasn't dead before he went up there. I just don't see how you'd get him up there without leaving more of a trace."

"Sounds like your cat'll be OK," Carla said.

Petra looked at her. "Not mine, believe me."

Carla returned her gaze. *Are they flirting?* Jade shook her head.

"Do we have photos of the site?" Carla asked, her gaze dragging away from Petra.

"We do." Jade handed over her mobile phone, with the Photos app open.

"Petra's right," Carla said. "Dragging a body up there would leave a significant trace. If the killer got him to walk up, possibly under coercion, it would look like just another walker. We'd never know the difference."

"That's what Jamie reckoned," said Stuart. Jade nodded.

Carla raised an eyebrow, looking at Petra. "Your girlfriend's cat is definitely safe."

"More's the pity," said Petra. She wrinkled her nose.

Jade had no idea what Petra was on about. Wasn't she dating an American? "You said there were two possible personality types."

Petra counted off on a second finger. "The other is the show-off. Someone who wants to get our attention. They know a bit of Macbeth, just enough to be familiar with the whole moving wood scenario. To be fair, that probably accounts for half the population. But the key thing is that they want this to become front page news. Kill a guy and leave him on a hill's one thing. Do it in a way that draws attention to one of the most well-known works in the English language is another."

"Which of the two do you think is most likely?" Jade asked.

"Does it make a difference?" Stuart said. "Not till we know who the victim is."

"I can work on that," Patty replied, "back in the office."

"No," Jade told her. "That's the other team's job. I want

you liaising with their DCs. Find out what's going on, what leads they have. We need to know if there's any overlap with what we're working on."

"Linking the victim to the killer," Mo suggested.

"Yes."

"And linking their forensics to mine," Carla added.

"Are you OK with being assigned to us?" Jade asked her. She was sensing antipathy from the woman.

"It's fine," Carla told her. "Squirrel me away in a lab and I'll be happy. I don't care about the internal politics of Police Scotland."

Petra chuckled. Carla glanced at her, cheeks reddening.

Jade sighed. "Good. Petra, given those two personality types, is there anything we should be looking for to pin it down?"

"If it's type two, the show-off, then he'll be keeping a close eye on the investigation."

"But not type one."

"Type one is too far up his own arse for that. He'll be more... unstable, I'd expect. To be honest, given the little we know about the crime, I don't think we're looking for a Macbeth obsessive at all. I think we're looking for a show-off. But one that knows a bit of Macbeth."

"Who'll be following the investigation," Jade said. "Trying to get himself involved?"

"Maybe. Are you planning to ask the public for help?"

"The other team are," Mo said. "There's a plan for a press conference in the morning."

"I'll go to that," Jade said. "Where is it?"

"Dundee."

"Of course."

Dundee was only half an hour from Perth by car. "Good. I don't want to rule out personality type one though, not until we know some more about the victim. Petra, I'd like you to come with me to the press conference. I want to watch the room, see if the killer turns up."

CHAPTER THIRTEEN

"I'm sorry I can't do any more, Mo."

Jade sat in the desk chair in her hotel room, Mo in one of the armchairs by the window. The sheer curtains were drawn and orange light filtered in from the street.

"It's not your fault," he replied.

"That doesn't make it easier."

He shrugged.

"Do you think Catriona will persuade you to move back down south?"

Another shrug. "I like it up here. I've got used to it. My old team in Birmingham's been disbanded, and I don't feel like getting my feet under the table in another one."

"I know that feeling." Jade had been forced to do that enough times. The worst of them had been when the eight Scottish forces had merged to become Police Scotland. Half the force had been reallocated, and the scars still showed in some teams.

"It depends if I can get another job up here, though." Mo

was slumped in the chair, his gaze on the garish chain-hotel carpet.

"I'll put in a word. And you never know, this case might lead to them keeping the CCU together."

He looked up. "You think that's a possibility?"

"One thing I've learned as a copper, and that's not to bother speculating about structures and politics. The only thing we have any influence over is how good a job we do. So we need to ensure we make a real contribution to this case. I want it to be the expert input that cracks it, not just the day-to-day evidence provided by Lyle's team."

"He's got three times as many people working on it as we have."

She leaned forward. "Twice as many, if you count Petra and Carla."

"Carla's going to be done as soon as she identifies those needles."

Jade shrugged. "Who knows? She may find more than she expects on the victim's clothing."

Her laptop pinged behind her. She checked her watch: 6pm. She was expecting a call from her mum, a chance to speak to Rory before he went to bed.

"Can we pick this up in the morning?" she asked Mo. "I need to take a call."

He stood up, brushing down the fronts of his already-clean trousers. "There's nothing to pick up. I'll do like you say, the best job I can. Then maybe things will work out."

She gave him a smile. "Let's hope so. We make a good team."

"We do." He headed for the door.

Not wanting to be late for her mum, Jade flipped her laptop open and jabbed at the keys to answer the call. After a few moments, Morag's face was on the screen. She could hear Rory's voice in the background.

"Sorry about that, Mum. I was in the middle of a chat with my DS."

"That nice Mo lad?"

"Not so much of a lad. He's in his forties."

"You know what I mean. Are you having fun up there?"

"A man died, Mum. It's not exactly fun."

"Sorry, love, that came out wrong. Is it going OK? Will you be home soon?"

Jade felt her stomach dip at the question. Her mum didn't mean to nag, but Jade felt like a neglectful mother every time she had to do something like this.

"How is he?" she asked.

"Hang on." Morag looked away from the camera. "Rory! Come here, your mam's on the phone." She looked at Jade. "Not phone, sorry. Video. Computer, I don't know."

Jade smiled. "Call it whatever you want."

Rory slid into view, wriggling his way onto Morag's lap. "Mummy! I was watching *Hey Duggee*. The squirrels built a sandcastle."

Jade rolled her eyes. "You and your *Hey Duggee*."

"It's good, Mummy. You should watch it, while you're away."

"I'll try to, sweetheart. You OK there?"

"Nanny cooked shepherd's pie. It was yum."

"Glad to hear it." Jade looked at her mum. "Thanks for feeding him."

"It's no trouble. I enjoy feeding a bairn who likes his food."

Rory shuffled off his gran's lap and ran off.

"No goodbye for Mummy?" Morag asked.

"Sorry! Bye!" came a shout.

Jade laughed and wiped away a tear. She missed her son.

Get this case cracked fast, and you can be back home with him.

"How long will you be there, love?" her mum asked again.

"I really don't know. But I guess we need long enough to identify the victim, and to talk to local witnesses. Not that my team's working on any of that."

"You're not in charge?"

"Not this time." Jade tried to hide the irritation in her voice. She appreciated Fraser bringing her team in, but she knew they were second fiddle to Lyle. "We're working on some more specialist aspects of the investigation."

"Ohh. Sounds fancy."

Jade nodded. No harm in her mum thinking her role was more impressive than it really was.

"I reckon a couple of nights," she said. "I can't see why they'll need us longer than that. There's a press conference in Dundee in the morning, then—"

"You could drive to that from home."

"It's a two-hour drive, Mum. More in the rush hour." And Jade still didn't enjoy driving unfamiliar roads, not since Dan's accident.

"OK. You know best."

Jade tapped the desk. She could hear Rory in the background, laughing at the television.

"Is he missing me?"

"You've only been away a few hours. He's fine. Stop your worrying."

"OK." Jade wasn't convinced.

"You're working on that murder on Dunsinane Hill, I imagine?"

"How did you know?"

"Saw it on the TV earlier. Don't worry, I switched it off before Rory saw anything. Helicopter footage, they had. Bringing that poor wee lad down from the mountain."

Jade nodded. "Hopefully we'll find whoever put him up there."

"How did he die? They aren't saying on the news."

"Mum..."

Morag put her hands up. "Sorry. Far be it from me to ask what my daughter's doing with her time. Anyway, I'm sure we'll learn more in the morning. They said there's to be a press conference."

"Yes, I just told you about that." Jade needed to prepare for it, too. "I'll have to go, Mum. You give Rory a goodnight kiss for me, yeah?"

"Of course."

Jade checked her watch. She needed to speak to Wallace, and she needed to find food.

"Thanks, Mum. See you both very soon."

CHAPTER FOURTEEN

JADE ARRIVED EARLY for the press conference, hoping she'd get the chance to have a chat with DI Wallace before it started. She'd called him four times the previous night but got no answer. After the third voicemail message, she'd given up.

Was he screening her calls, or did he just have a strict sense of work-life balance? The press conference was due to start at 8.45, it was 8.20 now, and she'd be justified in expecting the SIO on a murder investigation to be at work by this time.

But the Police Scotland building in West Bell Street was quiet. No sign of the press anywhere, no sign of the murder investigation team.

The lobby was a low-ceilinged space that felt as if it would have been sparkling and modern about sixty years earlier, but now smelled of damp and was too dark to be welcoming. A man scurried past as Jade entered, hurrying from one door to another.

"Morning," the sergeant on the front desk said. "Can I help you?"

Jade pulled out her ID. "I'm DI Tanner, this is DC Burns. We're here to see DI Wallace and attend the press conference."

"Oh, you don't want to be here, then."

"No?"

He shook his head and leaned over the counter, craning his neck to look back at the door she and Stuart had entered by. "They're holding it in the council house. DI Wallace and Superintendent Hamilton. And some bods off the council."

Jade knew of Superintendent Esme Hamilton, but hadn't met her. She had responsibility for CID in Tayside and clearly wanted to be seen leading this investigation.

How would Fraser feel about that?

She shook her head. *Sod the politics.* "Tell me how to get there."

"That's easy. Hook round the Sheriff's Court next door then straight down North Lindsay Street. Dundee House is on your right, looks like it was made from Lego."

Lego?

"Thanks." Jade touched Stuart on the arm. "We'll need to hurry."

"I run every week, boss."

"You do?" Stuart was short and squat, with a square face that didn't look like it belonged on a man who exercised regularly.

"You don't believe me."

"Sorry. Of course I do. Come on, then."

They hurried out of the building and followed the sergeant's directions, arriving at Dundee House ten minutes later. It was boxy and modern, but didn't quite look like Lego. The sergeant's directions had told her what she needed to know, though.

"Just a minute," she said. She checked her reflection in the tall windows. She didn't want to walk in looking dishevelled and out of breath.

"You look great," Stuart said.

She eyed him. "Less of the flattery."

He grinned. "I thought it would help if I reassured you."

"Now you're my mum?"

He blushed. "Sorry. Do I look OK?"

Jade looked him up and down. "You look like a man who runs every week, and wasn't the slightest bit phased by that quick sprint. I envy you."

He smiled.

She pushed open the doors and followed signs to the press room. Inside, journalists and cameras were gathering.

Shit.

A table had been placed at the front. People milled around it, and plenty of them: Wallace's twelve-strong team. Why were they here, and not out solving the case?

Someone moved to one side, and Jade noticed a squat grey-haired woman talking to Wallace. She approached, her hand held out.

"Superintendent Hamilton, I'm DI Tanner, Complex Crimes Unit. I'm working with DI Wallace on the investigation."

"I didn't know you'd been invited to the press conference."

Jade swallowed. "I didn't think an invitation was necessary."

"I suppose not." Hamilton looked past Jade at Stuart.

"This is DC Burns, one of my team. We were hoping to have a chat with DI Wallace before things kick off."

The Super raised an eyebrow. "A wee word, eh? You'd better be quick." She walked away.

Jade turned to Lyle. "I've been trying to contact you."

"At 8pm."

"It's a murder investigation. I might have had a key piece of information to share with you."

"I listened to your voicemail."

She pursed her lips. "Are we OK here, Lyle? I thought we were going to be fine, working together."

He glanced past her at the Super. *So that's the problem.*

"We'll be OK," he said. "Just try not to draw too much attention to yourself."

"Why, so you can take the credit when we find the killer?"

His brow furrowed. "You really think I'll do that?"

Jade felt heat rise up her neck. "Sorry. That didn't come out the way I intended it to. Let's start again, yeah? Can we grab a coffee after this, make sure we're coordinating our efforts?"

"I'm not so sure about a coffee, but there'll be a briefing immediately after." He glanced past her again; he was doing that a lot, she'd noticed. "I'll be leading it."

Jade turned to see Superintendent Hamilton talking to a man in a dishevelled suit, a council officer, perhaps.

Wallace clearly didn't feel comfortable around his senior officer. Well, that wasn't Jade's problem.

"I'll tag along, if that's OK," she said. "I can brief your team on what the experts have given me so far, and you can update me on what progress you've made on the victim's ID."

"Touché."

"I'm not having a go. Really." She could sense Stuart behind her, shifting from foot to foot. What was up with him? "I'm just eager to know who he is. Dr McBride is, too."

"I'm sure she is. And so am I."

Superintendent Hamilton was at the front table now, getting herself miked up.

"I'd best be off. We can talk after this." Wallace looked nervously at his boss.

"We can," Jade replied, and retreated to a seat amongst the press.

CHAPTER FIFTEEN

PETRA WOKE to the sound of her phone ringing on the bedside table.

She yawned and reached out for it, wincing when her hand hit something solid.

She opened her eyes.

Of course.

She wasn't at home in her West End flat. She was in Magdalena's flat in Dundee. And clearly, Magdalena's spare room had a bedside table that was higher than her own.

She pulled herself up and grabbed the phone: Jade.

What time was it?

9:30. She hadn't planned on staying in bed that late.

She put a hand to her forehead.

Magdalena and she hadn't got together for over a year. Petra knew that requesting a bed for the night, or maybe a few, was cheeky, but the two of them had been close when they'd both been working at Dundee University. Mags had welcomed her with open arms and an open bottle of very good Bordeaux.

"Jade," Petra croaked into the phone. "How's things?"

"We've just finished the press conference. I thought you'd be here."

Ah, hell. Petra poked her forehead again, then scanned the room for her bag. She needed painkillers.

"Sorry. I can be with you in fifteen minutes if you're at the police station."

"We're not. We're at the council house."

Petra screwed up her face. She couldn't remember where that was.

"There's no real rush now," Jade said. "If you're not feeling so well…"

Petra shifted down on the bed. Her chest ached, and her stomach was gurgling.

How strong had that Bordeaux been? She knew there'd been two bottles. And all they'd eaten had been a tube of Pringles.

Idiot.

"Let me get a shower, and I'll be right with you."

"OK. We're heading back to the police HQ in Dundee. I'd be grateful to know if you've had a chance to think any more about your two potential personality types. When you have your report—"

"Wait." Petra remembered a dim conversation with Mags the night before. Mags had mentioned a colleague.

"There's someone who can help," she said. "With the Macbeth references."

"I thought you said it wasn't so much about Macbeth, as about—"

Petra shook her head and immediately regretted it. "Have you got an ID yet?"

"No."

"That in itself is pertinent. I think the victim is supposed to be anonymous. He's random, just someone the killer picked out."

She heard a sharp breath on the other end of the line. "Which means…"

"Which means he may intend to strike again."

"That changes the nature of the investigation. Are you sure?"

"I need to work up some theories, and I'll let you have a full written report, of course. But yes. I think there's a good chance we'll see another Macbeth-related death."

"When?"

"That's where I need someone who knows the text and its context. My mate Mags has recommended someone."

"OK. Can you talk to her?"

"Him. His name's Anthony Urquhart. He's here in Dundee. I'll track him down, see if he can be of use."

"I have no more budget," Jade told her. "We already have two experts."

"I'll just be asking him for advice," Petra told her. "Not for consultancy. Don't worry."

A pause. "Very well. Don't promise him anything, though."

"I won't." Petra closed her eyes. She needed to get off the phone. "I'll be with you after that shower."

"You're sure you're well enough? Your voice is very quiet."

"All my own fault." There was a murder to solve. And another to prevent. Maybe. "It's fine."

Unable to say any more, Petra hung up and ran towards what she hoped was the bathroom.

CHAPTER SIXTEEN

JADE SAT at the back of the Dundee CID team room, fighting the urge to jump in and take over.

Lyle Wallace was methodical and thorough. But God, was he slow. He'd repeated the same pieces of forensic evidence three times, checking them with a DC and with Jamie's team, before moving on to the post-mortem.

"Very well," he said, turning from the team to the screen behind him. "The PM was conducted early this morning, by Dr Cooper. DC Shaw attended." Lyle gestured towards a male DC, then brought up a photo of the body lying on a post-mortem table. Murmurs spread through the room.

Lyle turned to face his team. "We've got a cause of death."

More murmurs. Jade, who'd been taking notes, stopped mid-word.

Lyle had spent the last twenty minutes talking about fibres found on a gatepost at the bottom of the hill. None of it was remotely useful. And all that time he'd been waiting to mention the cause of death?

She bit her bottom lip, stopping herself from speaking.

Hurry up. We've got a case to solve.

Glances were working around the room. It seemed she wasn't the only one who was frustrated.

She waited.

Wallace went to another photo, this one of the victim's torso. He pointed.

"Stab wound, right there. It's two centimetres deep and four across." He turned to the room. "Too shallow. Not the cause of death."

Jade couldn't hold it in any longer.

"What *is* the cause of death?" she asked.

He looked at her, his eyes narrowing. *Yes, you asked me to be quiet,* she thought, *but that was before I knew how you conducted a briefing.*

"DI Tanner." He cast a glance around the room. "Does everyone know DI Tanner? Complex Crimes Unit?"

More murmuring. Jade had been introduced right at the beginning. So yes, they knew who she was. Not that she recognised anybody else.

"The cause of death?" she repeated.

Lyle nodded. "Asphyxiation."

"But there were no marks on his throat." None that she remembered from the photos she'd seen.

"Internal," he responded. "Something was shoved down his throat."

"*What* something?"

"A scrap of cloth. It was still lodged in his windpipe, too far down to be seen until he was opened up."

"Where is the scrap from?"

"If we knew that, we'd be a lot further ahead."

Jade drew in a breath. "So the knife wound is post-mortem." So much for the Macbeth references, with all the blood and stabbing.

"Correct."

"Do we have a time of death?"

"You're full of questions, DI Tanner."

"I just want to know what happened."

"You're supposed to be working on the psychology."

"Knowing how the killer chose to end the life of his victim will help us understand his psychology."

"I can't deny that. The pathologist puts death between late Monday evening, around 10pm and Tuesday morning, around 10am. Ish."

"Do we think the victim went up there alone and was then attacked?"

Lyle put a hand on the desk in front of him, fist clenched. "Thank you, DI Tanner." He looked away from her, at his team. "Let's get back to the post-mortem report." He gestured, and another slide came up.

Jade resisted a yawn. Were they going to be here all day?

A phone rang, off to the right. A hand went up, belonging to a young woman in a smart beige blazer. "Boss?"

"Answer it, DC Graham," he told her. "We'll wait."

I bet you will. Jade waited while the woman took the call, spoke quietly, then listened. She put the phone down. "It's a development, boss."

Wallace nodded. "Share it, then."

At last, some urgency. Jade listened, along with the rest of the team. The room had turned silent.

"They've got an ID on the body," DC Graham said. "Name of Harry Nolan, twenty-three years old. He fits the description of a man who was reported missing on Monday."

"How long has he been missing?" Wallace asked.

"Only since Monday morning. The call came in from a Christine McTavish, who claimed to be secretary of the Perthshire Macbeth Society."

Jade pulled in a breath. "Say that again," she said.

The DC turned to her. "Christine McTavish called 999 on Monday evening. She reported Harry missing. The victim was a member of the Society."

CHAPTER SEVENTEEN

Mo WAS IMPRESSED that Jade had managed to obtain Wallace's agreement for him to be the first detective to visit the victim's family. He was in a squad car with PC Decker from Perth police, a trained Family Liaison Officer. Jade had called him as he drove to Perth from Stirling and told him to tell anyone who asked that he was already in Perth.

"Fair enough, boss," he'd said. "What's the angle?"

"We don't think the family is suspicious," she replied. "But be observant anyway."

"D'you want me to pick Stuart up?"

"He's with me, in Dundee. There's an FLO waiting for you at Perth nick. I'd get over to the house quick, before DI Wallace changes his mind and sends someone else in."

He'd thought working with the Dundee CID team would be smooth. Jade's team were focusing on the evidence of the two experts, while Wallace's were handling almost everything else. But something had changed while Jade had been at that press conference. He wondered what.

They pulled up outside the family's house. It was a modest semi on the outskirts of Perth, with a block-paved driveway and hedges flanking the front garden.

"Park a few doors along," he said. "Let's not make this too much of a circus."

PC Decker parked the car along the street and waited. Mo looked into the rear-view mirror. It was a quiet street, with a few cars parked outside houses and two family groups walking along the pavement. One group passed them and peered inside the car.

He was about to blow the Nolan family's world apart.

This never got any easier.

He looked at his watch: 10:13am. He waited until 10:15, then turned to PC Decker. "You know the drill, I assume."

"You'll break the news, ask them questions to establish more about the family and their relationships. Find out if there's anything useful they know and when exactly their son went missing."

"Yes."

"I'll put the kettle on and offer words of support, while looking out for any evidence in the house."

Mo gave her a tight smile. PC Decker knew what she was doing. "How many times have you done this?"

"This'll be my eleventh. And yes, I still hate it. But I'm glad to offer some comfort to people."

Mo raised an eyebrow.

"And to help with the investigation," the PC added.

"It's a tough balancing act we perform. Here goes." Mo opened his door and walked around the car, waiting for PC Decker to join him. The two of them made their way to the front door of the house, to find it already opening.

A woman stood in the doorway, wearing a pink sweater and faded jeans. She looked drawn.

"I saw your car," she said. "I was wondering what you were waiting for."

"I'm sorry," Mo said. He drew out his ID. "I'm DS Mohammed Uddin. You can call me Mo. This is PC Decker."

"Grace," PC Decker added.

"Are you Mia Nolan?" Mo asked.

"I am. My ex-husband's here, and my daughter."

The house behind her was silent. Mo wondered if she and her ex got along, and how old the sister was. "Do you mind if we come in?"

"Please." The woman stepped back to let them through, then closed the door behind them.

A man with thinning blonde hair wearing a threadbare cardigan appeared in a doorway. "We've been wondering how long you'd take."

Mo stopped beside him. "You must be Craig Nolan."

"I am. You are...?" The man looked Mo up and down.

"DS Mo Uddin. And PC Grace Decker."

A grunt. "You'd better come in, then. Get this over with." His eyes were rimmed red.

Mo followed him into a living room which contained a beige three-piece suite and little else other than a large TV in the corner. Mia was hovering in the doorway.

PC Decker turned to her. "You can sit down. I'll make us all a cuppa."

"Oh. Yes, alright. Tea, please."

"Coffee for me. Soya milk," the man added.

"I don't have it in," his ex-wife said.

A muscle in his forehead twitched. "Make it black, then."

Mia looked at him, then down at her feet. The husband

and wife – *former* husband and wife – were sitting on the sofa, but at opposite ends, almost as far as they could get from one another. Mo sat in the armchair opposite them.

So that's the nature of the relationship. He wondered how long they'd been divorced.

"From the fact you were expecting us, I assume you know your son was reported missing on Tuesday," Mo began.

"He'll be the person you found on Dunsinane Hill," Mia said. "Amelia got me to watch it."

"Amelia?"

"Our daughter."

"She should be here," Craig said. "Shall I?"

His ex-wife nodded. He crossed to the doorway and called out. "Amy!"

After a moment, there was the sound of a door closing upstairs. Craig took his seat again.

"Here we are." PC Decker entered with two mugs.

"You don't want one?" Mia looked at Mo.

"Maybe later. Thanks."

"You're here to confirm that it's Harry, aren't you?" she asked him.

Mo leaned forward. "I'm afraid so. Our officers weren't sure at first, but Mrs McTavish, who reported him missing, she described some distinguishing features. We believe from those that it's him, but we will need you or your husband to make an identification, if you don't mind."

"Ex-husband," Craig said. "We divorced three years ago. We still see each other. Kids' birthdays, graduation, that kind of thing. We get along. Harry wasn't damaged by what happened."

"Did Harry live with either of you?"

Craig narrowed his eyes. "*Did*."

"No," Mia said. "He's got a studio flat in Dundee. A poky place. He doesn't let us visit." A pause. "Wouldn't. Didn't. Sorry. I can't, not yet. He says it's not nice enough, so he comes here. Or to Craig and Charlotte's place."

"Charlotte is my wife," husband said.

Both parents looked withdrawn and pale. Glancing between them, Mo could see four eyes rimmed with red, and deep circles beneath them.

A young woman appeared in the doorway. She had a shock of spiky orange hair and a black nose ring.

Craig looked up. "Amelia. This is DS Uddin and DC Decker."

"PC Decker," the PC corrected.

He shrugged. "They're here because of Harry."

The young woman leaned on the doorpost. "Is he...?"

Her mother reached out an arm. "Come here, lovely."

The young woman went to her mother and sat on her lap. She buried her face in the older woman's hair and the two of them sobbed.

Mo swallowed. He watched Craig, who was looking at his ex-wife and daughter, his expression sombre.

He turned to Mo. "Amy is our daughter. She lives with Mia half the time and with me the other half. She's doing her Highers."

The young woman looked round at Mo. She wiped her face with the loose sleeve of her cardigan. "How did he die?"

Mo took a breath. "We believe someone killed him."

The girl broke into sobs again. Her mother put a hand on her shoulder and rubbed it.

"That's what we thought," Craig said. "When we saw your operation on TV."

"An operation like that can mean many things," Mo told

him. "But in this case, we believe your son was killed by another individual. We are obviously working to find out who that is."

"No one we know," said the mother.

"Harry was reported missing by the secretary of the Perth Macbeth Society," Mo said. "Was he a student of Shakespeare?"

The young woman snorted. Her mother gave her a wary look.

"He was obsessed," said Mia. "He went to that society every week. They organised walks up Dunsinane Hill, for people from outside the local area. They invited visiting speakers." She sniffed. "He went up that hill at least twice a month."

Mo nodded. That made a scenario in which Harry had been killed after climbing the hill alone more plausible.

"Was the study of Shakespeare something he shared with the rest of the family?" Mo had noticed no books in the house so far, but that meant nothing.

The victim's mother shook her head. "It baffled us. Harry was a computer programmer. He didn't even do English at school. But he met a girl at university, she got him into it. Then when he graduated, he carried on. He loves all the history plays, but particularly Macbeth."

"Macbeth isn't really a history play," Craig corrected.

"Harry thought it was. He was determined to discover the true story of the real King Macbeth, and to prove that Shakespeare had it right."

Mo exchanged glances with PC Decker. They'd been discussing the possibility of the killer being a Macbeth nut. It hadn't occurred to any of them that the victim might be.

"He had plenty of friends who were obsessed with just that

one play, though," Amelia said. "They re-enacted the scenes. Proper creepy, some of them were."

Mo made notes in his pad. *Macbeth Society. Visiting speakers. Tourist walks. Re-enactments.* Maybe they were looking for a Macbeth nut after all.

CHAPTER EIGHTEEN

"You ALRIGHT THERE, boss? You look a bit peaky."

"I'm fine." Jade sipped her coffee and gave Stuart a smile. Truth was, she was exhausted. She'd slept badly, the case tossing around in her head as they so often did in the early stages, and she was missing home. The hotel bed was hard and uncomfortable, and she wanted to cuddle up with Rory and sleep all day.

But now they had an ID and a concrete lead. The Perth Macbeth Society.

She and Stuart were in a Starbucks on Perth's main shopping street. The place was half empty, just a few mums with toddlers and a couple of students pretending to study as they sat round a large table at the back. The pensioners were all over the road, in the Costa. It had been fifty-fifty between the two establishments as they had approached, but the queue spilling out of Costa's door onto the street had decided it.

"We need to get the team together," she said. "Work out how to approach this Macbeth Society."

Stuart dipped his head and lowered his voice. "There might be members all around us right now."

Jade cast her eye around the coffee shop. The nearest table was occupied by a mum trying to negotiate with a red-faced toddler over whether he was going to eat an apple or a muffin first. The students had given up all pretence of studying and were engaged in throwing screwed up balls of paper at each other.

She shook her head. "I doubt it."

"We need to track them down though, surely."

"We do. First, let's find out what the victim's family had to say to Mo, then we can speak to this Christine McTavish."

"She must have been close to him, to report him missing."

Jade shrugged. "Secretary to a club like that, doesn't sound like another young person. So how did she know he was missing?"

"Maybe he didn't turn up to a meeting."

"That's quite a jump, to go from missing a meeting to calling the police."

Stuart shrugged. "Only way to find out is to ask her." He picked up his phone from the table, downing the last of his Americano. "I can check in with Patty, find out what she said on the call reporting his absence."

"Do that." Jade ran her finger around the rim of her mug. "Put me on speaker."

Stuart looked around the room. "You're sure?"

"I'm sure."

A few minutes later, Stuart's phone was on the table between them and Patty's voice was ringing out, tinny and distorted at the volume he'd set the phone to.

"That's right," Patty said. "She said she'd worried when he

didn't turn up to a regular meeting of the Society. She tried his mobile but got no answer."

"And when was that?" Jade asked.

"Tuesday night."

"So he was reported missing on Tuesday night, after he was killed." Jade's head was low over the table, but she looked up to check if anyone was listening. The toddler with the muffin was in full meltdown now, drowning out anything anyone might overhear.

"That's right," Patty said.

"Did she say anything else, about their relationship or any specific reason she was worried about him? I don't imagine it was taken seriously, after just one day."

"It wasn't," Patty confirmed. "She called again yesterday. And then I imagine someone put two and two together."

Indeed. "I assume we have an address for her?"

Patty read out an address in Perth.

"That's only a mile from here," Stuart muttered.

Jade nodded. "Good. We'll go talk to her. Stuart, can you call Mo as well? I want to know if the family has any connections to all this Macbeth business."

"No problem." He picked up his phone and frowned into it as he connected Mo to the call.

"Stuart," Mo said as the phone went back down onto the table.

"It's both of us," Jade said. "Patty's on speaker. Can you hear us? We're in a Starbucks in Perth and we don't want to shout."

"Heya, Sarge," Patty said.

"Hi, Patty," Mo replied. "Yes, I can hear you all."

"Good. How'd you get on with the family?"

"I don't think they're suspicious. PC Decker is in there now, offering sympathy and keeping an eye on them. The family dynamic is a bit odd, parents divorced but claim they get on."

"Could that be relevant?" Stuart asked.

"It could," said Mo, "but it didn't feel like it. They were all shocked."

"OK," said Jade. "I'm sure DI Wallace's team will watch them. What about the Macbeth Society? Are the rest of the family members too?"

"No," Mo replied. "They were slightly baffled by it all. Harry was a computer programmer, did a Computer Science degree at Glasgow. Apparently he met a girl, she got him into Macbeth, then when he came back home after uni he got in with this Macbeth Society lot."

"What did the family have to say about them?"

"Not much. I don't think they'd met any of them. But I got the impression the dad thought they were a bunch of nuts."

"In what way?"

"He told me the kind of things they do. Macbeth-themed walks. Re-enactments in the pertinent spots. Cauldrons, witches, that kind of thing. Dunsinane Hill featured large in it all."

"He'd been there before, then?"

"Regularly. Apparently Harry went walking up there about twice a month."

Jade nodded. "So that means he might have been up there already, when the killer came upon him."

"Boss," Stuart muttered, jerking his head. The woman at the next table, whose toddler was now quietly munching its way through the muffin and covering himself in chocolate, was listening in. She'd flinched at the word *killer*.

Damn. "Look, folks, we can't stay in here. We need to

follow up on this Society. Find out who the members were, who he was close to. Patty, can you do some digging?"

"Certainly, boss."

"And there's the ecologist's analysis too," said Mo. "We haven't had that in yet."

"No. Can you follow up on that? Have a chat with her. I want to know if any specific part of Birnam Wood is a potential crime scene."

"It's looking like Harry wasn't taken there," said Stuart.

"It is," Jade confirmed. "But let's just dot the I's and cross the T's, yes?"

"Yes, boss," Mo said.

"Good. Let me know when you've got anything new. Keep in touch, everyone."

CHAPTER NINETEEN

ANTHONY URQUHART OCCUPIED A LARGE, soulless office in a modern tower Petra had walked past many times but never entered. He had a view across the city to the Tay, which made the room feel even colder than it was. Petra sat in a flimsy chair at a Formica table as he pootled around with a kettle in the corner and made tea.

"Don't tell anyone I've got this thing," he said in an Edinburgh accent. "It hasn't been PAT tested."

She smiled, remembering her own time as an academic. She'd worked in the Scrymgeour Building, a couple of minutes' walk north of here and blessed with considerably more character.

Mind you, he still had a job, and she didn't. *Less of the smugness.*

She looked past him at the view. A stiff breeze, the kind English people would call a gale, pushed clouds over the Tay towards Fife. She'd been caught in a shower on the way in and had cursed the fact she hadn't brought an umbrella.

This was Scotland in April. She was a fool not to be prepared.

"Here you are," Urquhart said, placing a china cup and saucer on the table in front of her. "It's not the best. I had to go to the Premier for tea bags as I ran out of my usual."

"What is your usual?"

He raised an eyebrow. "Clipper organic English Breakfast."

"Ah." Petra nodded as if in agreement. Truth was, she had no idea what one brand of tea tasted like compared to another. But she found the psychology of people who did, interesting. Could they really taste a difference? Or was it just a way of seeking comfort, or perhaps marking themselves out as special?

She drank from her cup. He was right; it was bad. But that was mainly because the milk was turning. He might have smuggled in a contraband kettle, but it seemed Urquhart didn't have access to a fridge.

He settled down in the chair opposite her, shuffled a few times to get comfortable, and placed his hands on either side of his cup. He tapped out a beat on the table with a finger.

"You're a friend of Magdalena Kaminski?" he asked.

"She suggested you might be able to help me with something."

"Right." He glanced up at a clock on the wall. "I've got fifteen minutes before my next seminar. So fire away. You're a doctor in the Psychology department, if I remember correctly?"

Petra felt her heart sink. "Sadly, no longer."

"Budget cuts." Urquhart pulled a face. His skin was mainly grey, with pinpricks of pink on his cheeks. "Comes to us all, eventually."

Petra surveyed the bare room again. Maybe budget cuts took more than one form.

"What are you doing now, then?" he asked. "Some psychological study of elderly men, and you need my invaluable input?" His eyes twinkled.

"Nothing like that," she said, catching herself before uttering the word *dull.* Psychological studies of elderly men? Maybe someone somewhere undertook that sort of work, but certainly no one she'd come across.

"I'm working as a consultant for Police Scotland," she told him, noticing him perk up as she spoke. It always got people's attention: not a washed-up academic out of work, but a criminal profiler. "And they've asked for my opinion on a recent murder case."

"The Macbeth murder," he said, then cleared his throat. "Sorry, that was tasteless. That poor man."

Petra narrowed her eyes. "How did you know about the Macbeth connection?" Jade had told her there'd been no mention of Birnam Wood or the needles in the press conference.

He looked at her. "You haven't seen the news? The young man was a member of a club that celebrated all things Macbeth. Journalists have been doorstepping the officers of the organisation."

"Really?"

Urquhart nodded and stood to go to his desk. He fired up his desktop computer – elderly and attached by wire to a CRT monitor, Petra noted. Most academics she knew were no longer forced to use technology quite as antiquated as this. Which told her something about Urquhart.

"Here," he said, bringing up the website for the Dundee Courier. Petra stood behind him and read.

There was no real news, nothing of any substance. Clearly, the press was trying to learn more about any Macbeth connection, and the victim's links to the local Macbeth Society. But no one had picked up on the Birnam Wood link yet.

Good.

She looked at Urquhart as he scrolled down the screen, tongue between his lips. Could she trust him?

No. He was too intrigued by the whole thing. She'd ask him for information but offer none of her own.

"Bugger," he said. "I need to prepare for that seminar. Maybe we can pick this up later, if you're not too busy with your police work?"

"You don't know what it is I want to ask you about yet."

He span round in his chair, his foot brushing against her shin. "It doesn't take a psychologist to work that one out. You're investigating the death of a young man obsessed with Macbeth, in a key location from the play. I'm an English professor and one of Scotland's foremost experts on the text. You want my input."

Petra drew back, resisting the urge to rub her ankle. Her tights would be laddered.

Bloody man.

"Something like that," she said.

"Are Police Scotland paying for this kind of advice? I imagine they're compensating you generously, if you've given up your academic job."

She smiled. So that was what this was about. "All I need from you is some advice, not full-blown consultancy. I'm afraid there's no budget for that." She cocked her head. "But surely helping solve the murder of an innocent young man is reward enough."

Urquhart laughed. "You have such a way of putting things, Dr McBride. How is a man supposed to refuse, when you appeal to his conscience like that? 'Thus conscience does make cowards of us all'. Hamlet, Act III, Scene 3."

Petra wanted to roll her eyes. Instead, she carried on looking at him, waiting for an answer.

"I can give you some help," he said. "But I am a very busy man."

Of course you are. They all were. It didn't take a psychological study of middle-aged men in university departments to tell her that.

"Thank you," she said. "I appreciate it."

CHAPTER TWENTY

JADE AND STUART stood outside a slim terraced house on the western edge of Perth. The street had a mix of properties: smart, renovated houses and shabbier ones with multiple door-bells. This one had two doorbells, and Christine McTavish's was for the ground floor.

The door opened and a woman in her thirties with a shock of green hair appeared, her body language tense. She looked over their heads to the street.

"I'm not speaking to the press," she said.

Jade pulled out her ID. "We're from Police Scotland. DI Tanner and DC Burns."

The woman looked over their heads again. "Really? Only I've already had two journalists knocking on my door since your bloody press conference."

"I can assure you we are police detectives. I assume you're Christine McTavish?"

The woman looked Jade up and down. "That's me. What d'you want? I told them everything on the phone."

"You reported Harry Nolan missing."

"Like I say, I told them ever—"

"I'm very sorry for your loss. And I'm sorry to be disturbing you at this time."

The woman's face screwed up. "Too right."

"But we'd like to know about more about him. If you don't mind."

Another long look. "I've only got half an hour before I need to get to work."

"We'll be quick."

Jade exchanged glances with Stuart then followed the woman into the house. The hallway was tiny, with two doors leading off. Christine took them through one that led into an even smaller lobby and then a living room at the front.

She drew the curtains. "Don't want anyone watching."

"I can imagine," Stuart muttered.

The woman looked at him. "What did you say your names were, again?"

"I'm DI Jade Tanner. This is DC Stuart Burns."

"Hmm. OK. Get on with it, then." She sat down heavily in an armchair.

Jade and Stuart took the sofa opposite her. "Have you been told that we found Harry's body on Dunsinane Hill?" Jade asked.

"Yes."

"We have reason to believe that someone killed him."

"I know. I saw your press conference."

"I'm hoping you can provide us with information to help us find out who that was."

"It wasn't anyone in the Society, if that's what you're thinking."

"We weren't thinking anything." Jade felt out of breath just keeping up with this woman. Why was she so angry?

"You must be thinking something, or you wouldn't be knocking on my door."

Jade swallowed. "How well did you know Harry?"

"He was a good friend. A regular attendee."

"Of the Perth Macbeth Society."

"I know you think we're a bunch of obsessives. But we conduct rigorous academic work. We run tours and guided walks, we contribute to the local economy. We—"

"No one is questioning your Society's validity," Jade told her.

"Hmm."

"You reported Harry missing after he didn't show up for a meeting, is that right?"

"Tuesday night. We meet fortnightly, and we organise walks in the intervening weeks. Harry has been attending for four years and in all that time he's never missed a meeting."

"So you worried."

"Wouldn't you? I called his mobile, but there was no answer. So I called the police. Not that you took me seriously."

"It's normal procedure with an adult to wait twenty-four hours be—"

"If you'd listened to me on Tuesday night, Harry would be alive now."

Ah. So that was the reason for the anger.

Jade drew in a breath. "The pathologist has estimated that Harry died on Monday night. He was found on Tuesday lunchtime. I'm afraid there was nothing we c—"

"That's not what they told me the second time I called."

"That might have been before we had all the information. I'm sorry if—"

"I need to go to work. I think you should leave."

Jade took out her business card and held it out. Christine made no attempt to take it from her.

"It would be helpful if we could come back later, after you've finished work. If you can give us some background on the kind of man Harry was and his walking habits, it might help us t—"

"He went up there every week. He loved it. Is that enough for you?" Christine stood up. "Now, please leave."

She steered them towards the door. Unable to argue, Jade and Stuart allowed themselves to be ushered out onto the pavement.

The door closed behind them.

"Who ate her smarties?" Stuart said.

"She blames us."

"It's not our fault."

Jade shook her head. "People don't think logically, when they've lost someone." She knew that herself, from Dan's death.

"No." Stuart wrinkled his nose. "Sorry, boss."

Jade frowned at him. "You don't have to do that. Now let's just hope we can track down some other members of this Macbeth Society so we can find out more."

CHAPTER TWENTY-ONE

It felt strange, being back amongst the buildings of Dundee University.

Petra's first instinct was to head to her old department in the Scrymgeour Building. She wasn't sure if that was because she wanted to see her old colleagues, or purely out of habit.

Habit, most likely.

She paused outside the Tower Building, where she'd met Urquhart. Her old office was around a corner and down a narrow service road, invisible from here.

No.

She shook herself out, turned and started in the other direction. Magdalena's place was a twenty-minute walk and the sun was out, for once. She'd clear her head. Maybe ponder the case while she walked.

As she passed the Lemmings Statues looking out over the Tay, her phone rang.

She took it out of her bag: number withheld.

"Fuck off." She hit Ignore and shoved the phone back into her bag.

The calls hadn't come for months. She'd allowed herself to hope they were over. There'd been calls to her flat last year, and Petra had been convinced she'd seen someone. But that had only been the once; she might have been imagining things.

She realised her fists were clenched and her jaw was tight. She stopped walking and rubbed her cheeks. A headache was forming.

Aila. She'd call her girlfriend. That would cheer her up.

The phone was answered on the third ring.

"Hello, lovey," Aila said. "Can I call you back in a bit? I'm in the middle of something."

Aila was a banker. She'd be at work.

"Sorry," Petra said. "You in a meeting?"

"Oh no, nothing like that. I've had to take Monty to the vet. He got into a fight last night and there's a nasty wound on his ear." Her voice changed tone. "You've been in the wars, haven't you, honeybun? Mummy will get it all fixed for you."

Petra winced. When she'd met Aila, there'd been mention of a cat. But the cutesie voice...

Aila never spoke to *her* like that.

Stop it. Aila was gorgeous. She was funny, and clever, and she adored Petra. It was looking like this was a relationship that might last.

"Oh, Monty! Was that a furball? Poor baby."

"Are you still talking to the cat?" Petra asked.

"I should hope so," Aila replied. "Unless you've got a furball. How's your case going?"

Petra breathed a sigh of relief. Grown-up talk. Thank hell for that. "It's OK," she said. "I've brought in an academic who might be able to give some insight into the text."

"Macbeth."

"That's the one. It's odd though, being at my old university."

"Which one is that again?"

Petra paused for a step. She'd told Aila all about how she'd lost her job at Dundee. She knew she had.

"Dundee, hen."

"Ah. Yes, I remember. Oh! Monty is rubbing up against me, I think he's happier now. The vet's given him antibiotics, costs a fortune. But it's worth it, isn't it, gorgeous?"

Petra had a feeling it wasn't her who was being described as *gorgeous*. She felt her jaw clench again, tighter than when she'd been thinking about her old job.

"I need to go," she lied. "Another call."

"OK. When will you be home?"

"A couple of days I imagine. Looking forward to seeing you."

"Me too. And so is Monty."

Petra rolled her eyes and hung up.

She held her phone in front of her, wishing she hadn't lied to Aila. She needed to say something about that damn cat, tell her girlfriend that while she didn't have a problem with the existence of the thing, she didn't enjoy playing second fiddle to it.

Her phone rang. She dropped it in surprise, then bent to pick it up.

Number withheld. Again.

She gritted her teeth.

Answer it. Tell them to bugger off.

The police had told her to do the exact opposite.

What did the police know?

Petra hit Answer and held the phone to her ear, silent. She

was further along Perth Road now, shops and cafes on either side.

All she could hear was breathing.

"Who are you?" she snapped. "Why do you keep calling me?"

No response.

"I'll call the police again. They'll be able to track down your number. You're breaking the law."

She swallowed.

The person at the other end of the line cleared their throat.

Petra held her breath.

"Speak to me," she said. "Tell me what this is about."

"You know what it's about." A woman's voice. "And you know what you did."

The line went dead.

CHAPTER TWENTY-TWO

"IT's all bound up with this Macbeth Society, I'm sure of it," Mo said. Jade had him on speakerphone as she sat in the car park of a tractor company at the side of the A94 to Perth. She'd seen signs to Perth airport and wondered how big it was. No sound of any planes.

"What do the family say about them?" Jade asked.

"They aren't keen. Harry didn't live at home anymore, so they didn't know quite how often he went. But I think he talked to his sister about it."

"Does she still live there?"

"She does."

"Is the FLO keeping an eye on her?"

"PC Decker. She is, yes. I'm calling her every few hours, for an update."

"Good." Jade leaned back in her seat. Stuart was next to her, on his phone, investigating the Macbeth Society.

"Have you heard anything more from Petra?" Mo asked. "Do we need her to talk to the family?"

"I'm not sure about the family. But it might be useful to get her in a room with some of the Macbeth Society people. Not least Christine McTavish. She wasn't exactly pleased to see us."

Stuart looked up from his screen. "She practically kicked us out. I think it's suspicious."

"How so?" Mo asked.

Stuart shook his head. "She didn't want to be questioned. She said it was cos she'd been doorstepped by the press, but I didn't see any evidence of them."

"In that case," Jade said, "we need to speak to other members of the Society. See what they have to say, if they'll be more helpful."

"There's a meeting tonight," Stuart said.

Jade turned to him. "Of the Society?"

He nodded. "There's a statement on their website, and their Meetup page too. They're holding a vigil for Harry."

"What kind of vigil?"

"It's at the bottom of the hill."

"Good job it's not at the top," she said.

He looked up. "You're worried about contamination?"

"I'm worried about you having to trudge all the way up there."

His eyes widened. "I'm going?"

"You and the sarge. That OK with you, Mo?"

"That's fine. What time is it?"

"Six-thirty," Stuart said.

"Early," Mo replied. "That'll be fine."

"But first I'd like you to make contact," Jade said. She looked at Stuart. "I'm going to head back to base, keep Patty from feeling like we've abandoned her. We don't all need to be out here."

She didn't tell him that she was missing her son and felt bad for leaving him with her mum.

"That's fine," Mo told her. "You know I live just as close to here as to the office."

"Good. Stuart, I'm going to take you to where Mo is. The two of you can make more house calls, see if anyone else from the Macbeth Society might be willing to talk to us."

"There's a Chair," said Stuart. "Lachlan Kerr."

"Let's speak to him," Mo said. "See if he's more amenable."

Stuart put his phone away and sat up in his seat. "He's in Methven. Other side of Perth." He leaned forward and started typing the address into the satnav. "Sarge, shall we meet you there?"

"You're making yourself comfortable in my car," Jade told him.

His fingers stopped moving. "Sorry, boss. Would you rather do it yourself?"

She smiled. "No. I like that you don't need asking. Carry on."

"There's a Morrisons in Perth," Mo said. "I'll meet you in the car park."

"See you shortly," Jade told him.

Mo hung up.

"Stuart," she said. "You OK to hang around here, take over my hotel room?"

He smiled. "Course, boss."

"Good." She started the car.

"And I'll do another online search while you drive, see what I can find out about this Lachlan Kerr."

"You do that."

CHAPTER TWENTY-THREE

PETRA HAD BEEN at Magdalena's flat for all of ten minutes before she decided to go out again.

It felt odd being in someone else's deserted flat during the day. No matter how good a friend Magdalena was, and no matter how many times she'd told Petra it was fine.

She shrugged on her coat – a purple pea coat that matched her blouse – and headed down to the street. Magdalena lived in a converted terrace in Dundee's west end and there was a coffee shop a few minutes away. Petra had her laptop with her; she'd work on her report for Jade while enjoying an espresso.

As she joined the queue, her phone rang.

She pulled it out, hoping it wasn't her mystery caller again.

The number was familiar.

"Professor Urquhart," she said. "Good to hear from you."

"Dr McBride," he replied. "I've been thinking."

"You have?"

"I have a quiet week next week, it's reading week for the students. And my research project can be put to one side for a short period of time."

Petra had reached the front of the queue. She pointed to an almond tart and mouthed 'espresso'. The woman behind the counter nodded and turned to the coffee machine.

"You told me you were a busy man." Petra smiled. She'd piqued his interest.

"And that's still true," he replied. "But I can move things around to help a former colleague."

"There's no budget, remember."

"That's not an issue. This will be something to entertain my students."

Petra held her credit card to the reader and took her plate. She shuffled along the counter to wait for her coffee.

"You'll be required to keep details of the case confidential," she said.

"Of course. I won't provide them any detail. Cross my heart."

Could she detect excitement?

"A young man died, Professor Urquhart."

"Call me Anthony. And yes, I do realise that this is a tragic event."

His voice didn't echo his words.

Bloody academics, Petra thought. She knew; she was one of them herself.

"Well, that's good news," she said. "Can we meet again, later today?"

"We can do better than that."

Petra thanked the barista as her coffee was handed over. She wedged her phone under her chin and picked it up, heading for the nearest table.

"How d'you mean?" She plonked her bag onto the table and almost upended the coffee.

"Where are you?"

"A coffee shop in the west end. You want to meet here?"

"I want to take you for a walk. Are you wearing sturdy shoes?"

Petra sighed. *Not again.* "Not right now, Anthony, but I can fetch them."

"Send me your location and wait fifteen minutes. I'll pick you up."

He hung up.

"Dear God," Petra muttered. The elderly woman at the next table gave her a harsh look, which she returned with an insincere smile.

Anthony Urquhart fancied himself as the next Sherlock Holmes. And now he was treating a real-life murder case like some kind of adventure.

Had she done the wrong thing?

CHAPTER TWENTY-FOUR

"POOR LAD. It's just such a shame."

Mo and Stuart were in Lachlan Kerr's living room, sipping bitter coffee. Mo had tried to put their host off making it, but the man had insisted.

The house looked out over fields to the back, bounded by woodland. The living room had wide windows and chairs arranged to make the most of the view.

"Did you know him well?" Mo asked the man.

Lachlan shook his head, slurping his coffee. "Not really. He dealt with Christine more than me. Never spoke at the meetings, never took a role in the walks we run. Bit of a shrinking violet. But he was keen."

"He came to every meeting, I gather."

"He did." Lachlan stared out of the window. "The group will be horrified."

"You've got a special meeting tonight," Stuart said.

Lachlan turned to him, blinking as if he'd forgotten Stuart was in the room. "What's that?"

"A memorial," Stuart said. "I read about it on your website."

Lachlan sat forward. "Aye. Yes, we have. Wanted to remember the lad, you know."

"I was impressed by how quickly you managed to make that happen," Mo said.

"You were? Well, it's important to be timely with these things. Don't dawdle, that's what I always say." He slurped again and looked out of the window. "Birnam Wood is up that way, you know."

Mo made eye contact with Stuart. The information about Birnam Wood hadn't been released to the public.

"Can you show us?" Stuart asked.

Lachlan stood and crossed to the window, pointing. "Past Tavern Wood, to the north. Beautiful forested area. We run the occasional guided walk there, but the hill's more popular." He turned to Mo. "Last summer we had a weekend trip to Inverness. For the castle, you know."

"Is that in the play?" Mo asked.

"Inverness Castle," Stuart interrupted. "It's where Macbeth killed King Duncan."

Lachlan's eyes lit up. "So it is." He smiled, his expression pensive. "'I have done the deed. Didst thou not hear a noise?' The place feels like something momentous happened there, y'know? Like the walls are breathing history."

Stuart nodded. "The history of Scotland."

Mo was puzzled. "So did the real King Macbeth kill anyone in the castle?"

Lachlan turned to him. "Macbeth's forces killed Duncan alright, back in 1040. Not in the castle though; in battle."

"So it's the Shakespeare play people are interested in."

"Most of them, yes. Some like the history, and there's a fair few who are surprised to know there was a real Macbeth, and get very excited to think it might all have been true." Lachlan chuckled. "But he made it all up, the old bastard."

"Going back to Harry Nolan…" Mo said.

Lachlan looked up, as if suddenly remembering why the police officers were there. "Oh. Yes, of course."

"Did he have any particular friends in the group? Or anyone he'd fallen out with?"

"Not that I know of. Like I say, he kept himself to himself. Not sure he really made friends with anyone." He took off his glasses and wiped them with the hem of his sweater, then frowned before putting them back on. "Sorry."

"It's fine." Mo put down his unfinished mug of coffee and stood up. "Well, we won't be taking up any more of your time. But we will be coming along this evening. It would be nice to pay our respects."

Lachlan looked at him. "And watch our members, see if anyone's up to something shifty, eh?"

Mo said nothing.

"We won't intrude," Stuart said, still in his chair.

Mo jerked his head. "Come on, Constable."

"Sorry, Sarge." Stuart stood up. "Thanks for your time, Mr Kerr."

"My pleasure. It's not often you get this sort of excitement around here."

Not excitement, thought Mo. But he said nothing.

"Thanks for your help, Mr Kerr. We'll see you later."

CHAPTER TWENTY-FIVE

Patty didn't like being in the office on her own.

She'd never been much for working alone, and this office was so quiet when unoccupied that it was spooky.

She'd turned on all the lights when she'd arrived this morning, and was playing Radio 2 through the speakers in her laptop. It sounded tinny and inadequate in the large open plan office, but it was company.

She was looking into the Macbeth Society and its members. Stuart had sent her a membership list, provided reluctantly by Christine McTavish, and she was checking the system to see if any of them had a criminal record.

Chance would be a fine thing.

Most of them were retirees, nothing more to do with their time than obsess over a play written more than four centuries ago. A play that she imagined most people would never want to read again once they'd been forced to plough through it at school.

She'd had to read it, and write essays on the bloody thing, when she'd been doing her Nationals. *Compare and contrast*

Macbeth and MacDuff's actions in the fifth act of Macbeth. Give examples of blood references in Macbeth and describe what they signify. The memory of it made her shudder.

Still. She'd scraped a pass, and it had been enough to get her a police job. Funnily enough, she'd never once used her knowledge of Macbeth since.

She was pulling up a complaint made by an octogenarian member of the Society against his neighbour in Craigieholm when the buzzer sounded.

She looked up, puzzled. The DI was on her way, but wouldn't be back for another hour. And Stuart and the Sarge weren't due back for days.

Petra, maybe?

No. She was staying with a friend in Dundee.

Patty walked to the door and pressed the intercom button.

"Police Scotland, Complex Crimes Unit."

"Is that Jade?"

"It's Patty. DC Henderson. Who is this?"

"It's Dr Moreau. Carla. I was hoping to speak to DI Tanner."

"She's not here. Come in."

Patty pressed the button to open the door downstairs and waited for Carla to climb the flight of stairs leading up to their office. They occupied the first floor of this building, while the ground floor remained empty.

"Patty," Carla said when she arrived. "Good to see you."

"You too. You got news for us?"

"I have." Carla looked around the office. "Wow. This place is seriously empty."

Patty shrugged. "It's private. That seems to be what the high-ups wanted for us."

"Your unit is secret?" Carla walked towards the bank of

desks Patty and Stuart used. Beyond it was the meeting room, and the office the DI occupied when she was here.

"Not secret. But there's politics. Internal politics. I don't think the rest of Police Scotland really wants us around."

"Why not?" Carla ran her hand across the back of Stuart's chair.

Are you always this nosey?

"Not sure. I don't let it worry me. Long as I've got a case to work on, that's all that matters."

"And you have here." Carla nodded, her expression vague.

"We have. Like I said, have you got some news for us? Have you made progress on the plant evidence?"

Carla smiled. "I have." She lifted the laptop bag in her hand. "Can I show you?"

"Of course." Patty walked to her desk. "Sit here." She paused. "In fact, let's go into the meeting room. You can project it."

"It's only some soil analysis and a set of photos."

"That's fine. You show it to me, and we can take it from there."

"Good." Carla walked to the meeting room and pushed the door open. Patty followed her in as the ecologist plugged her laptop into the projector and scrolled through some images.

"Here," she said. The screen showed a graph with a series of peaks and troughs.

"You'll have to explain all this," Patty said.

"Of course. This is the composition of the soil attached to the needles we found in the victim's pocket. I found high levels of microorganisms and organic matter, and lower concentrations of nutrients like nitrogen and phosphorous. Compared to the Dunsinane Hill soil, the pH is more acidic."

"So the soil didn't come from the spot where he was found."

"No. I've also been to the three alternative sites I identified, and analysed samples from those." She brought up another screen, this time with three graphs, one in each quadrant except the top left. "See?"

"I do."

"Now let's fill in the gap." Carla clicked a button and a fourth graph appeared. It looked identical to the first one.

"That's the soil from his pockets," Patty said.

Carla turned to her, her eyes bright. "No. It's soil from the site of an ancient hill fort in Birnam Wood."

Right. "Go back to the last one," Patty said.

Carla smiled. "You're getting the idea." She clicked back to the previous graph. "Now let me go forwards."

She brought up the screen with four graphs, then clicked again to bring up two graphs, side by side. "The soil in Harry Nolan's pockets, and the soil from Birnam Wood. Identical, to within a ninety per cent margin."

"So that soil came from the wood."

"It did." Carla swivelled in her chair to face Patty.

"Good. There's a problem, though."

Carla's expression dropped. "There is?"

"I've been researching the Perth Macbeth Society. Harry Nolan was an active member."

"There's a local Macbeth Society?"

"There is. They meet once a fortnight, and on the intervening weeks they go for walks at the locations in the play. They act out scenes at the key spots."

"Fanatics."

"Some of them are. I think Harry was. But the reason it's a problem—"

"Is that those needles could have got there when he was at the Wood with the Society."

"Exactly," said Patty.

Carla clicked her laptop's trackpad and skimmed through a set of slides. She stopped at a photo.

"This is the contents of Harry's pockets," she said.

"Yes," Patty replied.

Carla pointed with a pen. "The needles are green."

"They are."

"If he'd picked them up from the Birnam Wood site a couple of weeks earlier, they would have been browning."

"It might have been more recently." Petra considered. "Wait a moment."

She went out to her desk and woke her PC. She brought up the schedule for the Macbeth Society's meetings.

Carla was behind her, leaning on the back of her chair. "Their walking schedule."

Patty nodded. On Tuesday night there'd been a meeting. The last organised walk before that had been to Moncrieffe Hill, the Tuesday before that. Not Birnam Wood.

"Why Moncrieffe?" Carla asked.

"It says the heath is similar to the one where Macbeth meets the witches."

"I've been there. It's nothing like it. And besides, wouldn't that be further north?"

Patty turned in her chair. "How would anyone know?" She remembered the descriptions in the opening scene: all it said was 'a heath'.

"Fair point."

Patty scrolled up to see earlier dates. The last time the Society had visited Birnam Wood was in February. Trips to

Dunsinane Hill were far more frequent. As were trips to the Three Witches tearoom, it seemed.

Even Macbeth nuts needed their fix of tea and cake.

"If he'd been there that long ago, the needles would have dried out," Carla said. "These were fresh."

"So unless he went there alone in the last couple of days before he died..." Patty began.

"... it was his killer who gathered those needles from Birnam Wood and put them in his pockets. And now we know which part of the wood they came from."

CHAPTER TWENTY-SIX

NOT AGAIN.

Petra looked out of the window of Anthony Urquhart's elderly red Jaguar XJS, towards Dunsinane Hill. The car park was quiet now, the police vehicles gone. The sun had disappeared behind a bank of clouds and the hill looked almost as eerie as Shakespeare would have imagined it.

Certainly just as forbidding.

"I'm not walking all the way up there," she said.

"We should," Urquhart replied. "It'll help us to understand the mind of the killer." He opened his door and sprang out.

Petra sighed. It had been bad enough, Jade wanting her to come here. She'd brought Anthony in for his knowledge of the play. Not for a hillwalking companion.

She sat back in her seat and folded her arms across her chest.

Urquhart opened the passenger door.

"Have you seen the length of these legs?" She pointed down at her feet.

"You fetched sturdy shoes specially. Why else do you think I drove you all the way up here?"

She clenched her jaw.

He shrugged. "Fair enough. I'll head up there on my own." He closed her door.

She watched him stride towards a metal gate and push open the kissing gate beside it. He glanced back and beckoned as he went through, a smile on his face.

Why is everyone so happy about this poor wee guy getting himself killed?

Urquhart paused to watch her for a moment. Petra turned to look out of the front window. He shrugged and continued walking.

She watched him recede up the hill. After five minutes, during which he didn't turn once, she threw open her door in irritation.

"Professor!" she called.

He continued walking.

"Anthony!"

No response.

"Fuck him." She grabbed her phone and dialled.

"Dr McBride." Urquhart stopped walking, his phone to his ear. He turned and waved.

"Wait for me," she said.

Truth was, she'd been regretting not going up there yesterday. Petra never missed an opportunity to visit a crime scene and try to see it through the eyes of the killer, to feel it through their skin and bones. And yesterday, thanks to her lack of fitness, she'd missed out.

"Stay right where you are," she told him. "I don't want you gallivanting up there without me."

"I swear I will remain in this exact spot until you join me."
There was laughter in his voice.

Insolent bastard.

Petra plunged her phone into her pocket and went to the
boot of the car. She pulled out a waterproof jacket. Urquhart
hadn't stopped to put on anything more than the tweed coat he
was wearing, and those clouds looked ominous.

Coming up here in the first place was one thing. Letting
the weather get the better of her was something else entirely.

She squeezed through the kissing gate – *damn these things*
– and started up the hill, deliberately taking it slowly. All her
instincts were screaming at her to hurry up and catch him, but
she knew she'd regret it if she did.

When she arrived at the spot he'd stopped in, she was only
a little out of breath and secretly quite impressed with herself.

"I'm coming with you," she said.

"Glad to hear it." He fished in the inside pocket of his coat.
"Fancy a mint?"

She took a mint, glad of an opportunity to rest. When she
was halfway through sucking it, he clapped his hands.

"Chop, chop," he said. "Let's not let those clouds catch us."

"Your coat will be ruined," she told him.

He waved in dismissal. "Coats can be replaced."

Really? It looked expensive. Maybe she should have
worked her way up to Professor.

They took the hill slowly, Urquhart occasionally stopping
to wait for Petra to catch up. To their left was a wood. Ahead of
them, nothing but interminable hill.

Petra stopped. "Jesus Christ, this hill is a bastard."

Anthony laughed. "It's a bit steep, yes. But you're making
good progress."

"Doesn't bloody feel like it."

He offered a hand and pulled her over a muddy patch. "You'll be fine. It'll be worth it."

Petra grunted but didn't stop walking. *Keep moving*, she told herself. If she stopped, she might never start again.

"So," he said. "Dunsinane Hill. There was a fort up here, in the iron age. Not in Shakespeare's day, or even King Macbeth's."

"Is that how you differentiate?" she asked. "By using the title?"

"The fictional version of Macbeth was a king, too. But it's true, we don't think of Shakespeare's villain as King Macbeth, do we? So yes, I suppose that's what I do." He cocked his head. "You're perceptive, aren't you?"

"It's my job. Tell me more about the play."

"Macbeth has a castle in Inverness before he becomes king. He has land in what was Morayshire, and possibly another castle near Forres. Inverness is where we tend to assume the murder takes place. But after becoming king he moves here, to Dunsinane."

"And the witches make their prophecy."

"They do indeed."

They reached the end of a wood they'd been following to their left. Ahead of them was thick gorse. Petra steeled herself.

"Keep going," she said, walking ahead of him.

"The witches said Macbeth would be safe on two conditions. First that Birnam Wood doesn't come to Dunsinane. Second that he isn't challenged by a 'man of woman born'."

"But those things come true."

"They do indeed. In Act 5, Scene 5, Macduff's forces use branches from the wood as camouflage. It makes the wood appear to move. And then in Act 5, Scene 8, Macbeth is slain by Macduff, who was, as he says, 'from his mother's womb untimely ripped', in other words, born by Caesarean. In modern times one certainly wouldn't describe that as 'not of woman born', but in Shakespeare's time, Caesareans were extremely rare and regarded as unnatural."

Petra paused, turning to watch him. He was walking calmly, displaying no sign that he realised how relevant what he was discussing was to the case.

"In our murder case, how much do you know about how the body was found?" she asked. "Did you watch the press conference?"

"Heavens, no. I was working. Why? Is there something I should know?"

"The man had needles from Birnam Wood in his pockets."

Urquhart stopped walking. "He had *what*?"

"Needles and soil. From the wood."

The professor laughed. "*Now* I know why you brought me in."

Petra said nothing, but continued picking her way through the gorse, trying to ignore the scratches on her hands.

"'Great Birnam Wood to high Dunsinane Hill, Shall come against him'," he called out from behind. "The killer recreated it."

I know. Petra continued to walk.

"Clever bugger." Urquhart was walking again. "Well, I can help."

Petra reached the end of the gorse. *Thank God*. She turned to Urquhart.

"This is confidential information," she said. "The police aren't releasing it to the public. You are *not* to talk to your students about it. Or your colleagues."

He raised his eyebrows. "What kind of man do you take me for? Of course not." He looked past her. "Nearly there now."

Petra turned and walked, wishing she'd never set out from the car. At last they crested a rise, and now she could see the cairn at the top. A man was next to it, bending over.

"Who's that?" Urquhart asked.

"How am I supposed to know?"

He paused, squinting. The sky was darker now and Petra had felt drops of rain already.

She was going to regret this.

They approached the cairn and the figure straightened. A man, wearing a forensic suit.

"Hello," he said. "Dr McBride. And...?"

"Who are you?" she asked.

He shook his head at her. "Jamie Douglas. Crime Scene Manager."

"You're up here on your own."

"We've been clearing up. Heather's on her way over here to pick me up, once she's finished up at Birnam Wood."

"That's where we need to go next," said Urquhart.

"I'm sorry," Jamie said. "Are you involved in the case?"

"I'm a Macbeth consultant."

Petra snorted. "He's a fellow academic. I've asked for his input on the literary aspects of the crime."

Jamie nodded. He glanced down at Urquhart's walking boots, which looked at least twenty years old. "You came prepared."

"I keep boots in my car. I'm a keen hill walker."

"Hate the things, myself," Jamie said. "I spend much too much time tramping around at work."

"Are you nearly finished?" Petra asked. "I was hoping to get into the mind of the killer."

"And you need the place to be quiet." Jamie gave Urquhart a quizzical look. "No problem. Nice to see you."

He trudged down the hill, leaning sideways under the weight of a large holdall.

"Nice young fella," Anthony said.

"He's just doing his job."

A sniff. "Indeed. So, what do you think? Does this help you get into the mind of our killer?"

"Not so much of the *our*." Petra was irritated with Anthony Urquhart. He wanted to ask her questions, while she wanted silence. Jamie had had the right idea.

"I get it," he said. "I'll leave you alone." He walked off and began to wander around the top of the hill. He approached the cairn and examined a stone. He found another stone about five metres away and brought it back to place it on top.

Interfering.

Petra closed her eyes. She breathed in the damp air. She'd put up her hood against the rain, which had now become a light drizzle.

Scotland in the spring. She needed a holiday.

She lowered herself to the ground, keeping her eyes closed. What would it feel like, to be up here with someone you'd killed?

Powerful. That's how you'd feel. Like you owned the world.

She opened her eyes to take in the view. Perth to the south, Dundee behind her. The mountains to the north.

You'd feel like a giant. Like you were invincible.

She stood up.

"Useful?" Anthony called across to her.

"Yes," she told him.

He was holding his stone, trying to stop it tumbling off the cairn.

"I'm getting wet," she said. "Shall we go back down?"

CHAPTER TWENTY-SEVEN

JADE THREW her bag onto the floor as she entered the office.

"My God, I'm knackered." She rubbed her eyes. "That bloody hotel bed. And the M9 was stationary near Bannockburn."

She looked up to see Patty and Carla staring back at her.

She swallowed and recomposed herself.

"Carla." Jade smiled and took a step towards the ecologist. "I'm sorry, I didn't know you were coming."

"I didn't exactly give any warning."

"Carla and I have worked out that the pine needles in Harry's pockets had to come from Birnam Wood," Patty said. "And from a specific spot."

"Oh?"

Patty glanced at Carla. "Well, Carla did most of the work. The scientific work, anyway."

"Patty checked the schedule of the Perth Macbeth Society," Carla added. "Confirmed that they didn't visit the wood recently enough to get fresh needles in his pockets.

"He might have gone there under his own steam," Jade suggested.

"I spoke to PC Decker," Patty said. "She asked his mum if he had a car."

"And?"

Patty shook her head. "No. That was why he joined the Society at first, apparently. So he could tag along on their trips."

"Did they use buses?"

"People gave each other lifts. They held their meetings in the Three Witches tearoom."

"Of course they did." Jade yawned. "Are Mo and Stuart going there tonight?"

"Yes."

"And..." she looked at Carla, "you said you had a specific spot in Birnam Wood?"

"There's an ancient fort, or the site of one. Near a spot called Duncan's Camp."

Jade frowned. "More Macbeth? King Duncan, that's the one he killed, right?"

"It was," said Patty.

"I took samples from various spots," Carla continued, "and the needles from that location are a perfect match."

"So either Harry Nolan found a way of getting himself there in the days before he died, or the killer brought needles from there and placed them in his pocket."

"Exactly."

Jade nodded. "It's not a hundred per cent conclusive, but given his membership of the Macbeth Society, I think we can safely say we need to look at its members closely. Who have we got?"

"I've been checking them all on the system," Patty said. "There isn't much to be going on with."

Jade turned back towards her desk just as the door buzzer sounded.

"I'll get it." She walked to the intercom. "Police Scotland."

"I thought I'd never find you. I've got a delivery for you."

Jade frowned. "It's open." She pressed the button.

She opened the door to see a young man in a DPD uniform climbing the stairs. He held a Jiffy bag.

"I didn't know there was anyone in these buildings," he said as he handed it to her. "I've been looking for fifteen minutes."

"Sorry." She took the envelope.

The man retreated and Jade went back into the office. "We've got mail."

"That's odd," Patty said. "All of our post goes via Dalmarnock."

Jade shrugged. "Not this time."

She turned it over. It was addressed to her. Typewritten.

"Hang on," she said. "Pass me some gloves."

Patty opened a drawer and handed Jade a pair of blue gloves. Jade pulled them on before picking up the envelope again and opening it.

A single sheet of paper fell out.

Jade looked inside the envelope. It was an A4 Jiffy bag, now empty.

"Overkill for one sheet of paper," she said.

She could feel her chest constricting. This wasn't any ordinary letter.

"Patty," she said. "Don't go anywhere." She wanted backup in case the paper had been contaminated.

She unfolded the sheet. Carla and Patty watched, their eyes wide.

"Does this happen a lot?" Carla whispered.

"Never," Jade replied. She licked her lips as the paper unfolded.

Inside was a note, composed of lines cut out from a book or newspaper and stuck onto the sheet. But it wasn't what she'd been expecting. Instead of individual letters making up words, each piece of paper contained a single line.

She read the first one.

"Is this a dagger which I see before me, The handle toward my hand?'"

She frowned. "Is this...?"

"It's from Macbeth," Patty said. "I did it for my Nationals."

"Shit." Jade swallowed as she read the second line.

"'To be thus is nothing, but to be safely thus.'"

"That's when he decides to kill Banquo," Patty said.

Jade nodded, reading the third line.

"'I'll make assurance double sure, And take a bond of fate: thou shalt not live.'"

Patty frowned. "I'm not sure about that one." She hurried to her computer. After a moment, she looked up. "It's a threat. Against Macduff, but it could be... against the police?"

Jade could feel the blood draining from her face. "There's one more. 'Something wicked this way comes.'"

"Even I can work out what that one means," said Carla.

Jade looked at her colleagues, her mouth dry. "There's going to be another murder."

CHAPTER TWENTY-EIGHT

PETRA FELT like her legs might fall off at any moment. She sat sideways in the passenger seat of Anthony Urquhart's Jaguar, her feet on the ground of the car park, removing her boots.

"I already said you don't have to," he told her.

She shook her head. "I'm not bringing mud into your car. How old is this thing, anyway?" The footwell had been pristine when she'd got in, and she wasn't about to change that.

"Twenty-eight years." He put his hand on the bonnet and stroked it. "But you really don't need to."

She ignored him and continued removing her boots. Her stilettos were in the boot.

Damn. She should have got them out first.

"D'you mind fetching my other shoes from the boot?"

"Of course." He smiled, then opened the boot. Five minutes later her 'proper' shoes were on and they were driving away.

"What next?" he asked. "I can take you back to my flat, walk you through all the scenes in Macbeth that reference the wood or the hill."

She stretched her legs, trying to relieve the ache. "Not today. If you can take me back to Magdalena's, she'll be wondering where I am."

"It's only just gone five."

"Which is when she gets in from work."

He shrugged. "Fair enough. But I think we should go to Birnam Wood on the way."

"There's no need."

He glanced at her. "From what you've told me, it sounds like your killer went there too, before committing the deed. In which case, that site can give you an insight into his mind too."

"Why is everyone assuming it's a he?"

"Sorry."

Petra grunted. But he was right. The more she imagined the killer, and the kind of person who might have done the things she'd seen, the more convinced she became that it was a man.

Not a young man. Not an uneducated man. A man who took the time to plan the removal of the needles, the placing of them in the victim's pocket, and the crime itself.

From climbing that hill, she could be confident that Harry Nolan hadn't been carried up. Even a fit young man would struggle with that. And they weren't looking for that kind of killer. Their killer was older and more cerebral. He found it clever and amusing that he'd got them thinking about Macbeth.

A member of the Perth Macbeth Society? Maybe. She'd need to know more about the group's membership before passing judgement.

"So are we going?" Urquhart asked, accelerating out of the car park towards Collace.

"You seem to have already made your mind up," she said. They were driving in the wrong direction for Dundee.

He grinned. "Who knows? The killer may have driven this way."

"But in the opposite direction," she said.

"True."

He had a point. Maybe driving the route would help.

Petra stared out of the window. The rain had cleared and a low evening sun was breaking through the clouds, illuminating the Cairngorms in the distance. It was quite beautiful.

She sighed. "We can't wander around there, though. We'll contaminate the scene."

"We've already been to one scene. Besides, they've got our boot imprints and DNA."

"They don't have yours."

"I can provide them."

She looked at him. "I only brought you in for advice. Not to play at amateur detective."

But he was right. Visiting one site after the other would help her.

She pursed her lips. "Very well. But we don't stay for long."

CHAPTER TWENTY-NINE

"OK," Jade said. "Don't let this scare you." She looked at Patty. "It isn't a threat against the police."

"Read that second line again."

Jade frowned at the DC. "'To be thus is nothing, but to be safely thus.'"

"They sent it here," Patty said. "Whoever it is, they know where we're based. They want to be sure they aren't caught. And they know how empty this building is." She stood up, staring at the door.

"Patty," Jade said, "we've got a job to do here. Regardless of who any threat may be against, we need to investigate." She crossed the room and put a hand on Patty's arm. "Do I need to send you home?"

Patty looked up at her. She shook her head. "No, boss. Sorry. Of course, I'll..."

Jade glanced at Carla, who was standing by the window, watching them.

"Is anyone outside?" Jade asked.

Carla shook her head. "Delivery guy went straight away."

They had no reason to assume he was suspicious. But still...

"I don't suppose you got his registration number?"

Carla smiled at her. "I did." She went to Patty's desk and grabbed a Post-it note. She scribbled a registration number and handed it to Jade.

"Patty," Jade said, "PNC check."

Patty drew in a deep breath, her whole body rising and falling in her chair. "Right." She typed, then deflated. "It's legit. DPD, registered to their Glasgow office."

"Well, that's something. Call that office and find out how the parcel came in. Tell them this is urgent."

Jade turned to Carla. "I'm afraid there isn't anything I can ask you to help with here."

Carla looked at the note, now sitting in an evidence bag on an empty desk. The Jiffy bag was in another. "I can analyse those."

"It's fine. We'll give it to Jamie."

"If you pass it to Jamie, it'll go straight to Lyle Wallace in Dundee. That team may be bigger than yours, but they're busy."

"You're right. You think you can tell us something about the killer, by analysing it?"

Carla picked up the evidence bag. "There are four elements to this, as physical evidence. First, there's the Jiffy bag. That's going to have the most contamination, as it went through the whole delivery system. Then there's the paper itself. Third, the glue used. And finally the quotes themselves. Are they typed out, or are they taken from books?"

Jade picked up the evidence bag containing the note. "It looks like the kind of typeface you'd get in a book."

"In which case, we might be able to identify the specific book it came from."

"You specialise in ecology," Jade said. "Surely this isn't…"

"My lab can analyse the chemical composition of any sample provided. Paper is a natural substance, and different papers have different properties. That paper will have chemicals in it which will help us to identify the printing processes used, and lead us to the publisher. We can try to date it, too."

"All that could take weeks."

"If I bring it in myself, we can fast-track it. Find out where this came from, and you might prevent a second death."

"Very well."

Patty was beside them. "I'll need to take photos of it. See if we can pass it round Shakespeare experts, find out if one of them can identify the edition."

Jade felt her eyes widen. "Petra's man."

"Sorry?"

"Petra has been talking to an academic, from Dundee. He's a Macbeth specialist."

"That gives us a head start," Patty replied.

"He can examine the content of the text more closely, too," Carla suggested. "See if it points to where the next murder might take place."

"And who the victim might be," added Patty.

"OK," Jade said. "I'll give Petra a call. Carla, can you take a sample of each of the four elements without significantly degrading the item as a whole?"

"I can."

"Good. And we need to look at the collections of the Macbeth Society members. See if any of them own a book like this."

CHAPTER THIRTY

Mo PULLED up along the road from the small car park at the bottom of Dunsinane Hill. Up ahead, the car park was full. People milled around, moving from car to car, talking to each other.

"All very pally," Stuart said.

"Don't be so sure," Mo replied. "Any one of those people could be a killer."

Stuart sniffed. "So... do we go and join them, or do we watch from a safe distance?"

"We get closer, but stay at the edge. Observe the group, see if you spot any unusual activity. Anyone hanging back from the crowd, keeping themselves apart. Any extreme displays of emotion."

"No problem." Stuart opened his door and stood next to the car.

Mo reached into the back seat and grabbed his waterproof. It was getting dark, and there'd been rain on the journey here. He noticed umbrellas going up in the car park.

He got out of the car and looked at the DC across the roof. "You want my brolly?"

"It's OK." Stuart reached into the pocket of his coat and brought out a flat cap, which he wedged onto his head.

"A flat cap?" Mo asked. "That's very hunting and shooting."

"Well at least you're not accusing me of being a hipster." Stuart smiled.

"No."

Stuart was many things. Bright, keen, at risk of being promoted out of the team. But a hipster, he was not.

"OK," Mo said. "Let's see if we can spot Lachlan Kerr and Christine McTavish."

"She's the one with the rainbow umbrella."

"How can you tell?"

"I heard her voice."

"Good. Come on, we can find Kerr when we get closer." Mo started walking towards the group. People were passing through the kissing gate, moving up the hill.

Surely they weren't going to head all the way up to the summit? It would be pitch black by the time they got there.

"Ah, DS Uddin." Lachlan Kerr was waiting for them at the edge of the crowd. "I wondered if you'd be here."

"We won't impose," Mo told the man. "We just want to pay our respects, and take the opportunity to meet some of your members."

"Interrogate them, you mean." Lachlan smiled. "It's alright, Sergeant, I know how these things work. My brother's a detective in Edinburgh."

He hadn't mentioned that before. Mo made a note to check the HR system for a Kerr in Edinburgh CID.

"I'll leave you to whatever it is you'll be doing," Lachlan said.

"Are you heading all the way to the top?" Stuart asked. "It's probably not safe."

"Have you seen our demographic? I'd have half the Society dead from exposure or falls. No, don't worry. We've identified an open spot just beyond the wood, up there." He pointed. "There are views from there, it feels appropriate. Christine has prepared a kind of service. Nothing religious of course, even we don't have any ecclesiastical members yet, but it'll be a fitting way to remember poor Harry."

He turned away and walked up through the kissing gate, the last of the Society members to do so.

"We follow them," Mo said. "Keep far enough away not to draw attention to yourself, but close enough to be able to hear."

"The darkness will help," Stuart added.

"It will." Mo headed for the gate and the two detectives passed through.

They trudged up the hill in silence, following the dim group of people ahead. To their left was a wire fence and a wood; to the right, open fields. At last they reached the edge of the wood and the landscape opened up.

The group had stopped ten metres or so ahead of them.

Mo's phone rang. In the quiet of the night, the ring tone echoed like a siren.

"Damn," he muttered. He fumbled for it in his pocket: Jade.

"Boss," he whispered.

"You OK?" she asked. "Your voice..."

"We're at the memorial service for Harry Nolan. Partway up Dunsinane Hill. It's very quiet."

"Of course. Sorry. This can't wait, though."

"What can't wait?" Mo met Stuart's gaze and shrugged.

"We've received a note," she said. "A threat. It's not entirely clear, but I think it's telling us there'll be another death."

Mo swallowed. "Another? Where?"

"We don't know. I'm going to ask Petra to analyse the text, with the help of her Macbeth expert."

"Sorry, what text?"

"It takes the form of lines from Macbeth."

Mo felt his skin run cold. "More Macbeth."

"Yes. I'm assuming the location will be another from the play."

Mo looked at Stuart. "We need to talk to Lachlan Kerr."

"You want me to go get him?" Stuart asked.

"Not yet." He could hear voices, from the group. The ceremony had begun.

"We think it's been cut out from a copy of the play," Jade told him. "Can you check the collections of members of the Society, see if any books have been defaced?"

"Not without a warrant," Mo replied.

"It's worth trying for goodwill first." There was a brief pause. "I know it's clutching at straws, Mo, but we're desperate here. Anything you can do will be helpful."

"I'll try," said Mo.

"Good. Keep me posted."

Mo put his phone in his pocket. "There's been a threat. A letter," he told Stuart.

His phone buzzed: a message from the DI, with photos attached. He showed them to Stuart.

"She thinks it's one of this lot?" Stuart asked.

"That's the most likely possibility, isn't it? They knew him, and they're obsessed with the play."

"But surely it's too obvious. If you're a member of this club, you know the police will be looking at you."

"Still," Mo said. "It's what we've got to go on."

The group was breaking up, people walking past them to head down the hill. They were moving much more quickly this time.

"Already?" Start said. "That was quick."

"It's cold and wet," Mo reminded him. "And most of them are elderly."

Lachlan Kerr stopped beside them. "I hope you caught some of that. Our members are most distraught."

"A lovely ceremony," Mo told him, despite having not heard a word of it. "Over very quickly, though."

"Well, you know what it's like with the old biddies. Can't have them dying of exposure."

Mo winced. Was it really appropriate for Kerr to be making jokes like that, in the circumstances?

"Anyway," the man told him. "I thought you'd want to know that one of our key members didn't show up tonight."

"Someone you were expecting?"

"Indeed. Our treasurer, Frank. I've tried to call him, but he's not picking up."

Mo felt his stomach drop. The letter. The threat.

"Where does Frank live?"

"Dunkeld. Why?"

"And can you give me his full name?"

"Frank Drummond. Why, Detective Sergeant?"

"No reason." Mo looked at Stuart, gesturing towards the DC's phone. Stuart walked away from them, his phone to his ear. Calling Patty to get an address for this Frank Drummond, hopefully.

He gave Lachlan what he hoped was a reassuring smile.

"Do you mind if we come back to your house? We need to check the text of the play, and I was hoping we might be able to use your copy."

"I'm sure you can get it online." Kerr narrowed his eyes. He looked across at Stuart, who was muttering into his phone, heading down the hill. After a moment, he turned back to Mo.

"No problem, Detective. I'm only too happy to help."

CHAPTER THIRTY-ONE

URQUHART PULLED into a lay-by and stopped the car. Petra sat next to him, drinking in the quiet of the woods at dusk.

"It's a bit late to be going into the forest," she said at last.

He turned to her. "We don't need to go far. What if your killer came here at night? It's likely, wouldn't you say?"

She shrugged. It was possible that the killer would visit at night to collect his needles, to avoid being seen. But then, if he was spotted here at night, that would be more suspicious.

She thought through her observations about the crime so far and shook her head.

"No," she said. "He's confident. He knows these spots. He wouldn't have felt the need to come here under cover of darkness."

"Still," Urquhart said, opening his door. "Let's take a look."

He closed the driver's door, making the car shake. Petra's boots were on the floor next to her feet, her socks tucked inside them. She sighed and pulled them on over her tights.

When she left the car, he was nowhere to be seen.

"Anthony!" she hissed. "Where are you?"

"Up here," came a voice. "Along the road."

She walked in the direction of his voice and found him standing at the mouth of a path leading into the woods. The path led past a cottage on the right and over a cattle grid that had long since been filled with soil.

"You want to go in?" He didn't wait for her reply, but started walking.

"Stop!" Petra called after him. He ignored her and continued walking.

She hurried to catch him up.

"This is pointless," she said. She felt uneasy, and that was impairing her ability to empathise. "Let's go back."

Urquhart turned to her, a finger against his lips. She listened, watching his expression. He looked thrilled and fascinated in turn. By the case, or by the woods at night?

"It's marvellous, don't you think? The Scottish countryside, when there are no humans to disturb it."

"There's us," she reminded him. "We're disturbing it."

"We're being quiet. The birds don't care about us."

"I wouldn't be so sure." She wondered what Dr Moreau, the ecologist, would say to him. No doubt she'd put him right.

"Dr McBride, what are you smiling at?"

Am I smiling? "Nothing. I'm going back to the car."

She turned and walked away from him.

CHAPTER THIRTY-TWO

"Are you sure you can't get a copy somewhere else?" Lachlan Kerr asked as he let Mo and Stuart into his house.

"Not at this time of night," Mo replied. "But we're very grateful for your help."

Lachlan shrugged. He moved around his dining room, turning on lamps. Bookshelves lined one wall.

"Here," he said, standing next to a section full of Shakespeare plays. "Which one would you like?"

Mo stepped in closer. Stuart was outside in the car, talking to Patty. "You've got five editions of Macbeth."

"Six." Lachlan reached up and pulled a book down. "Here. This one's the least valuable." He handed the paperback to Mo. "Now, what did I do with the Arden?"

Mo opened the book and leafed through it. He brought out his phone and looked at the photos Jade had sent him.

"What's that?" Lachlan asked.

"Just some lines I need to check."

"You've had a clue."

Mo stepped away from the bookshelves, uneasy at Lachlan breathing over his shoulder. He pinched his screen to zoom in.

How was he going to find these lines, in the play? He had no idea of the context.

He looked up at Lachlan. "Can I borrow this for a moment? I need to call a colleague."

"Feel free." Kerr gestured towards the dining table. It was covered with maps and books. "Here, I'll clear some space for you. I've been planning the next residential."

"Your society goes on residential trips?"

He shook his head. "No. We coordinate them for visitors. Small groups, other societies, the occasional academic. It helps fund our group."

"When was the last residential?"

"About... three months ago? Yes, it was before Christmas. There was a young woman who insisted on talking about Dickens all the bloody time." He huffed.

"You run them yourselves?"

"We do." Lachlan puffed his chest out. "With visiting lecturers. Local people, mostly. Sometimes from further afield."

Mo nodded. "Thanks. I'll just borrow this book, then I'll be right back."

He headed outside to stand by the car and dialled Petra.

"DS Uddin, to what do I owe the pleasure?"

"I hope I haven't disturbed your evening."

"Oh no. I'm just on my way home after a wee trip with Professor Urquhart."

"That's handy," he said. "We need his advice on something."

"Fire away."

Mo told her about the note Jade had received and read out the lines.

"They mean nothing to me," she said. "And he's driving. I'll ask him when we stop."

"Thanks. I'll send you the photos."

"No problem." She hung up.

Mo knocked on the passenger door of his car. Stuart wound the window down.

"Any joy?" Mo asked.

"I'm trying to track down an address for Frank Drummond. No sign of him on any of our systems."

Damn.

"Give me a moment, and I'll return this book." Mo walked back to the house. The front door was open.

"Hello?" he called as he walked through the hallway. "Just returning your book."

Lachlan was standing in the doorway of the dining room. "I can't find it."

"Sorry. Can't find what?"

"The Arden edition of Macbeth."

"Could you have lent it to someone?"

"That one's special. It's the second series. I never lend it out."

None of this meant anything to Mo. "Maybe you've taken it into another room."

Lachlan gave him an angry look. "That's where I've been looking. It's gone." He pushed a fist into the door frame.

"It's just a book," Mo said. He handed out the paperback. "Here, have this one."

Lachlan took it off him then tossed it aside. "You don't understand. The missing one is valuable." He blew out a shaky breath. "DS Uddin, I'd like to report a theft."

CHAPTER THIRTY-THREE

Jade blinked as she took the flyover near Old Kirkpatrick. It was 9pm and she was struggling to stay awake. She'd returned to Glasgow in the hope of being able to spend the evening with Rory and here she was, driving home after his bedtime.

You're a terrible mother.

Her phone rang. She glanced at it: DI Wallace.

She frowned and hit the button on her steering wheel to take the call.

"Lyle," she said. "Have you received the details of the letter that arrived at the CCU offices earlier?"

"I have," he replied. "I gather you have a Macbeth expert trying to figure out the significance of those particular quotes."

"A Professor Urquhart from Dundee University," Jade replied. "I'm hoping for an answer first thing."

"That'll be too late."

She blipped the brake, then caught herself and put her foot back on the accelerator. "It's the best I can do. I spoke to Petra McBride just half an hour ago and—"

"Stop talking, Jade."

Jade clenched her jaw. "What's happened, Lyle?"

"There's been a death. A security guard found a body."

Jade blinked again. She slowed at the Dunglass round-about. "Where?"

"Inverness Castle. It's a young man, covered in blood. He's been stabbed twice."

"You think it's related."

"Inverness Castle is where Macbeth killed Duncan."

Jade nodded. "OK. Is there a team up there dealing with it, or is it being subsumed into our investigation?"

"I'll be SIO. We'll need you to liaise with the experts again."

"Of course. You're sure it's linked?"

"There's a note next to the body. With a quote stuck to it. 'Sleep no more! Macbeth does murder sleep'."

CHAPTER THIRTY-FOUR

JADE PULLED in a lay-by to read the report Lyle had sent her. She scanned it, then grabbed her phone. Mo picked up after three rings.

"Boss," he said. "I'm with Lachlan Kerr. He's got a missing edition of Macbeth, and he reckons it's been—"

"Stop right there," she told him. "There's been another murder."

"What?"

"Inverness Castle. The body was found this evening, by a security guard."

"It's connected?"

"A note was left next to the body. With a quote from Macbeth stuck to it."

"Just like the note that arrived at the office."

"Exactly. Mo, did you say there was a missing member of the Macbeth Society, at the memorial this evening?"

A pause. She could hear voices.

"Yes," Mo said. "Stuart's managed to get his contact details. There's no answer on his phone."

Jade felt her heart rise into her mouth. "He lives alone?"

"We don't know. All we have is a name and an address. I can ask Lachlan Kerr, get more background."

"Do that. I'll wait."

She hung up and started driving. Murder or no murder, she wanted to kiss her son goodnight.

She was approaching Alexandria when her phone rang. She hit hands-free.

"Any news?" she asked Mo.

"Yes." His voice sounded shaky.

"Tell me."

"OK. So Frank Drummond is in his forties. He matches the description in the report you sent me. He lives alone, his wife left him just after Christmas. And he's not at home."

"Stuart's been to check?"

"He's walked all round the man's house, knocked on all the windows. Even broke into the back garden."

"Has he gone inside?"

"We were waiting to speak to you."

"For God's sake, Mo. If he isn't the victim, he might be in there, needing help. Or..." she clenched a fist on the steering wheel. "Or he might be the killer. Stuart needs to break in. Get uniformed backup."

"They're already there. I'll message him." The line went quiet.

Jade passed the roundabout for Balloch and went straight on, up the western shore of Loch Lomond. She was slowing for the turnoff to her home when Mo spoke again.

"He's not there. No sign of him."

"OK," she said. "The report says there were no identifying objects found with the body. No wallet or phone. Can you find a photo of him?"

"There's nothing in the house. But Patty's found his Facebook account."

Jade turned into the service road leading to her house. She parked in the front drive. The front door opened and her mum appeared.

"I've got to go, Mo. We need to head up to Inverness. You stay in Perthshire, see if you can track Frank Drummond down. I'll take Stuart up."

"He's in the hotel in Perth."

"I know. He can head up first thing, check the place out before I get there."

Jade got out of her car, her limbs heavy. She wanted to sleep. She'd need to be up early to catch a train. There was no way she was driving to Inverness.

"Everything OK, love?" Her mum looked worried.

"I'm so sorry, Mum. I've got bad news."

CHAPTER THIRTY-FIVE

JADE CLIMBED down from the train and surveyed Inverness Station. It was a medium-sized station with seven platforms. Stuart was waiting by the ticket barrier.

"Hey, boss," he said. "Good journey?"

"Fine," she said. She'd slept for as much of it as she could, after getting up to catch a 6am train from Balloch. Two changes and four hours later, she felt like it was time for bed.

"I spoke to the sarge," Stuart said. "He's talking to the members of the Macbeth Society. No one's got any idea where Frank Drummond is."

"Are we any closer to identifying this body?"

"The pathologist is with him now, SOCOs are on site. The castle is boarded up, being renovated."

"That's something," she said. "Means the scene is less likely to have been contaminated. A security guard found him?"

"Yeah." He pulled out a notepad. "Arjun Bhatia. He's there now, waiting for us. Bit of a state."

"Poor man. We'll have a quick chat with him, then he can go home to recover."

"It's going to take him a while."

She winced. "What state is the body in?"

"Not good. Deep stab wounds, lots of blood."

"Like in Macbeth." She'd found a digital copy online and started reading it on the train, before tiredness had overwhelmed her.

Stuart nodded. "Petra said she'd talk to Professor Urquhart, try to establish the significance of the quotes we've been sent."

"I'd have thought that was pretty obvious."

They walked out of the station and Stuart led her to the road. A squad car was waiting.

They slid in and Stuart leaned forward to speak to the male PC driving. "We can go back to the castle now, mate."

The PC turned. "No problem. I've been told to come back, after that. There's another member of your team on their way."

Jade frowned. Mo was in Perth, and Patty was back at the office. Lyle?

"Who?" she asked.

"An expert witness, I've been told. That's all I know."

"Petra McBride," she said. At least, she hoped it was Petra.

"Her train doesn't get in for another forty minutes," the PC said. "So I can take you to the castle."

"Good." She turned to Stuart. "We need to focus on two things, before we can even start to think about those notes."

"You're right. The ID of the body."

Jade nodded. "And if the body isn't Frank Drummond, we need to know where the hell he is."

CHAPTER THIRTY-SIX

"I've been called away at short notice," Petra said, keeping her voice low to avoid being overheard by her fellow passengers. "But I do still need your advice."

"Glad to hear it," Urquhart said. "Fire away."

She pressed her phone closer to her ear. "We think there's a chance there's been a second... incident."

"Incident? You mean murder?"

"I'm on a train."

"Ah. I see. How great a chance?"

"Let's just imagine he were to repeat what he did." Her gaze flicked up to the woman opposite her, who was reading a book but hadn't turned a page since Petra had started her call. "Where would he do that?"

"Locations from the play, of course."

"I know that. But where? I'm no expert, Anthony. That's what you're here for."

"Indeed. Well, there's the heath, where it all kicks off. Scholars believe that's probably somewhere in Moray, near Cawdor, Macbeth's seat before he becomes king."

"A heath in Moray?"

"It's a possibility. Impossible to pin down which one, though, and the chances are it would no longer be heathland. Don't forget, Shakespeare never travelled to Scotland."

"OK. Anywhere else?"

"The obvious location is Inverness. Wait a moment, Dr McBride."

She closed her eyes. *Have you been reading the news today, Professor Urquhart?*

"One of my colleagues mentioned it, in the cafeteria. There's been a body found. Inverness Castle."

"There has." She'd been hoping to keep it from him in the hope his advice might not be coloured by prior knowledge. "That's where I'm headed."

"Good for you. Going to stand next to Flora McDonald's statue and breathe in the air the killer inhaled before committing his dastardly deed?"

"It's not a day trip, you know."

"No. I can see some logic in thinking this might be the same killer. Are there any more clues to go on?"

She looked out of the window, at the Cairngorms speeding past.

"I'm on a crowded train, Professor. I'd rather not."

"I see. Very well. You send me what you can when you arrive in Inverness. All the best of luck with it."

"Thanks."

"But if you do find yourself wondering where the killer might have gone inside the castle, try the dungeons."

"The dungeons? Why?"

"It tallies with some of the descriptions in Macbeth. Might be worth a shout. Good luck."

CHAPTER THIRTY-SEVEN

FRANK DRUMMOND still hadn't come home. In the absence of an ID on the body in Inverness, his house had been declared a potential crime scene and the SOCOs were inside, checking for signs of a break-in or a struggle.

Mo stood outside, pulling on his forensic suit. Heather walked out, carrying a box of evidence bags.

"What have you got?" he asked.

"Not much," she told him. "We've been dusting for prints, taking samples for DNA. But there's no blood anywhere we've looked yet, and no sign of forced entry. Your man might have just decided to go on holiday."

"I spoke to the chair of the Macbeth Society who told me Frank Drummond had said nothing about going away. He's the treasurer."

She shrugged. "Voluntary post. He's not obliged to tell anyone."

Mo shook his head. Lachlan had informed him that Frank, despite being younger than most members of the society, was an 'old soul'. He never failed to submit monthly financial reports and attended almost every meeting. When he wasn't able to attend, he gave apologies.

"There is one thing, though," Heather said.

"Yes?" Mo felt his breathing pick up.

"He left his passport. And there's a mug of tea on the kitchen table that's not warm, but the milk hasn't gone off yet. I'd say he left that there within the last forty-eight hours."

"So he was here a couple of days ago."

She nodded.

A car pulled up and a man in a black donkey jacket and check shirt got out. There was mud on the hem of the jacket; not the sleeve, as Jade had warned.

Mo approached him. "DI Wallace. I was told to expect you."

"This scene has nothing to do with your expert witnesses," Wallace replied. "You can go."

"Frank Drummond was a member of the Macbeth Society. Which connects him to that line of enquiry. If you don't mind, I'll stick around."

Wallace looked him up and down. "Haven't you got anything better to do?"

"I won't stay any longer than I need to."

"Hmm." Wallace walked inside without putting on a protective suit.

Moments later, he was being pushed out again, Heather Reynolds behind him.

"What the hell d'you think you're doing, contaminating the scene like this?" she shouted at him.

"I'm the SIO. It's my job to—"

"I don't care if you're the goddamn Queen of Sheba. This is a crime scene, and everyone wears protective gear." She turned to a colleague. "Nick, get DI Wallace here a suit."

Wallace shot Mo a disdainful look. Mo was fully suited up, his hood still up.

"You might as well stick around," Wallace said. "I've got a briefing to run."

Mo resisted a smirk. Heather watched Wallace get back in his car, then waved.

"Good riddance. Do you work with him a lot?"

"Never met him before."

A grunt. "Now I'll have to run his DNA and prints against all my samples. Bloody hell." She stormed back inside.

Mo stood watching the street, wondering if the neighbours had heard all that. Jamie Douglas had been in charge of most of the crime scenes Mo had worked on, and his approach was far calmer than that of his colleague.

Still... it meant Mo was still here, and Wallace wasn't.

He turned to go into the house, just as a squad car pulled up and PC Decker got out.

"Grace," he said. "What's up?"

"I've been assigned to assist at the crime scene. Is DI Wallace about?"

"He just came and went. You're not busy with the Nolans?"

"They insisted they didn't need anyone watching over them. Can't blame them, really. What can I do?"

"You got a forensic suit?"

"In my car. Why?"

"Get yourself suited up, then you can come inside with me."

CHAPTER THIRTY-EIGHT

INVERNESS CASTLE WOULD HAVE BEEN impressive, had it not been surrounded by seven-foot-high red hoardings.

Jade and Stuart left the squad car at the main entrance, taking in the building site inside and the views in the other direction. The castle looked out over Inverness, the River Ness and the countryside beyond. It must have been quite the vantage point.

But today, it was a mess. Construction vehicles and vans were lined up outside the main gate, and a wide area that Jade imagined had once been grass was now mud.

There was no sign of any police presence.

"Why isn't there a PC on the gate, taking a log?" Jade asked.

Stuart shrugged. The squad car was manoeuvring to drive away, en route to pick Petra up.

She strode towards a portacabin and peered inside. A lone security guard sat with his back to them, watching CCTV screens.

She rapped on the window and he looked round, his eyes wide.

He put a hand on his chest. "Bloody hell, you gave me a right scare." His accent was London, not Scotland.

She held up her ID. "We're here to investigate the body that was found here yesterday. Where is everyone?"

He smiled. "Ah, yes. Come with me."

He left his hut, locked the door behind him, and started walking into the site towards the castle. A statue loomed ahead of them: Flora McDonald, hand raised to her forehead, peering out over the Highlands. Or over the hoardings, for now.

Up ahead was an archway. Through it, a uniformed officer was walking towards them.

He broke into a run. "Stop right there, please. I'll need to know who you are."

Jade held up her ID, which still hadn't found its way back into her bag. "DI Tanner, DC Burns, Complex Crimes Unit. Are you in charge of the log?"

"I am. I just had to go for—"

"Where is everyone?"

"Wait," he said.

She turned. "Sorry?"

He blushed. "I've got a list. Your names aren't on it."

"What?"

"I'm sorry, I can't let you in."

"In that case, find someone who can. Is there a senior officer on site?"

"Yes. DI Murphy. But she's... she's inside."

"You've got her mobile number, haven't you?"

"I have."

Jesus Christ. "Well, call her. Tell her we're here."

"Right. Sorry, Ma'am."

Jade tapped her foot as the PC dialled. She glanced at Stuart, who looked embarrassed.

Was she being hard on the PC? She was tired and irritable, and it wasn't his fault her name wasn't on his list.

She hoped that whoever emerged from inside the castle would be more competent.

CHAPTER THIRTY-NINE

"Don't go wandering around," said Heather.

"Don't worry," Mo assured her. "We'll only go into rooms where there's a member of your team."

"Good." She turned away, working through kitchen drawers.

"So who lived here, then?" PC Decker asked.

"Frank Drummond. He's the treasurer of the Macbeth Society. He's missing, and there's a possibility he's the body they found in Inverness yesterday."

"They haven't got a definite match yet?"

"We're working on it."

"What are we looking for?"

"Anything to help us identify why he left. And if he's planning on coming back."

"Or if he's a body in a castle."

"Exactly," Mo replied. "Signs of a struggle, forced entry. If he was taken by someone, then that might have happened here."

"I assume the SOCOs are looking for prints, DNA, that kind of thing."

He smiled. "Of course."

She nodded. "Where d'you want me?"

"Let's take a look upstairs. I want to get a feel for the man. There'll be personal belongings in his bedroom."

Grace nodded and headed up the stairs, her footsteps heavy on the wooden treads. The wall running alongside the stairs was a party wall, shared by the house next door. Mo would need to speak to the neighbours when they came home.

A white-suited tech was in the large room at the front. Mo stepped inside. "OK if we come in?"

The technician nodded.

Mo stood to one side of the bed and looked around, making sure to examine the room in three dimensions and not just focus on eye level.

"This all looks pretty normal to me," PC Decker said.

Mo nodded. There was a book on the bedside table, and a glass of water. No watch or phone.

"What would you leave behind, if you weren't planning on going anywhere? If someone took you or made you leave in a hurry?" PC Decker said.

"In a bedroom, it's hard to tell," Mo said. "But downstairs, there might be keys, a phone. We haven't found anything like that."

"Can I open the bedside drawers?"

Mo looked at the tech, who nodded. "We've already been in there."

PC Decker opened a drawer. She sifted through the contents with a single glove-clad finger. "No keys. Some cash, envelopes. Bills maybe? Nothing much."

Mo nodded. "Three dimensions," he said. He bent to look

under the bed.

"Careful," said the tech. "We haven't examined the floor in detail yet."

"You haven't gone under the bed?"

"No."

Mo approached the bed, still bent double. He could make out an object.

"There's something under here," he said.

The tech turned to him. "Give us time."

Mo frowned, shuffling towards the bed. He was squatting now. He could make out a shape. Cylindrical.

"I'm extracting an object from under the bed. It's the only thing I can see under there."

He hunkered down to get closer. He reached out. It was just at the tip of his fingertips.

"D'you want me to have a go, Sarge?" PC Decker was next to him. Her arms were shorter than his but she was slim and already had a shoulder under the bed.

"Careful," said the tech. He was standing behind them, watching.

Mo looked up. "There's something under there," he repeated.

The area under the bed had been tidy. Clean. Except for this one object.

"Got it."

He turned to see PC Decker holding the object out. It was leather, almost cylindrical, and in two parts.

She looked at the tech. "It's..." She pulled the two sections apart. One was a sheath.

Mo looked down at the object. "A knife."

PC Decker looked back at him. "Why would he have hidden it under there?"

CHAPTER FORTY

JADE AND STUART were returning to the security guard's cabin just as the heavens opened. They huddled inside, watching the water beat at the flimsy windows.

"This thing won't get blown down the hill, will it?" Jade asked the guard.

He grinned. "No chance. It's anchored down."

She grimaced at the thought of taking shelter in a structure that someone would have thought to anchor down. Stuart was chatting with the guard, seemingly unconcerned. They were discussing unusual finds during the refurbishment of the castle.

"Baby's skeleton in the dungeons," the guard said. "That put me off my dinner for a few days."

"D'you go in there, as well as being out here?"

"I did, at the beginning. I had a job hauling rubble out. Bloody knackering, it was. Then I got this job. Right cushy number." He grinned again.

"Where's DI Murphy?" Jade muttered, looking out at the rain.

"She'll be inside the castle," the guard said. "No one comes outside when it's lashing it down like this."

She shuffled towards the window, wiping it to get a better view. The glass was misted up, making the world outside appear foggy. Maybe it was.

At last she saw movement outside.

"Finally." She walked to the door as it opened.

A short woman in stilettos, flourishing a Rangers umbrella, darted inside.

"Bloody hell, my shoes'll be ruined!"

"Petra," Jade said. "Good to see you."

Petra looked up. "Aye, you too. I thought you'd be in there by now. Inspecting the body."

"Long story."

Petra shrugged. "Sorry to hear it. What do we know about the crime scene?"

"We don't know much at all," Stuart answered. "They won't let us in."

"What d'you mean, won't let us in?"

"There's an officious PC out there with a list," Jade said.

Petra laughed. "List, schmist. Let me at him." She made for the door, pulled on it then almost fell backwards as the wind blew it back into her face. "Shit. Maybe not."

The guard got up to help close the door. "Cuppa, anyone?"

Jade shook her head.

"Don't mind if I do," said Petra with a smile. "What have you got?"

"Err... tea."

"Well in that case, I'll have tea. All the sugars."

He smiled. "I'll give you three."

"Fantastic."

"I'll have the same please, mate," Stuart said. "But without the sugar." He patted his stomach.

The wind was dying down, the cabin not moving as much as it had been. Jade looked outside to see two figures heading their way. One was the uniformed constable. The other was a slim woman in a grey suit, ducking to get under the PC's umbrella.

The door opened and the pair entered. The woman looked around.

Her gaze landed on Jade. "You must be DI Tanner."

Jade stood up. "DI Murphy?" The woman nodded. "I'm working on a murder case in Perthshire. We have reason to believe this death is connected."

"Well I'm from local CID, and no one has told me anything of the sort."

Jade sighed. She went for her inside pocket, then realised her ID was no good here. "One moment," she said.

She grabbed her phone and dialled Fraser. Normally asking her boss to wade in was the last thing she'd do, but today she didn't have the energy. There'd been the sleepless night in the lumpy hotel bed in Perth, followed by a late night and early morning today.

She put her hand to her mouth as he answered.

"Jade? Are you yawning?"

"Sorry, Sir."

He chuckled. "You're clearly working too hard."

You could say that. "I'm in Inverness, Sir. At the castle."

"Ah. Yes, Perth have told me about that. Why haven't I heard anything from you, though? I don't recall telling you to go up there."

"DI Wallace thought it would be a good use of resources.

And given that this cements our theory that the killer is a Macbeth fanatic, it made sense to—"

"It's OK, Jade, You don't have to explain yourself to me. I authorised three nights' hotel in Perth, you can transfer one or two of them to Inverness."

"We might need more than another night or two."

"You'll have to come back to me, if that proves to be the case. I'm not made of money."

"No." She took a breath. On the other side of the cabin, Petra was talking to DI Murphy over a cup of tea. Jade couldn't make out the words over the rattle of raindrops on the roof.

"Sir," she said. "We're having some problems here. Local CID won't let us into the crime scene. I was hoping—"

"You want me to vouch for you."

"I wouldn't normally, but—"

"It's fine, Jade. You need to make use of me more often. You sit tight, and I'll get you access to your crime scene. Is there anything else I can help you with?"

Did she detect sarcasm in his voice? "I need to debrief you on the situation in Perth. DS Uddin attended a memorial for the victim last night, and another member of the Macbeth Society has gone missing."

"Can you put it in writing? I've got a budget meeting in five minutes and I need to prepare if I'm not going to have to axe your unit."

Jade felt her chest constrict. "Of course."

She hung up. So the threat was still there.

DI Murphy was standing over her. "Come on, then."

"That was quick."

Jade stood up. She'd been off the phone for all of ten seconds. There was no way Fraser had had the time to call Murphy's senior officer already.

The DI looked back at Petra. "Your Dr McBride explained everything to me. She can be quite persuasive."

I bet she can.

"OK. Good." Jade stood up. The rain was easing on the roof; hopefully they wouldn't get too wet.

The uniformed constable had the door open.

"OK," Jade said. "Petra, thanks."

Petra nodded acknowledgement.

"Put your tea down, Stuart," Jade continued. "We've got a crime scene to examine, and I don't know how long we'll have access to it."

CHAPTER FORTY-ONE

DI Murphy led Jade, Petra and Stuart past the statue of Flora McDonald to the castle. The rain had eased but the wind was picking up again, and Jade wished she'd brought her sturdy waterproof, the one she kept in the boot of her car. Instead she was wearing the thin one she used for travelling.

"It's not pleasant," DI Murphy said.

"We've seen plenty of murder scenes."

"OK." Murphy gave Jade a blank look. Jade smiled in return and followed the woman further into the castle.

"I'd like to see the note," she said as they walked further inside.

Murphy continued walking. "It's been submitted into evidence."

"Another note was sent to our team. I'd like to compare them."

Murphy glanced back. "All in good time."

The castle was dark and dank here, bags of cement and sand piled up against the walls and scaffolding surrounding the building. Jade wondered what it would look like when it was finished. Better than what she could see under the scaffolding, she hoped.

"Here." DI Murphy had stopped by a low doorway. She gestured for Jade to go through.

Jade pushed the door open and stepped past her, Stuart behind. Petra kept pace.

"I'm not sure she's allowed," said Murphy.

"She's part of my team," Jade said. "She's allowed."

The DI gave Petra a calculating look but didn't object. Jade wondered what Petra had said to her, to talk her into letting them come up here. And was Fraser on the phone to her high-ups right now, demanding that they be let in?

"OK. No further," Murphy said, standing behind them in what Jade supposed was some kind of lobby area. The walls were made of stone and the floor was concrete.

"There's a plastic curtain up ahead," the DI told them. "Put there by the builders. I'll pull it to one side for you and you can look through. But I can't let you go in unless you get suited up."

"We've brought suits," Stuart said. He reached into the rucksack he was carrying.

"Put them on, and you can go in." She gave Petra another look, but didn't exclude her.

Once in her suit, Jade waited for Murphy to pull aside the plastic curtain. She was looking into a white-walled room about twenty feet square. The floor had been partially covered in wooden parquet, and there were boxes of flooring materials stacked up to one side. At the far end were two ladders leading up to a mural about eight feet up on the wall. The ceiling was vaulted stone.

At the centre of the room was a man. His body was twisted

at an unnatural angle, his face pointed towards the ceiling. His eyes stared blindly up.

"The blood," Petra said.

"Don't step in it," came Murphy's voice through the curtain.

"No." Jade put out a hand to stop Petra and Stuart from going any further. The blood had travelled at least three metres towards them from the man, spreading out in all directions and seeping into the parquet.

"Wow," Stuart said. "I don't think I've ever seen so much blood."

Jade nodded. "That's from a chest or neck wound." She stepped forward to approach the body, but was prevented from getting too close by the blood at their feet. Even in protective overshoes, there was no way she was going to step in it. "A deep wound. From a sharp blade. Front of the abdomen, by the looks of it."

The man's chest was soaked in blood. So much so that she couldn't make out the colour or fabric of the clothing.

She turned to Petra. "Does this fit with the profile you're building from the earlier crime scene?"

Petra wrinkled her nose. "Depends."

"On what?"

"On how long the killer stuck around after doing this. I've got him pegged as a coward. He killed Harry Nolan in a spot where the young man walked regularly, then left him up there for the birds. There was no blood there. But here..."

"There was no blood at the site," Stuart corrected her. "That doesn't mean no blood somewhere on that hill."

"But yes," Petra said, "I think there's a good chance it's the same man."

"Have you looked at the wall behind you?" DI Murphy's voice again.

Jade turned towards the voice. She pulled in a breath.

"Oh my God. Why did no one tell us about this?"

"We didn't spot it at first." Murphy folded her arms. "Yes, I know. But until you're done with the body, and you turn round..."

Stuart and Petra turned with her.

Stuart whistled.

Petra coughed. "Bloody hell."

Jade nodded. She stared at the wall.

"Don't touch it," came Murphy's voice.

Jade rolled her eyes. *What d'you think I am, stupid?*

But still she reached out her hand, stopping a foot short of the wall.

The wall between them and DI Murphy was white, just like the others. But this one wasn't plain. It had been written on.

In blood.

"'Out, damned spot'," Stuart breathed.

Petra shook her head. "It's him, alright."

CHAPTER FORTY-TWO

"THIS NEEDS TO BE ANALYSED," Mo said, dropping the knife into an evidence bag that Heather held out.

"Don't worry," she said. "I'll get it straight back to the lab."

"Frank's DNA will be on it, I'm sure."

"But the question is whether we'll find that DNA on the handle or the blade," she added.

"There's no blood on the blade."

A shrug. "No reason it wouldn't have been cleaned."

"But if the killer cleaned it," PC Decker said, "why would they just leave it here?"

"If someone attacked Frank, then leaving the knife here might be safer than taking it somewhere else," Mo said. "This way, it's associated with the victim and not the attacker."

"So it's unlikely that Frank used it to attack someone else."

"Exactly." Mo took out his phone. "I need to call the DI."

"Come in here." Heather was in the next room along.

Mo pocketed his phone and followed the sound of her voice. "What is it?"

"See this room?"

The second bedroom was small, taking up the rear quarter of the house, next to the bathroom. There was a single bed in a corner, a small bedside table, and a wall covered in photos.

"Who are they?" PC Decker asked.

Mo leaned in to get a better look. The wall contained dozens of pictures of young men. They varied: white, black, Asian, thin, chubby, tall, short. There was no one type. But they were all men, all in their twenties or thirties. Every one of them looked as if they'd been photographed in secret.

Not one of them was facing the camera. Not one of them was posing. And many of the photographs were grainy, as if they'd been taken from a distance.

"Frank Drummond was a pervert," PC Decker said.

Mo studied the photos, saying nothing. He was picturing Harry Nolan's face from the crime scene photos and the ones the family had provided.

"There he is." He pointed.

Near the bottom of the display, not far from the bed, was a photo of Harry.

CHAPTER FORTY-THREE

Jade was outside the castle heading for the security hut when her phone rang.

"Mo," she said. "Have you managed to track Frank Drummond down yet?"

"No. But I'm pretty certain he's our suspect."

"Why?"

"First, we found a knife under his bed."

"That could mean he's the victim."

"And then we found a wall of photos in the spare room. Young men, all taken in secret. One of them's Harry Nolan."

"One of them? How many of them are there?"

"Dozens. I'm not sure how many are duplicated. Grace is up there now, attempting to catalogue them."

"Who's Grace?"

"PC Decker, from Perth police. She's been sent over to help."

"By Wallace?"

"She's alright, boss. You don't need to worry."

Jade sighed. She needed to start trusting people. They were all doing a job here. All trying to solve a crime.

And now, it seemed that job was to stop a killer, and possibly a stalker.

"It doesn't make sense," she said. "These photos... Petra would say this indicates a sexual motive. Following people, photographing them. Killing them. But there's no sexual nature to the crimes. The body here was stabbed, twice, in the chest."

"Has the pathologist been?"

"No. But the victim is fully clothed. No sign of an assault. Apart from the obvious, of course. And there's writing, in blood by the looks of it."

"Writing?"

"Lines from Macbeth. 'Out, damned spot.'"

"So it's one of ours then."

"It is."

"You want to send me photos, and I'll see if he's on this wall?"

Jade considered. "I'll see what I can get. I can barely see his face for blood. And we still haven't ruled out the possibility that this victim *is* Frank Drummond."

"Having seen these photos," Mo said, "I think it's more likely he's the killer."

"Do you have photos of Drummond?" Jade asked.

"I haven't seen any in the house. I'll ask Patty to trawl social media."

"Lachlan Kerr might have one."

"Yes."

"OK. Tell me if you find a photo. I'll talk to the forensics people here, their van has just arrived. See what they can tell me. And I'll find out what's happening to the pathologist."

"You're not in charge?"

"Local CID have sent someone in. DI Murphy."

"Never heard of her."

"Nor me. And she's not happy about us being here." Jade looked past the forensics van that had just pulled in, towards the security hut. DI Murphy had disappeared inside it, along with Petra and Stuart.

"OK," she said. "Send me photos of the wall, and anything you can find of Frank. I'll get photos from here. First thing is to establish whether Frank is the victim, or the suspect."

"Will do, boss."

"And less of the boss, yes? I'm Jade."

CHAPTER FORTY-FOUR

"WHO ARE YOU, ANYWAY?" DI Murphy asked. Petra and Stuart were with her and the security guard in his hut, sheltering from the weather.

"Dr Petra McBride," Petra replied. "Didn't we already go through this? This here is DC Stuart Bur—"

"That's not what I mean. I'm not sure why there's a psychologist here."

Petra was used to explaining herself. Convincing people she wasn't a quack. "You'll know about the body they found on Dunsinane Hill, in Perthshire?"

"Yes."

"The victim had pine needles in his pockets, from Birnam Wood." Petra watched the DI, waiting for realisation to hit.

Nothing.

"Are you familiar with Macbeth, Detective?"

"I know it's Shakespeare, but that's about as far as it goes."

"Right. So at the end of the play, there's a scene where the wood moves to the castle on top of the hill. It wasn't a real castle, the bard made it up. And the wood doesn't really move, it's just branches tied to soldiers. I'm not explaining it very well. The point is that when DI Tanner realised that the crime had a Macbeth theme to it, she called me in to analyse the psychology of someone who might commit that kind of crime."

"Does that explain the writing on the wall inside the castle?"

"Those are lines from the play. Lady Macbeth says them, when she's struggling with her conscience after killing King Duncan."

"Which she does on Dunsinane Hill."

"No. Right here, at Inverness Castle."

Petra hesitated. There had been no murder at Dunsinane in the play. Macbeth himself died there, slain by Macduff in the final battle, but neither he nor his much-maligned wife had murdered anyone else there.

But here... here at Inverness Castle, they'd committed the crime that had kicked the whole sorry saga off.

And they'd done it by stabbing someone.

Petra stood up. "He's getting complacent."

Stuart turned to her. "Sorry?"

"The first crime was more oblique. We might not have spotted the literary reference in it. But this one... this one we can't miss."

"What does that mean?" DI Murphy asked.

Petra bit her bottom lip. "It means he's laughing at us."

"Why?" asked Stuart.

"Either he doesn't know we've spotted the Macbeth connection from the first crime, or he does know, and he wants to confirm it for us. He thinks we're stupid, for not being closer to catching him."

"How d'you get all that, from some lines from a play?" Stuart asked.

"It's not the lines. Well, it is. The lines are the most obvious ones he could have picked. They're famous. Anyone would recognise them."

DI Murphy cleared her throat. "I didn't."

"Well, almost anyone. But the first crime, that was more subtle. We could have missed it. This one, no chance. Even the method of killing..."

"Maybe he thinks we haven't worked out the connection from the first murder, so he's done this to make sure we figure it out and then go back to that one and make the connection," Stuart suggested.

"Maybe. I still think he's laughing at us." Petra looked at DI Murphy. "How long ago was he killed?"

"The pathologist hasn't been yet. He was found yesterday afternoon."

"And the pathologist *still* hasn't been?"

"Dr Cameron is off sick, he's the Inverness pathologist. We've had to get someone from further afield."

How long would it take to drive here, from pretty much anywhere in Scotland? Petra shook her head.

"Do you have any idea of when he was killed?" she asked the DI. "From your own experience?"

DI Murphy flushed. "This is only my second murder that's not drugs-related."

"Only your second?"

Murphy looked at her. "You may think Inverness is a sleepy wee city at the northern edge of the world, nothing more than a stopping off point for the loch and the monster. It's not."

"How so?"

"We've got a major drugs smuggling problem up here. It's out of the way, gets less attention than Glasgow and Dundee. And that kind of thing comes with murder."

"But not stabbings like this."

"Most of our crimes involve overdoses, or guns." DI Murphy coughed. "So that means I don't have a lot of experience in estimating time of death for someone who's bled out like that."

"Gunshot victims bleed out."

"They tend to be found quicker."

"So you reckon he's been there a while." Petra's mind went to the crime scene. The blood had pooled on the parquet floor, but it had been brown around the edges. Only at the centre, nearest the body where the pool of blood was deep, was it red.

But even that wasn't the bright red she might expect from fresh blood.

"He might have been killed before Harry," she said.

Murphy stood up. "Harry?"

"The first victim."

"Let's not jump to conclusions." Murphy turned to the security guard. "All of what you've heard here is confidential. Please don't go repeating it to your colleagues."

He flinched, visibly irritated by her assumption. "Of course not. But you might want to see this."

The door opened and Jade walked in. She looked between Petra and the DI. "What's up?"

"We were discussing the case," Petra said. "I've had some thoughts."

"Good." She looked at Murphy. "I need photos of the victim. We need to go back in there."

"No," said Murphy. "The SOCOs are working on spatter analysis. I don't want you contaminating it."

"Excuse me," the guard said. "But you really want to see this."

Petra turned to him. "Sorry, pal. What is it we want to see?"

"While you two have been chatting, I've worked my way backwards through the security camera footage in that room." He grimaced. "And I think I've seen your man dying."

CHAPTER FORTY-FIVE

JADE WENT to stand behind the guard. "Sorry, what's your name?"

"Arjun. I was wondering when someone might ask."

"Sorry." She stifled a yawn. "We've all been a bit preoccupied. What have you got?"

He turned to his screen. It was black and white, split into four sections.

"So we've got cameras all over the place," he told her. "You should be able to track the killer's route in and out. The victim's, too." He glanced at Murphy as if wondering why she hadn't already done this.

"How many cameras do you have?" Jade asked.

"Twenty-three, in total."

"That'll take hours to go through." Stuart had joined them at the screen.

"It will," Jade said. "Which ones have you looked at?"

"The room where I found the body, of course." Arjun made a sucking sound. "Seems pretty obvious to me."

She smiled. "I agree. Show us."

Murphy was behind Stuart. "Can you email those to Inverness CID, please?"

Jade turned to her. "I'm sure he'll do that. But let's just watch them first, yes?"

Murphy's forehead twitched. "OK."

Jade nodded. "Good."

She knew she needed to follow up on the photos Mo had sent her. But there was a chance the CCTV would give them an image of the killer, as well as the victim.

Her phone pinged: a message from Patty. *Emailed you photos from Frank Drummond's Facebook profile.*

Thanks, Patty. Jade opened the email to find images of a man in his thirties, with brown hair and an unremarkable, roundish face. The victim had had a thin face, with sunken cheekbones. But that might be related to the sudden nature of his death.

She showed the phone to Stuart.

"Can you go back to the crime scene, check his face against this. I don't think it's him but we need to check."

"No problem, boss."

"I've forwarded Patty's email to you."

He nodded and left the room.

Jade turned to Arjun. "Sorry about that. So, what's the timeframe for the images you've found?"

"Thursday morning, around 3am."

The murder had taken place more than twenty-four hours ago.

Jade clenched a fist. "That's brilliant, Arjun. Sorry, that sounded patronising. But you have no idea how long it can take us to find useful footage."

"How did you know to look at that time?" Murphy asked.

He shrugged. "Well, I skipped the bits where I was on. I

know there's a chance someone might have got past me, but I didn't think anyone had, so I missed out the day shifts, y'know?"

"And then you looked in that room," Jade said.

"Don't put words in his mouth," said Murphy.

Jade looked at her. Did the DI think Arjun was a suspect?

"I did," Arjun confirmed. "Rewound, luckily we've got good cameras now so you can scan the footage on ten times the speed and still see what's going on."

"Ten times the speed," said Murphy. "How d'you ever find anything useful in the middle of that?"

"No one's supposed to have been in that room since last week. So I stopped when I saw someone in there." He scratched the stubble on his cheek. "D'you want to see it, or not?"

"Yes," Jade and Murphy replied in unison. Jade wondered what Petra was making of all this. Probably conducting her own private psychological analysis of all three of them.

"Right," Arjun said. He'd stopped the four cameras at the same time: Thursday morning, two forty-eight am.

"OK." He pointed. "So that one at the top left is inside the room. It's empty, see?"

Jade nodded.

"The one next to it is the next room along, the one I saw you go into and put on your protective suits. And the two at the bottom: one's the corridor by the entrance to the castle itself, which is the only way through to that space, and the other is the front entrance. My hut's there, see?"

He bent to look out of the window and upwards. "You can see the camera there."

Jade followed his gaze. A camera was attached to a high

post outside, with a vantage point over the entrance and the vehicles parked on the mud.

"OK," she said. "Play it then."

He hit a key on his keyboard and the four screens flickered. There was no movement for a few moments, then a van appeared in front of the main entrance, caught by the camera over the hut.

It was a plain white van, not much bigger than a car. There were no markings, and the registration plate was just out of shot.

"Do you know if there's any other footage with the registration plate?" Murphy asked.

"Not that I can find," replied Arjun.

Jade nodded and watched the vehicle. A man got out of the driver's side. He wore a cap and a hi-vis jacket not unlike Arjun's.

"He one of yours?"

"That's not one of our vans. But he might be working on the castle. I can't see his face."

She nodded as the man went to the passenger door. Another man got out, also wearing a high-vis jacket, but with no cap.

"I don't recognise him," Arjun said.

With the black-and-white image and the distance of the van from the camera, it was difficult to make out either man's features, however clear the pictures were.

"We'll send it to digital forensics," Murphy said. "Get it enhanced."

Jade was about to interrupt, but then she remembered that her role here was purely to work with the expert witnesses. She had no authority to work on forensics.

Apart from ecological forensics, and there was certainly no sign of those.

They crowded around the screen, trying to get closer to it, as the footage played. The man in the cap helped the other man out of the van, supporting him as the two of them walked towards the castle.

They walked past the portacabin. The first man waved towards it as they passed. No one challenged them.

"Who would have been on shift at that time?" Murphy asked.

"Kai," said Arjun. "Don't blame him."

Murphy pursed her lips and said nothing.

The two men approached the castle. They rounded Flora's statue, still unchallenged, and disappeared behind it.

Jade's gaze shifted to the footage from the corridor between the castle entrance and the room where the body had been found. Sure enough, the two men passed under the camera. They were closer now, and she could make out words on the back of their hi-vis tabards.

"That's just like mine," Arjun said, "but they don't work here."

Jade nodded. At 3am, all they'd had to do to convince the sleepy security guard that they were legit was don a pair of jackets.

They disappeared from view and entered the room where she'd put on her forensic suit. As they did so, the man in the cap let go of the other man, who slumped to the ground.

The first man turned away from his companion and walked towards the camera. Keeping his head bowed and his face out of shot, he reached up and adjusted it to face the ceiling.

"Did it stay like that?" she asked.

Arjun shook his head. "He comes back and fixes it. That's why no one thought to look at that camera."

Jade watched as shadows passed across the ceiling. "I don't suppose there's any audio."

"No. Sorry."

"Boss," Stuart said, pointing to the top right image. Another man in a high-vis tabard was running under the camera in the corridor.

"Did we see this one in the outside footage?" Jade asked.

Arjun rewound to the point at which the man had adjusted the camera. At the same moment, a guard emerged from the portacabin and ran towards the castle.

"Skip forwards," Murphy said. Arjun took them back to where they'd left off.

Jade shifted her gaze to the top left camera, which showed the room where the body had been found. She'd spotted movement to one side.

A foot appeared at the edge of the shot, then a leg, then the full body of a man wearing a high-vis jacket.

She hadn't seen the faces of any of these men, and didn't know which one this was. But he was wearing a cap.

"Was the guy from the cabin wearing a hat?" she asked.

"Kai normally wears a beanie on night shift. He feels the cold."

Sure enough, another man appeared, wearing a beanie. Now there were two men in shot.

"That's not him, though," Arjun said. "Neither of those men is Kai. Look, they're white."

Jade nodded. "So that's the other two men." The intruders.

"Why has one of them put Kai's hat on?" Stuart asked.

"Camouflage," said Petra. Jade turned, having forgotten she was there.

Jade turned back as the two men fell on each other. There was a struggle, then one of them brought something out of his pocket.

"A knife," breathed Arjun.

"Are you sure?" Murphy asked.

He shrugged.

The man in the beanie drew back his arm and stabbed the other man.

"That must be the victim." Murphy said. "He's wearing the cap, but it was the other man wearing that before."

"It's not exactly clear," Jade muttered.

"It makes sense, though," Petra said.

Jade turned to her. "Why?"

Petra's gaze was intent on the screen. Jade turned back to see the man with the cap go down. He slumped to the floor, his vi-vis jacket blooming with dark blood.

She pushed out a breath.

"It's Macbeth," Petra said. "The fight in the castle. The guards who are blamed. He's staged it. He wanted it to look like your guy Kai was the killer."

CHAPTER FORTY-SIX

Stuart hurried towards the castle and made his way inside, then stopped.

He knew the body had been left in a large, white room. But he couldn't remember how they'd got to it.

He brought out his phone, uneasy.

I don't want the boss thinking I'm incompetent.

He put his phone away and stood still, listening. He'd seen the SOCOs go inside, and they'd be at the crime scene.

Sure enough, he heard voices off to the left.

He followed the sound, whistling to alert them to his approach. As he entered a room filled with equipment, two women standing at its centre looked up.

"Who the hell are you?" the shorter of the two asked.

He held up his ID. "DC Burns. I've been sent by my boss to get photos of the victim."

"Why?" The other SOCO straightened up. She was tall and thin, and looked like she might snap in a strong wind.

"We've got a potential ID, a man in Perthshire who's gone

missing. I need to send photos to my sarge so he can compare them."

The tall SOCO sniffed. "Alright then. Wait there." She disappeared through a curtain of black plastic.

Stuart stood at the threshold to the room, feeling uncomfortable.

After a few moments, he couldn't resist. "Are you going to let me go in, then?"

Her short colleague glanced up from her laptop. "Just be patient."

He shifted between his feet. "It's urgent. If our guy isn't the victim, then he's probably the suspect."

"How can you get a victim and a suspect muddled up?"

"He's either been killed, or he's absconded." Stuart cocked his head. *Surely you can work that out?*

At last the thin one reappeared. "Give me your email address."

He gave her the address for the CCU team inbox.

She nodded to her colleague, who frowned at her laptop then clicked the trackpad. "Sent."

"You've sent me photos?"

"We have. I cleaned him up a bit for you, too. Didn't want *you* doing that. You shouldn't have any problem checking if he's your guy."

"Why not?"

"Because he's got a dirty great burn mark on his neck. If your missing person hasn't, then chances are he's your suspect."

CHAPTER FORTY-SEVEN

"Boss."

Jade looked round to see Stuart entering the portacabin.

"You'll want to see this." He held out his phone: photos of the victim.

"Is that blood?" Jade asked.

He shook his head. "It's a burn. Whoever this guy is, he's got an historic burn injury."

"Which Frank Drummond doesn't."

"No."

She looked back at the screen. They'd run through all the footage now, and she still hadn't seen the face of the man in the cap.

"I didn't see the burn mark on him in the CCTV," she said.

"Maybe the quality isn't good enough," suggested Petra.

"The quality is fine," said Arjun.

Jade inhaled, staring at the frozen screens on the CCTV footage. All four aspects were empty now, apart from the man lying in the middle of the top right screen in a pool of blood.

"It's not Frank Drummond. Which means he's most likely

the killer." She tapped her fingers on the desk next to Arjun's monitor. "Mo needs to know about this. I want to check if our victim is on Frank Drummond's wall." She looked at DI Murphy. "And we need to talk to Lyle Wallace."

"Who's Lyle Wallace?"

"He's SIO on the Harry Nolan murder. If Frank Drummond killed Harry as well as this victim, then he needs to know about it."

"You're not the SIO on that case?"

"I'm heading up the expert witness input. Petra here, and the forensic ecologist."

"What even does that mean?" Murphy asked. "You're just a middleman. Why can't the experts talk direct to the SIO?"

Jade looked away. She didn't have a good answer for that. *Because my boss is trying to protect the future of my team* wasn't something she was prepared to say out loud.

She sighed. "All three of us will need to work together."

Murphy shook her head. "You've given me the name of a potential suspect in a crime committed on my patch. No one has said this isn't Inverness's to investigate. Now I'd be grateful if you could hand over the details of your Frank Drummond."

Jade shook her head. "I'll work with you, yes. But you're not forcing us out. Your senior officer will have called you."

"I've had no call."

Jade narrowed her eyes. Fraser would have made the call, surely?

Maybe he had done. But whoever he'd spoken to might have chosen not to pass it on.

Shit.

She wasn't about to call Fraser and check if he'd acted on her behalf. That would be like a kid in the playground getting her mum to stand up to the bullies for her.

Her mum.

She checked her watch: 5.30pm.

She'd missed Rory last night, and this morning. Hadn't even had a chance to tell him she was going away.

I'm sorry, wee man. I'm a godawful mum.

"I need to make a call," she said.

"You need to leave," Murphy replied.

"I'll go outside, get some privacy. Then I'll be back. We need to—"

"Uh-uh." Murphy had her arms folded across her chest. "It's time we all got out of here for the day, anyway. The SOCOs'll be off in a bit."

"They need to continue. There's work to—"

"We don't have overtime authorised. We'll be back in the morning."

What if the killer struck again?

Where was Frank Drummond, anyway?

Jade took Stuart by the elbow. "Come outside with me."

"Boss?"

"Just come with me."

He nodded, giving Petra a confused look, and followed her.

Outside the portacabin, Jade stopped. Her legs ached and she longed for sleep.

Forget about that. This is more important.

"I need you to look for other sources of CCTV," she told him.

"But DI Murphy. She—"

"Don't worry about DI Murphy. If we find anything, we'll show it to her. To Wallace, too. But just take a walk. See if you can spot any cameras that might have caught Drummond as he was arriving or leaving. I want to see his face."

"You definitely think it's Drummond?"

"Who else can it be?"

He looked at her, his brow furrowed. "OK, boss. Where will I find you?"

"The hotel. I'm going to have a chat with Petra."

"No problem, boss."

CHAPTER FORTY-EIGHT

"THANKS, STUART," Mo said as he pulled up outside Lachlan Kerr's house. The DC had called to tell him what they'd learned about the second victim, including the fact that it definitely wasn't Frank Drummond.

Which made Drummond their suspect.

He got out of the car and shook himself out to try and alleviate the stiffness in his limbs.

Having a suspect was a good thing. It helped hone their efforts and increased the chances of making an arrest.

So why did he feel so uneasy?

He rang the doorbell and Kerr appeared a few seconds later.

"DS Uddin," he said. "Come in. Have you found Frank yet?"

Mo stepped inside and closed the door behind him. Lachlan looked at his watch. "It's getting on," he said. "You want to join me in a beer? I need something to steady my nerves."

Mo shook his head.

"Ah, sorry. You're a Muslim."

Mo clenched his teeth. "No. I mean, yes I am Muslim. But not strict. I drink."

"But not when you're on duty."

"Exactly."

"Very sensible. Mind if I have one? I can get you a glass of water."

"Please." Mo had been hit simultaneously with both a headache and the realisation that he was thirsty. He followed Lachlan through into the kitchen and watched as the man got a bottle of Tennent's lager out of the fridge and poured a glass of water. He leaned against a counter and swigged.

"So. Frank."

"Bad news, I'm afraid."

Lachlan's face fell. "No."

"Not that."

"So he's still alive." Recognition passed over the man's face. "Which means he's a suspect."

Mo nodded. "Certain evidence has come to light which means we'd very much like to speak to Frank." He resisted telling Lachlan what kind of evidence it was, and took a gulp from his water. "You say Frank was a regular attendee of the society?"

"Was? Still is. You really think he could have killed Harry?"

"I can't say anything for sure, not without talking to him. But I need your help tracking Frank down, so we can speak to him."

"And exonerate him."

"And find out the truth."

Lachlan stopped mid-swig. He looked at Mo for a long

moment, then swallowed. "Fair enough. What d'you need to know?"

"I need a list of members. With contact details."

"Christine can give you that."

'We've asked her. She hasn't provided it."

"I'll put pressure on her."

"I'd rather you did it yourself."

Lachlan eyed him. "I don't have that information. I'll go to her house first thing, refuse to leave until she's given me a print-out. Is that good enough?"

"I'd rather it was sent by email."

A sigh. "OK. I'll ask her to do that. It'll be quicker, I suppose. What else?"

"Do you know if there's anywhere Frank might have gone? Family members, friends outside the area?"

"His ex-wife lives in Glasgow now." Lachlan wrinkled his nose. "But no, she's got a new fella. He won't go to her."

"Does he have any children?"

"Two teenagers. They live with their mum."

"Full time?"

Lachlan considered for a moment. Then he nodded. "Yeah. He talks about them a lot, but they never stay with him. I never thought to wonder why."

Mo felt his heart pick up pace. If Frank Drummond either hadn't wanted or hadn't been allowed to share custody of his children after his divorce, that might have been for a reason.

And that reason could be related to what he'd seen on the man's bedroom wall.

CHAPTER FORTY-NINE

PETRA WAS ABOUT to ask the security guard about his colleagues and the CCTV when Jade opened the door to the cabin.

"Petra, are you OK to have a chat? I want to go over some of the psychological aspects, now we know more."

Petra looked at DI Murphy, who had her eyebrows raised in encouragement, clearly keen to get the newcomers out of the way as soon as possible. Petra put a hand on Arjun's shoulder.

"Thanks for your help, lad. You've been brilliant."

He smiled and shrugged.

"Right then, see you in the morning." Petra put out a hand. DI Murphy took it reluctantly and shook.

She emerged from the portacabin into the chill of a spring night in the Highlands.

"Jesus Christ. It's bloody freezing."

"Let's find a warm pub," Jade suggested.

"Hang on." Petra went back into the portacabin and grabbed her wheelie suitcase. She bumped it down the step from the cabin and looked at Jade.

"Where's yours?"

Jade looked down at Petra's case. "I had Uniform drop it at the hotel."

"Ha! You're a bright kid, you know that."

"I'm only three years younger than you."

"You know what I mean."

Jade smiled and turned to walk down the hill towards the centre of Inverness. Petra followed, cursing the uneven pavements and drop kerbs as she dragged her case behind her. She needed to bring fewer shoes when she travelled. And it would help to know exactly how long they expected her to be away.

"Where are we staying? You've booked a room for me?"

"The Premier Inn. It's only a fifteen-minute walk according to Google Maps."

"Fifteen minutes in these shoes, on these pavements?"

Jade turned to her. "D'you want me to take your case?"

Petra hesitated. She didn't like accepting help. But Jade was younger than her, even if only by three years. And she was certainly fitter.

"There you go." She pushed the case towards the DI.

"Thanks." Jade took it and started walking.

"You got a particular pub in mind?" Petra asked.

"No. I don't know Inverness." Jade looked at her. "Have you been here before? Any recommendations?"

"I've been here, yes. But I can't remember any pubs. Let's go in that one."

They were approaching a bridge over the river. Blue and yellow lighting reflected off the water. Jade paused to shift the suitcase between hands.

"Come to think of it," Petra said, "I haven't eaten since a slice of toast at Magdalena's. Let's get some food."

"Works for me." Jade gestured towards an Italian restaurant on their right and Petra followed her in.

Inside it was warm and bright. Just what Petra needed. They took a table and ordered drinks before perusing the menu.

"So," Jade said, "any theories yet?"

Petra leaned back in her chair. She could see the waitress approaching with a glass of wine and a Coke. She took her wine and raised it before sipping and placing it on the table.

"You've got two bodies," she said. "Two very different ways of connecting them to Macbeth. The first is subtle. There's every chance we could have missed it."

"There are no conifers near the top of Dunsinane Hill." Jade drank from her Coke.

"No. But even so, Harry Nolan was a keen walker. It was perfectly possible that he'd just failed to clean out his coat after picking up some stuff on a previous walk."

"Those pockets were stuffed full."

"Which is how the whole thing came to your attention. So yes, the killer wanted us to notice them. He wanted us to think he was referencing the play."

"You still think it's a man."

"He's a show-off, Jade. He wants us to know how clever he is."

Jade regarded her. "And you don't think women do that?"

Petra snorted. "You think I'm a show-off?"

"I said nothing of the sort."

"Women can show off too, but it tends to be different." She waved a hand in dismissal. "I know the dangers of drawing conclusions. But even if Harry wasn't dragged all the way up that hill, he was carried some of the way. And besides, you've got your CCTV from the castle."

"True." Jade put her glass down. "A man, wearing a cap."

"Exactly."

"So what d'you think about the castle? Is he showing off there?"

"The castle is ridiculous. He attempted to re-enact a scene from the play, and he wrote its most well-known lines on the wall in blood. It's so glaringly obvious as to be laughable. Which is what makes me think he's laughing at us."

"Unless it's a copycat."

"You haven't released information about the pine needles."

"True," Jade replied. "So he might not be aware that we got the Macbeth reference from the first body."

"Don't forget, this body's been there a couple of days. Even if he's watching us, even if he knows we know now, he might not have known at that point."

"So he decided to make sure we did."

"Exactly."

"We're going to have to buy a copy of Macbeth. I don't know enough about the scene with the guards."

"Nor do I," Petra said. "But I can talk to Anthony Urquhart about it."

"I feel uneasy about you bringing him in."

"Ach, don't. I made it very clear to him that he's not getting paid. He seems to enjoy taking me on jaunts to the crime scenes."

Jade glanced upwards and smiled. "Here we are."

The waiter set their food down in front of them. Jade inhaled, wafting the smell of her lasagne towards her. "It's so good to eat proper food."

"What d'you normally eat?"

"Whatever I can get my son to eat. Fish fingers and chips, mainly."

"Nothing wrong with fish fingers and chips."

"There is when it's three times a week."

"There is that." Petra took a bite of her pizza. "I'd like to consult Anthony about this latest crime scene," she said. "Particularly the whole business with the guard. The killer was trying to make out that there was a security guard in the room with the victim."

Jade nodded. "DI Murphy is trying to get hold of Kai. Find out if he saw anything."

"He even swapped the hats around," Petra said.

"Is that relevant?"

"There's a bit where Macbeth tries to pin one of his crimes on a couple of guards. Anthony will know the details."

"Or like I say, we can just buy ourselves a copy of the play." Jade brought out her phone and swiped at it. "Leakey's bookshop. I can go there in the morning."

"It's about more than reading the words, though," Petra told her. "Anthony understands the context. He can help me get around the psychology."

Jade wrinkled her nose.

Petra leaned over the table. "If you think buying a copy of Macbeth is as effective as consulting an expert, then you might as well watch *Mindhunter* instead of talking to me."

Jade shook her head. "It's different."

"Not entirely."

Jade sighed. "Alright, then. But I'm getting my own copy of the play too."

"That's your prerogative."

CHAPTER FIFTY

"You AGAIN?" Heather Reynolds asked as Mo entered Frank Drummond's house. She checked her watch. "Don't you have a family to get back to?"

"Don't remind me." It was Friday night and he and Catriona would normally be getting a takeaway. He'd called and asked if she could keep his warm, but it wasn't really good enough.

"What can we do for you, then? Nick and I'll be off in about half an hour."

"I need to check that wall again."

"We've taken photos of it."

"It'll be quicker if I can look at it in the flesh."

Heather stood back and extended an arm towards the stairs, gesturing for him to go up. "Be my guest. What are you looking for?"

"I've got photos of the Inverness Castle victim. I want to see if he's up there."

She whistled. "Good call. I'll help."

They hurried up the stairs, Mo's stomach rumbling as he

reached the top. He was looking forward to his sweet and sour chicken.

He entered the room and pulled out his phone, bringing up the clearest of the pictures. He showed it to Heather.

"This is the victim."

She winced. "Ouch. I can see cyanosis to his lips, and his cheeks are sunken." She looked at him. "I assume there's a lot of blood at the scene?"

"A whole roomful."

"He'll have gone into haemorrhagic shock, I imagine. If he lost the blood that fast. You'll be able to tell from the state the blood is in at the scene. There'll be minimal drying, it'll be like a lake."

"They tell me it is."

"Who've they got on it, doing the Forensics?"

"I don't know. But there's a team."

"Good. Let me know if they need help."

"You're busy here."

Heather shook her head. "We're almost done. I don't think an actual crime took place here."

"What about that knife?"

"There's nothing around it, nothing in that room. I reckon Drummond disposed of it under there."

"After he killed his victims?"

"Now you'd have to have more than natural powers to know that. All we can do is find evidence of who touched it. I can't tell you when it was left."

"Fair enough." Mo turned to the wall.

"Show me that picture again," Heather said.

He held out his phone. She squinted at it then approached the wall. "Here." She pointed at an image at one end. "And there." She indicated another photo, near the top.

Mo got closer and took pictures of them both. "Thanks," he said.

He looked at the images. A young man, older than Harry, but still in his thirties. He was white, with brown hair and a slim face. The burn mark was more prominent in one of the photos than the other, but it was unmistakeable in both.

In one of the photos the man looked like he was on a shopping street, a distance away from the camera. He was unaware of it, looking off to one side. In the other photo, he was smiling, in front of a backdrop of greenery. A fleece had been pulled up at the collar, possibly to hide the burn. The image looked as if it had been cropped at one side.

Mo stood back to scan the rest of the wall, searching for the rest of the image. Nothing.

He could feel his breathing, shallow and tight.

Frank Drummond, where are you?

Harry was on that wall just the once, and the second victim twice.

Did that have any significance?

CHAPTER FIFTY-ONE

Petra didn't feel like going back to the hotel yet.

It meant lugging that bloody suitcase herself, but staying out for another drink was just too tempting.

She waved Jade goodbye outside the restaurant and turned into the city centre. There had to be somewhere that did a decent whisky.

Five minutes later she was in a pub, the kind of place that smelt of beer and had a stage for live music. There was a decent array of whiskies behind the bar.

She dragged her suitcase towards it, catching a loose patch of carpet and cursing. She peered upwards.

"You after a whisky?" the barmaid asked.

"That I am. What d'you recommend?"

"I'd go for the Glen Ord myself. It's flirty and malty, goes down easily."

Petra eyed her. "I don't need something that goes down easily."

"Oh. Sorry. Well, how about the Dalmore? That's more robust."

"Sounds like just the ticket. I'll have that with ice and a jug of water please."

"Of course."

The barmaid poured her a shot of the whisky in a plain tumbler, placed two cubes of ice in another tumbler and filled a metal jug with water. She placed all three on a tray. "Enjoy."

Petra winced at the Americanism. She took her tray to an empty table then returned for the bloody suitcase.

At last she was sitting down, sipping at her whisky. It was good; full-bodied enough to count but not so much it blew her hair off.

She kicked off her shoes under the table, and put her phone down beside her drink. She hadn't checked her email all day. There was the possibility of a job helping out the police in Marseille, a potential series killer case. She knew they were talking to another psychologist in London, and she wanted to be sure of landing the job.

The Mediterranean would be a welcome change from the Highland cold.

She scrolled through her emails, scanning for a French address. Nothing. She went back up to the top and opened the most recent message, working her way through them one by one and deleting most of them.

She stopped at an email that had no text, just a photo attachment.

The address it had come from was gmail gobbledegook: random letters and numbers. Nothing that made any sense and certainly nothing she recognised.

She should delete it.

Anything might be in that attachment. It might be a virus.

But Petra knew it wasn't.

She took another swig of her Dalmore, then coughed. This was the sort of whisky that demanded you drink it slowly.

Open it.

She wouldn't sleep if she ignored it. She'd end up waking at 3am and dragging it out of her trash.

She clicked on the attachment.

It was a scan, of a newspaper article.

Prominent Psychologist Accused of Perjury.

She jerked her head up, suddenly worried that everyone in the bar had read this thing and would be staring at her.

She looked back at the piece. The Dundee Courier, just two days ago.

How had she missed it?

She shoved her phone in her pocket.

How was she going to explain this to Jade and Fraser?

CHAPTER FIFTY-TWO

IT WAS GETTING DARK, and Stuart was starting to wish he'd brought a thicker coat. He'd forgotten just how cold Inverness was, compared to Glasgow.

He shivered. Why anyone chose to live up here at the arse-end of nowhere was beyond him. Stuart was a city boy, and although Inverness was officially a city it wasn't a patch on Glasgow.

Still, he wouldn't be here for long.

He walked along the pavement alongside the hoardings that surrounded the castle, scanning the area around them for CCTV cameras that weren't in or on the building site, and didn't belong to the castle. Anything like that would be covered by Arjun.

The pavement took a route away from the castle and down-hill from it, eventually reaching a point where he had to cross a car park and climb some dismal steps to reach the castle again. He mounted the steps two at a time, as much to warm himself up as for speed. It wouldn't do him any harm to move quickly.

He might warm up, and the sooner he got this done, the sooner he'd be inside, in the warm of the hotel.

He followed a path back along the walls of the castle until he reached a gate in the hoardings. So there was another entrance. He wondered if Arjun had checked the cameras around here.

The guy seemed pretty thorough, though. And there was no sign that the killer had tried to enter the castle another way. Stuart was secretly impressed by the killer's nerve, just parking up and walking in like that, with nothing more than a wave in the direction of the security hut.

He retraced his steps back down to the car park. There might be cameras on the shops across the road. All he needed was a registration plate. And even if those cameras hadn't caught that, they might show which route the van had taken, and from that he could speak to the Highland Council and get access to numberplate recognition cameras.

That was what he needed: a bus lane, or a traffic light. Somewhere with a camera designed to capture plates. But a traffic light camera would only catch the van if it had gone through a red light, and a bus lane camera would only have fired if a vehicle had entered the lane.

He needed more general CCTV. A speed camera, maybe.

He stopped at a pedestrian crossing and made a note of the location. He'd speak to traffic control in the morning and see if they'd caught the van on film. It would probably have been speeding away.

There was a bar along from the crossing. He approached it, and saw a camera attached to the front.

The door was locked. Stuart tugged at it, but it didn't give. He knocked.

Shivering, he waited a few moments. No answer.

This street was quiet, and would be especially so with the castle locked up. It looked like the businesses along here were struggling and closing down as they lost the fight.

He stood back, standing at the edge of the pavement, and looked up.

There were windows above the shops. A Highland-themed gift shop, a fishing supplies shop and a grocery that had closed for the night. Two other shops that looked permanently closed.

One of the windows above was lit.

Flats.

Maybe the people living up there would have seen something.

He walked along the shop fronts, trying to work out how to access the flats. There was no sign of a door along the frontage.

Shit.

Stuart had nothing else to do this evening. He would find a way in.

In search of an alleyway, he walked further along the street. He'd find a way to speak to the people living in those flats, even if it took him all night.

CHAPTER FIFTY-THREE

JADE PRESSED the buzzer at the hotel reception and a young woman emerged from a doorway, smiling.

"You must be DI Tanner."

Jade frowned at her.

"The constable who brought your bags is my cousin. He described you."

Small world. "That's great. Have you got my bag?"

"I took the liberty of putting it in your room. I hope you don't mind."

"Mind? That's wonderful. Thank you."

"No problem." Another smile. Jade wondered if the woman was always this welcoming, or if she was getting special treatment.

She picked up her key and took the lift to her room. Once inside, she threw herself onto the bed.

She closed her eyes, wishing she could sleep. But there were calls to be made.

Sit up, woman. Jade pushed herself upright and checked

her phone for the time. She might be just in time to catch Rory before he went down for the night.

Using her image on the phone screen as a mirror, she tidied her hair while waiting for her mum to answer.

"Hello, hen," her mum said. "You're just in time."

Thank God.

Rory pushed onto his gran's lap. "Hiya, Mummy."

"Hi, gorgeous. How's things?"

"Good. The squirrels went camping."

Jade laughed. "Still watching *Hey Duggee?*"

"I told you, it's awesome. Did you watch it?"

"Not yet, little man. But I will, soon as I'm back home with you."

She was hoping that would be tomorrow night. It was the weekend, after all. But she wasn't about to tell Rory that. She knew the impact of a broken promise on a child.

"I've got to clean my teeth, Mummy. Bye!" He climbed down and ran away.

Jade wiped away a tear. "Is he missing me?"

"From time to time, love. But most of the time he's too busy. He's a bundle of energy, isn't he?"

"I'm sorry, Mum. Is it too much for you?"

Her phone buzzed. She checked it, trying not to make it look too obvious. It was Mo.

"You know I love spending time with him," her mum said. "But I won't deny I'm looking forward to you coming home."

"I'm expecting that to be tomorrow. I'm sorry, Mum. I know it's tiring for you. I'll find proper help when this case is done. A nanny."

"No grandchild of mine is having a bloody nanny."

Jade smiled "We'll see. Tomorrow. I'll be home tomorrow."

"Don't make promises you can't keep, love."

"I'll try."

Her phone buzzed again. "I'm sorry, Mum," she said, for the third time. It seemed to be almost the only thing she ever said to her. "I've got to go. Sleep well, both of you."

"You look after yourself, girl. Make sure you're eating properly."

Jade rolled her eyes – *I'm not sixteen any more* – and switched to Mo on voice call.

"Boss. I'm not disturbing you, am I?"

"No. How did you get on with the photos?"

"The victim's on Frank Drummond's wall."

Jade sat up straighter on the bed. "He's what?"

"There are two photos of him. I'm sending them to you now."

"Shit." She waited for the email to come through. "That's him. OK, so we have a suspect. Where the hell is Frank Drummond?"

"I spoke to Lachlan Kerr, and he had no idea. But Drummond's got an ex-wife in Glasgow. His teenage sons live there with her. Full time."

"He didn't get shared custody?"

"No. That might be relevant."

Jade lay back on the bed, staring at the ceiling. "OK," she said. "We need to access court records, find out if there was a hearing. If Frank Drummond abused his kids, or anything like that."

"You think he did?"

"I don't know what to think, Mo. But the man's got a wall covered in photos of young men, he's disappeared after two of those men have been killed, and he wasn't allowed to live with his sons."

"We'll never access the court records tonight."

"And it's Saturday tomorrow." She thumped the bed. "Damn."

"What d'you want me to do?"

"You go home. Have your Friday night Chinese with Catriona. I'll call Fraser, and I'll work out what to tell Wallace and Murphy."

CHAPTER FIFTY-FOUR

JADE WOKE to the sound of knocking on her bedroom door.

She turned over, her body heavy with sleep. "Rory? Sweetie, come in. Have a cuddle."

Rory never knocked. He woke up early and would run into her room and slip into bed with her, burrowing his small limbs into her side for warmth and comfort.

She turned over. "Rory?"

It wasn't like him to wait.

More knocking.

She opened her eyes.

The room was dark. No light seeping around the curtains.

Jade slumped back into the pillows. She wasn't at home. She was in a Premier Inn in Inverness.

She yawned. "Who is it?"

"It's Stuart, boss. Sorry to wake you."

"Stuart?" Jade reached out for her phone on the bedside table. 6.30am.

She groaned. "Right with you."

She heaved herself out of bed and dragged on a sweater

over her pyjamas. She opened the door, blinking at the bright light in the corridor.

"Sorry to wake you, boss, but I've got something."

Jade sniffed and pulled the sweater tighter around her. "What kind of something?"

"I went looking for CCTV, like you said. I checked the shops opposite the castle. There were some cameras there but obviously I couldn't get into the shops. I managed to find a way round the back and into some flats above them."

"What did you find, Stuart? I don't need the whole story." Jade yawned again, wishing it *had* been Rory who'd woken her.

"A woman in one of the flats heard a loud noise, early hours of Thursday morning. A car driving up towards the castle, revving its engine. She said there'd been a few of them lately and she was getting sick of it. So she grabbed her phone and when it came back, she managed to get a photo."

"Tell me you got a registration plate."

He smiled. "I did."

Jade scratched her cheek. "PNC check?"

"Not yet, I can't get through. I'll send it to Patty when she's in, see if she can match it to Frank Drummond."

Jade leaned against the door post. She'd had a good night's sleep for the first time in days. In bed at ten. Woken at six-thirty. That was over eight hours. So why was she so exhausted?

"OK," she said. "Give me half an hour. When does breakfast start?"

"Seven."

"Perfect. Meet me down there. We can plan for the day."

She shut the door and threw herself onto the bed, wishing she could just sleep.

CHAPTER FIFTY-FIVE

JADE HAD A QUICK SHOWER, deliberately not washing her hair, and dressed in one of the two blouses she'd brought with her. She was hoping this stint away from home wouldn't last much longer.

She checked the time after putting on some mascara: 6:48. She had time to make a call.

Fraser picked up on the second ring.

"Jade, did you try to call me last night?"

"It was late, Sir. Sorry if I bothered you."

"You didn't bother me. Sorry I didn't hear the phone. What can I do for you?"

"We have reason to believe that a member of the Perth Macbeth Society killed both Harry Nolan and our Inverness victim."

"Have you got an ID on the Inverness victim yet?"

"Not yet."

"Your suspect, is this the Frank Drummond who's gone missing? He's not your body?"

"He's not. And we found photographs of the two dead men on the wall of Drummond's spare bedroom."

"What kind of photographs?"

"Nothing obscene. But they look like they were taken without the men's permission. There's more of them, too, a whole wall full of young men."

"And there's no trace of Drummond?"

"No, Sir."

"OK. You don't need me to tell you that we'll need to work closely with Dundee and Inverness on this one. DI Wallace is already—"

"I sent him an email last night. I'm waiting for a call from him."

"Good. I'll do what I can to make sure you have a key role. Is it your team who found this new evidence?"

"With the help of the SOCOs."

"Good. And do we have any indication of where Drummond might have gone?"

"He's got an ex-wife in Glasgow. Teenage kids there, who it seems he never sees."

"Do we know why?"

"Apparently he talks about them a lot, but they aren't on the scene."

"We can't jump to conclusions about that. Dundee will want to look into it, find out more from the ex-wife."

"I've got Mo and Patty in the office in Glasgow. One or both of them can pay her a visit."

"OK. But make sure Wallace is in the loop." Fraser sighed. "I'm trying to save your unit, Jade. The best way to do that is by ensuring you make a valid contribution to this investigation. Not by pissing everyone off."

"What will you have me do?"

"Is Petra McBride with you?"

"She's here in Inverness. She's been consulting a Macbeth expert at her old university, wants to show him the writing from the second crime scene."

"What writing?"

"Someone, presumably the killer, wrote one of the most best-known lines from Macbeth on the wall. In blood."

"Don't tell me. 'Out, damned spot'."

Jaded smiled. She wedged her phone under her ear and shrugged on her jacket. "That's the one."

"OK. I'd like you to contact this Macbeth guy direct. Having one expert working through another makes me uneasy."

"OK."

"And do you need to stay up there any longer? I'm worried about you."

Jade straightened up. "I'm fine."

"I can hear it in your voice. You're tired."

Jade hated the idea that the Detective Superintendent didn't think she could do her job. "I got a good night's sleep last night. I'm fine."

"This isn't your Super talking now, Jade. It's your friend. Dan used to talk about how tired you'd get. He felt like he only got half of you."

Jade tightened her grip on the phone. "When did he tell you that?"

"About ten days before he died."

Jade wasn't sure how she felt about her late husband discussing her with her boss. Even if Fraser had been their friend for almost six years.

"I appreciate your concern, Sir. But I'll be fine. We'll get this wrapped up by tomorrow, then we can continue the case from the office."

"Good. Don't overdo it. And please…"

"Yes?"

"Don't piss too many people off."

CHAPTER FIFTY-SIX

Mo DODGED past Catriona as she reached into the fridge for a carton of apple juice.

"Isla's gone off it," he told her.

She turned to him. "No, she hasn't."

He nodded. "She has. She told me yesterday on the way into school."

Catriona sighed. "Bloody hell. Why do they keep changing what they eat?"

He shrugged. Isla had woken them quarter of an hour earlier and was now sitting in front of the TV watching *iCarly*.

"Just do her some Coco Pops and a glass of milk and she'll be fine," he said.

"I don't want to give her Coco Pops. I'm a GP, for God's sake. How can I look my patients in the eye and tell them to eat a healthy diet when I fill my own children up on sugary breakfast cereal?"

He put a hand on her shoulder. "It won't kill her, Cat. Give her some Coco Pops and you can go back to bed."

Catriona leaned on him. "I will. Sorry you have to go into work."

He shrugged. "We're in the middle of a double murder investigation. It's what I do."

She shifted her angle to look into his eyes. "When you moved to CID, I thought you'd do more regular hours."

"And I do. Remember how many nights I had to work when I was in Uniform?"

"I suppose so." She yawned. "Anyway, I can't talk. I've got a mountain of paperwork to do this morning, and there's a management meeting on Monday to prepare for. One of our GPs has handed in his resignation."

"Another one?"

She nodded. "God only knows how we'll replace him. I might have to work late for the next few weeks. Cover more Saturday morning clinics."

"It's OK." Mo stroked his wife's face. "We both have demanding jobs. We'll cope."

"Mum! Where's my breakfast?"

Catriona threw a look towards the living room. She stuck her tongue out and Mo laughed. "What does she think this is, the Ritz?"

"Make her wait," he said. "Maybe she'll get her own."

"Chance would be a fine thing. You get off to your murder case. How far do you have to drive today?"

"I'm in the office with Patty. On a Saturday, it'll only take me half an hour."

"I worry about the amount of driving you do."

"It's fine." He kissed her cheek and grabbed the bag with his packed lunch in it. He'd prepared it after eating the takeaway last night. "I like the scenery. It's a sight better than driving around the West Midlands."

She grunted. "It's still driving. Long hours."

"Which both of us do. Don't worry about me." He kissed her. "I'll see you later. Have a good day and don't miss me too much."

"I'll try not to." She gave him a playful smile.

Mo smiled back then turned for the door. He might have been working, but it still felt like the weekend.

CHAPTER FIFTY-SEVEN

"Any joy with the PNC check?" Jade asked as she sat down opposite Stuart at the breakfast table, a mug of coffee in hand. The restaurant was quiet at this time on a Saturday morning, just an elderly couple at the opposite end and a dad with a toddler a few tables along. The dad was still in his pyjamas.

"I've sent the details through," he told her. "Patty'll be in an hour and she can follow it up."

"Good. I don't suppose there was any report of a car being left at Frank Drummond's house?"

"Nothing in the driveway, boss. I've sent a message to Lachlan Kerr asking if he knows what Drummond drives. He's being pretty helpful."

She nodded. "At least someone is. That Christine McTavish still isn't answering the sarge's calls."

"You think maybe she's covering for Drummond?" Stuart asked. "She could have something to do with it."

"It was her who reported Harry Nolan missing. I can't see why she'd do that if she was covering for the murderer."

Stuart leaned in, anxious for the man with the toddler not to overhear. "It's a good way to cover her tracks. Being the person who reports him missing makes her look innocent. And she did report his disappearance very quickly."

"She said he always turned up at meetings."

"It's not like she lived with Harry, or anything. Who's to say he hadn't just decided not to show up?"

Jade gulped down a mouthful of coffee. It was bitter. "OK, let's go back to her. See if we can find out what she knows about Frank and what she says when we ask her about the second victim."

"The pathologist has arrived, apparently. He's on his way to the castle."

"At seven am?"

"He turned up late last night. Staying over somewhere."

"Here, maybe?" Jade looked around the breakfast room. None of their companions looked likely to be the pathologist.

"I doubt it," Stuart said.

"No. Right. I'll go to the castle, you go back to Perthshire and pay a visit to Christine. I want to follow up Frank's ex-wife in Glasgow, see if she knows anything about his whereabouts. I'll ask Mo to talk to Wallace, let him know about her, then visit her too."

"What about the Macbeth stuff?"

She put down her mug. "Petra's brought in an expert. We can show him a photo of the blood writing, see what he thinks."

"He's not going to come up here?"

"I don't see the need." Jade slumped in her seat. "But we can't do any of this until I've had a conversation with DI Wallace."

"No."

"He'll want to allocate resources. But it's a Saturday morning, chances are he isn't in the office yet. And I don't want that to hold us up." She gave Stuart a long look. "If you know what I mean."

"I do, boss." He raised an eyebrow.

"I don't like working like this," she told him. "But..."

"But?" Stuart leaned forward.

"You might as well know." She'd only spoken to Mo about this. "There's a threat to our unit. We might be broken up. I see this case as an opportunity to prove ourselves."

He nodded. "Is that why you're not the SIO?"

"Don't remind me. Yes, it is. I haven't told you about this, yes?"

He touched a finger to his lips. "I won't tell a soul. You think we'll be OK, though?"

"If you're asking if I think you should apply for another job, no. I'm going to fight for this team, and the Super is too. You're a good detective, Stuart, and I don't want to lose you."

His cheeks had turned pink. "Thanks."

I don't tell my team that enough. Jade had to change her ways.

Now she'd told Stuart about the threat to the team, she should tell Patty. She couldn't risk her finding out through Stuart. Not when the two women had worked together for so many years.

"Let's just get on with the case, Stuart. Go and see Christine, tell me how she reacts. Keep what you tell her to the minimum so you can better judge what she already knows."

"I know what's needed."

"Of course you do. Call me when you're done and we can plan our next steps according to what the wider team says."

"No problem, boss." Stuart scooped up the last of his cornflakes and grabbed his coat from the back of his chair.

CHAPTER FIFTY-EIGHT

THIS ROOM WAS a bloody awful place to work.

Petra got up from her chair for the twentieth time and went into the bathroom to fill her water glass.

The water was tepid. The coffee was instant, and stale. And she'd long since run out of teabags.

As she ran the water to try to get it at least slightly cold, she contemplated the report she was writing.

Jade wanted to understand the psychology of a person who could commit these crimes. And Petra was struggling to come up with answers.

The first crime had been subtle. Clever.

The second was a mess. Writing on the wall in blood. A staged fight between guards. It was melodramatic, over the top.

The work of an idiot.

Or a fool?

What was that line from Macbeth again?

She went back into the bedroom and picked up her phone. She wasn't supposed to be calling him. But she needed to tell him that.

"Dr McBride," Urquhart said, picking up as it rang, "I was wondering when I'd hear from you again."

"Anthony, is there a quote in Macbeth about an idiot?"

"There's one about life being a fool. 'It is a tale told by an idiot, full of sound and fury, signifying nothing'."

She tapped her chin. The second crime had certainly been full of sound and fury. But signifying nothing?

"Can you give me the context for that?"

"It's from Act five, Scene five. Macbeth ponders his guilt and paranoia. One of Shakespeare's grandest soliloquies."

"What else does Macbeth say?"

Urquhart cleared his throat. "'And all our yesterdays have lighted fools

The way to dusty death. Out, out, brief candle!

Life's but a walking shadow, a poor player

That struts and frets his hour upon the stage

And then is heard no more. It is a tale

Told by an idiot, full of sound and fury,

Signifying nothing.'"

Dusty death. Lighted fools. Had the crime scene been dusty? And the lighting? Petra would need to ask Jade about that.

"That's not much help," she said.

"Apologies. I gather you're at Inverness Castle. Fine spot for a crime, it's being renovated."

She grunted.

"You're trying to understand the mind of the killer, yes?"

"Yes." But what could Urquhart tell her about that? He was an English professor.

"I think you're looking for a private person," Urquhart said. "He killed Harry Nolan on the top of a hill where no one would see him, and now he's chosen a venue that's out of sight as far as the public are concerned. Hidden by those huge red hoardings."

"A coward, you mean."

"Not necessarily."

"The nature of this second death isn't exactly private."

"It was done in a private place, a part of the castle that's rarely visited."

"You seem to know a lot about the castle."

"I was in the area a couple of weeks ago. Research trip. I'm working on a book about the royal palaces and castles in Shakespeare's work, and it gave me the perfect opportunity to take a trip north. Rather disappointing, finding it boarded up like that."

Petra inhaled. "We found writing by the victim. In blood."

"What writing?"

"'Out, damned spot.'"

"Maybe your killer is feeling remorse. Guilt. Lady Macbeth uttered those words at the height of her torment over what she'd done to King Duncan."

"Was it Lady Macbeth who killed Duncan, or her husband?"

"Ah. Good question. In the play it's Macbeth, with his lady's encouragement. They fit up some guards though."

Petra thought of the guards, at the castle. The CCTV.

"Anthony, what do you—"

"I'm going to come up and join you."

What?

"You don't need to do that."

"You're looking for insight on this writing. Seeing it in person would help me to help you, as it were."

"It's fine," she told him. "I'll send you photographs."

"I believe that being there would be beneficial."

Petra knew that refusing the professor would only make him more determined. "You visited the castle recently," she said. "How do you think a person would set up a murder there?"

"You're trying to get me to do your job?"

"I'm thinking aloud. The method he used was brash, no attempt to hide."

"Hiding in plain sight, as they say. Clever."

Clever, or stupid.

Or wanting the police to think one or the other.

CHAPTER FIFTY-NINE

DI Murphy was standing at the entrance to the castle when Jade arrived.

"DI Tanner," she said. "I thought we'd got rid of you."

"I hear the pathologist is here."

"He is." Murphy cocked her head. "Not that it's anything to do with you."

Jade looked at the woman. She thought of her conversation with Fraser: *don't piss anybody off*.

"You're right," she said. "I came to tell you my team is moving on."

Murphy couldn't resist a smirk. "You're leaving us?"

"Heading back to Glasgow."

Should she mention Frank Drummond, or his ex-wife?

She took a breath.

"We're following up on a suspect from Perthshire. He's got an ex-wife not far from our base in Glasgow. It makes sense for us to visit her."

Murphy took a step forward. "You're supposed to be

managing the external consultants. Leave the proper police work to me."

"Perhaps it should be DI Wallace's team who deal with this. They are closer, after all."

"I've already spoken to DI Wallace. I'm sure he'll be pleased to know that there's a new lead."

"Have you got an ID on this body yet?"

"We're looking at dental records. There are only two NHS dentists in Inverness; we're starting with them."

"What makes you think the victim wouldn't go private?"

"Have you seen the state of his clothes?"

That hadn't been easy, what with them being soaked in blood. Jade shrugged.

"His jeans are torn," Murphy said, "and his t-shirt has ingrained dirt that has nothing to do with his death. He's not going to be using a private dentist."

"If he was seeing a dentist at all."

"There is that. Let's hope he was."

Jade caught movement behind the DI. The pathologist was emerging from the castle, stripping off his forensic suit.

She smiled. One advantage of Inverness having to call for someone from further afield.

"Dr Pradesh," she said. "Fancy seeing you up here."

He pulled back the hood of his suit and smiled at her. "DI Tanner. Is this your case?"

"No," interrupted Murphy.

Jade smiled. "It isn't, but we've been assisting with it. And another case we believe to be linked."

"Ah, right. Well in that case I can tell both of you the cause of death: blood loss after being stabbed in the chest."

"Anything else?" Murphy asked.

"From the look of his eyes, I think he was drugged beforehand. I'll do a toxicology analysis and let you know, but there are signs he was given a sedative."

Jade nodded. From the way the man had been manoeuvred into the castle by his killer, that made sense.

"And we've received matching dental records," the pathologist added. He held out a file.

Murphy grabbed it. "We have an ID?"

"We do. He's not local. Not anymore, at least."

"Not anymore?" Murphy asked.

"He's originally from Inverness but was living in Dundee more recently."

Dundee.

That meant Wallace.

Jade held out her hand. Murphy pulled back the file, then sighed and handed it over. "You might as well see."

Jade opened it. Callum Ferguson. An address in Dundee.

She needed to pass this to Wallace. And she needed to speak to Petra.

CHAPTER SIXTY

"Heya, Sarge." Patty looked up from her screen.

"Patty." Mo put his jacket over the back of his chair and smoothed it down. "It's good to see you again."

"Good to see you too. This place is bloody spooky when it's empty."

Mo looked around the empty office space. "I can imagine. What's been happening?"

"Oh, all sorts. I had a party on Thursday. I got the Chippendales in and everything."

He smiled. "The case?"

Patty snorted. "Oh, the case. Well, I've got PNC results on that van Stuart sent me."

"And?"

"It doesn't belong to Frank Drummond."

Damn. "Any idea who it does belong to?"

Patty smiled at him, her eyes twinkling. "You're not going to believe this."

"Try me."

"It belongs to another Drummond."

"His ex-wife?"

"No. Adam. His son."

"I thought his kids were teenagers."

"He is. He's nineteen years old and there's a van registered in his name."

Mo sat down.

Frank Drummond was estranged from his family. His boys lived in Glasgow with their mum.

So what was he doing, using his son's van?

CHAPTER SIXTY-ONE

"You AGAIN." Christine McTavish stood at the door to her building, her face sour.

"I'm sorry to bother you," Stuart said. "But there are a few more questions I need to ask."

"You could have phoned me."

I could, but you wouldn't have picked up.

He smiled. "I thought it would be easier to chat face to face."

She lifted her wrist and made a show of checking her watch. "I've got work in ten minutes. You'd better be quick."

Why was it that every time they visited Christine McTavish, she had somewhere to be?

"Can I come in, or would you rather have this conversation on the doorstep?" He'd already noticed a neighbour peering out of the window of the flat above.

A grunt. "Come in."

Stuart followed her through to the living room at the front of the house. She didn't offer him a seat, nor did she sit down herself.

"We're investigating a second murder," he told her.

"Oh." Her expression didn't change.

"A young man, found in Inverness."

"Where in Inverness?"

Stuart ignored the question. "You're a member of the Macbeth Society. We're working on a link between the play and these crimes. Is that something you've considered?"

She laughed. "You're trying to get me to say something incriminating. Just because I haven't rolled over like a good puppy and helped you do your job."

"I just wanted your input on the Macbeth connection."

She took a step towards him. Stuart held his ground.

"When was this second victim killed?"

"Early Thursday morning."

"Well in that case I can tell you exactly where I was, and who I was with."

Stuart pulled out his notebook. "Please."

"Lachlan Kerr. I was at Lachlan Kerr's house, having sex with him."

Stuart flinched. He looked up from his notepad.

"Surprised?" she asked. "Shocked?"

"No. Just... why did neither of you tell us this?"

"You didn't ask. Maybe Lachlan's trying to protect my honour." She smirked. "Idiot."

"OK." Stuart put his pen away. "Obviously we'll be speaking with Lachlan to confirm this."

"I promise I won't phone him and get him to vouch for me, if that's what you're thinking."

Stuart met her gaze. Why was this woman so cynical?

"I'm not trying to interfere with your job, DC Burns. I'm just not a fan of the police. Look me up, when you get back to your office. Then maybe you'll see why I'm not lapping it all up the way Lachlan is."

"I will."

"Now if you don't mind, I need to go to work."

CHAPTER SIXTY-TWO

GAIL DRUMMOND LIVED in a modern semi in Broomhouse. Mo could hear the roar of the M73 less than five hundred metres away, as he and Patty got out of the car.

"I could have done this on my own," Mo said as they approached the house.

"There's nothing to do in the office. I keep calling Lyle Wallace's lot and asking if they'll pass me any jobs, but they won't."

"They've refused?"

"They tell me they're going to send me something, then they never send it. Flippin' annoying, it is."

"I'll speak to one of the DSs in that team."

"Don't. I'm here with you now, aren't I? Two heads are better than one. And she might speak more freely to a woman."

Patty had a point.

Mo pressed the buzzer for the second time and heard it sound somewhere inside the house.

"It's working," he said.

"Maybe she doesn't want to talk to us."

"She won't know why we're here, or at least, I assume she won't. I don't see any reason why she wouldn't come to the door."

"She could be out."

"I can hear music."

Patty cocked her head. Mo watched her face as she registered the music playing somewhere inside: Blondie.

"Good taste," she said.

The door opened just as Mo was about to ring the bell again. A short blonde woman dressed in jeans and a silk blouse stood before them.

She looked from Mo to Patty and back again. "Are you the police?"

"We are." Mo held up his ID.

"At last. I've been wondering when you'd turn up."

"You were expecting us?"

"Of course I was." She grabbed Mo's elbow and started tugging him inside. "Now come in, so we can get started."

CHAPTER SIXTY-THREE

JADE PHONED Petra as she was arriving back at the Premier Inn.

"Petra, I'm at the hotel. Are you still in Inverness?"

"Of course I am. I'm working on your report."

Good. "How's it going?"

"Almost done. But if you keep interrupting me, it'll never—"

"This is the first time I've called you. Is there anything new? We've got an ID for the second victim."

"Hang on. I'm coming downstairs." Petra hung up.

Jade found a chair in the foyer and sat, fidgeting with her wedding ring as she waited. At some point she'd have to stop wearing it. But not yet.

The lift doors opened and Petra emerged. She was wearing a t-shirt that didn't fit and her hair was down.

Jade smiled. "You look like you've been working hard."

Petra pushed her hair up. "Damn. You haven't seen me like this. Now," she took the chair next to Jade, "tell me about this victim."

Jade leaned in. The foyer was quiet, not even a receptionist on duty. But she didn't like the quiet. Whatever they said would be audible to anyone who might come through the front door or down the stairs.

"Callum Ferguson," she said. "He's got a record."

"What kind of record?"

"Intent to supply. He was stopped by Dundee Police last autumn and arrested with ten wraps of heroin on him."

"He was a user?"

Jade shook her head. "I don't think so. The pathologist has said nothing about track marks." But she'd need to send him the man's record, so he could check. "He might have been dealing but not taking."

"Only a quarter of dealers manage that," Petra said. "It's even lower for the ones farther down the chain. That's how they're recruited."

Jade gave her a look.

"Sorry," Petra said. "You know all this stuff."

"I do."

"OK." Petra turned away, deep in thought. She turned back. "You say he's from Dundee."

"Inverness, originally. That's how we found his dental records. But he was living in Dundee more recently. As a post-graduate student."

Petra frowned. "Of what?"

"History. Seventeenth century England."

"Which is when Shakespeare wrote Macbeth."

Jade screwed up her face. "He was a historian, though. Macbeth was fiction. It made a mockery of the historical record on King Macbeth."

"Callum wasn't the killer, remember. He's a victim. Who's

to say he even knew the killer was seeking out these Macbeth connections?"

"You've got a point," Jade conceded.

"I spoke to Professor Urquhart again," Petra said. "He gave me more lines from the play, that might be useful."

"I meant to tell you, I need to deal direct with Urquhart from now on. Fraser doesn't like the fact he doesn't have a direct input to the team."

Petra looked at her. "I'm not part of your team?"

"Officially, no. You're a freelancer bought in on an ad hoc basis."

Petra smiled. "I'm joshing you, lass. Of course I'm not part of your team." She shuddered. "A copper, me? Fat chance."

Jade felt the tension leave her shoulders. "So you'll let me deal with Urquhart from now on?"

"If you insist. The man's annoying me anyway. Too many questions about the castle."

"What kind of questions? Questions linking it to the plays?"

"More quotes, mainly. He thinks the castle crime scene might be an attempt to mock us. To compare us with the foolishness of life."

"So the killer's not just being obvious."

"He is that, but he's trying to impress us with his cleverness at the same time."

"It feels like that's the whole point."

Petra nodded. "It's an important part of the psychology of this bastard. He's impressed with his own intellect, and he wants us to be as well. If he kills again, I think he'll go off on a tangent. There won't be a quote from the play, or even a location that features in it."

"What kind of location, then?"

"I need to do more thinking about that."

"You think he *will* kill again?"

"He's taunting us. We didn't catch him after the first death, and as far as he knew we hadn't spotted the Macbeth link. So he committed another, more obvious, crime. But even then his message was intelligent, or at least he thought so. We still haven't caught up with him, so I believe there's reason to think he'll strike again."

"And we still haven't tracked him down. Mo and Patty are talking to his ex-wife, but—"

"Whose ex-wife?"

"Frank Drummond's. She's in Glasgow, with their sons. He used the eldest son's van to bring Callum Ferguson to Inverness Castle."

"He did?" Petra asked.

Jade nodded. "It's not Frank Drummond's vehicle, but it's the next best thing. We've got our man."

"And we need to catch up with him, before he kills again."

CHAPTER SIXTY-FOUR

"Have you found it yet?" Gail Drummond asked. Mo and Patty were in her kitchen, having been all but dragged inside the house.

"Found what?" Mo asked.

"The van. Adam's van was nicked on Tuesday."

Mo rubbed his chin. "I'm sorry. I don't know what you're talking about."

She blew out a breath. "It went missing from outside the house on Wednesday night. Adam left it here on Monday, he's got nowhere to park at his girlfriend's place. When I got up on Wednesday morning it was gone. But you know all this. I gave a statement."

"Adam is your partner?" Mo asked.

"My son. He needs that van, for his theatre work."

Mo exchanged glances with Patty. He looked back at Gail.

"I'm sorry," he said. "But we aren't here about your van."

She slumped back against the kitchen cabinets. "So what are you here about?"

"Your husband. Frank."

"Ex-husband." Her face darkened. "What's he done now?"

"We want to speak to him in connection with a double murder inquiry."

"Frank killed someone?" She laughed. "Frank's a bastard and a fucking pervert, but he's not a killer." Her brow furrowed. "Well, he wasn't when we were married."

"How long is it since you've lived with him?" Patty asked.

"Our divorce was finalised in November. We split up last January."

"Does he see your sons?" Mo asked.

Gail's jaw clenched. "Frank is not the kind of man you want spending time alone with vulnerable teenagers. No, he does not see my sons."

"Are you aware of any places he might go, if he's looking for somewhere to hide?"

"There's his brother's."

"Where's that?" Patty asked.

"Edinburgh. Jake was the clever one, the one with a career. Frank was the fuckup, but I didn't know that when I met him."

"Can you tell us where Jake lives?"

"I've got his address somewhere. Wait."

She walked past the two detectives and left the room. Moments later she was back, phone in hand.

"Here you are." She read out an address in Edinburgh's Southside.

"Thanks." Mo wrote it down. "Anywhere else? Has Frank lived in Glasgow in the past?"

"Briefly, when he was a student. That twenty-five years ago, though. I'm pretty sure he hasn't got any friends here from those days."

Mo nodded. Frank Drummond was still eluding them.

"If he came to Glasgow, would he come here?"

"He's not supposed to. But yes, he does. He was here on Wednesday night."

"I'm sorry?"

"He came here in the middle of the night. Waking the whole street. I could have killed him."

"On Wednesday?" Mo glanced at Patty. "What time?"

CHAPTER SIXTY-FIVE

"Professor Urquhart," Jade said. "My name's DI Tanner. I head up Police Scotland's Complex Crimes Unit."

"Yes," a thin voice replied. "Petra told me about you. Is she alright?"

"She is. But I wanted to make contact myself. It's not often we have one expert bringing in another."

"Ah. You want to keep a tighter leash." A chuckle. "Well, I can't blame you."

"Petra tells me you've been advising her about Macbeth and how it relates to our murder inquiry."

"Double murder inquiry, she tells me."

"Yes." Jade pursed her lips. She was at Inverness Station, waiting for a train south. Petra was still in the hotel, finishing her report. "So is there anything we need to know about? Anything that can help us identify a potential third crime scene?"

"You think he's going to strike again?"

"That's not what I said."

"It sounded like it."

She clenched her teeth. "We've had a murder on Dunsinane Hill, with plant material from Birnam Wood. Another in Inverness Castle. What are the other significant locations in the book?"

"Play."

"Sorry?"

"It's a play, not a book. Shakespeare would never have intended it to be published in book form."

"Ah. Right." Jade had visited Leakey's secondhand bookshop in Inverness, but their last copy of Macbeth had been sold the previous day. So her knowledge of it was still limited to the snippets she'd picked up over the years. "So are there any other significant locations in the play?"

"Well..."

Silence.

"Professor Urquhart?"

"Sorry. I was looking something up. If your killer is looking to stage a re-enactment again, he might try to set up the whole three witches scenario."

Jade remembered something. "There's a Three Witches tearoom near Dunsinane. Could he potentially target that?"

"DI Tanner, with respect, there are certainly no tearooms in Macbeth, and the killer is unlikely to lower himself to such a thing."

Jade smiled.

Her train was pulling in. She stepped forward, dragging her wheelie suitcase.

"OK," she said. "So where else might he go, that's linked to the witches?"

"You really don't know?" he asked.

"Please." She stepped onto the train. "Enlighten me."

"The witches encounter Macbeth on a heath. The bard

doesn't say where this heath is, he likes to be vague. Probably near Macbeth's castle at Cawdor, but no one knows exactly where."

Cawdor. That wasn't far from Inverness.

Jade checked the train's information screen, scrolling through its destinations. First stop was Carrbridge. She would be leaving Cawdor far behind very soon.

Did she need to go back?

"Do you think we need to be looking at a heath near Cawdor, Professor?" She found a seat and parked her suitcase beside it.

"Even if the heath was up there," he replied, "it wouldn't be there now. Three quarters of Scotland's heathland has been lost since Shakespeare's time."

He was right. And even if a heath was the next target, who was to know which one?

They had a concrete lead. Frank Drummond, and his family in Glasgow.

"Are there any locations near Glasgow that might be relevant?" Jade asked.

"Glasgow? Why?"

"Humour me. Does any part of the play take place in Glasgow?"

"Glasgow was a small town back then. So no, Shakespeare did not write about the place. You're not looking for a location in Glasgow."

She sighed. "You can't help us with anything else?"

"There is Macduff's castle. East Wemyss, near Kirkcaldy. In the play, Macduff's wife and children are slaughtered there, by Macbeth's men. Given that your man has re-enacted the Duncan murder scene with those guards in Inverness, he might choose to do the same again."

Jade felt a shiver run across her skin.

Wife and children.

Might Drummond target his own ex-wife and estranged teenage sons? Might he take them to East Wemyss so he could act out the scene?

"Thank you, Professor. That's very helpful."

CHAPTER SIXTY-SIX

Mo RAN through the timeline in his head. The CCTV images Jade had sent to the team inbox.

"Correct me if I'm wrong. You said Frank came here on Wednesday night. Do you mean Thursday morning?"

Gail frowned. "You're right, yes." She chewed her bottom lip. "At two am.

"At two am?"

"Yes. I checked the alarm clock next to my bed. He woke the boys. Davey was bloody terrified."

"Are you sure about the time and day? Thursday morning at two am?"

"Yes. I've got a Ring doorbell, if you want to check it. Why, do you think he'll come back?"

Mo licked his lips. "I doubt it."

She stood up. "I'm more worried about the van, to be honest. Adam needs it. He works backstage at the Tramway theatre. There was equipment in that van, he's hoping he won't have to explain it to his boss. Or worse, pay to replace it."

"We'll do what we can." Mo doubted there was any

theatrical equipment left in that van. It had been used to transport a murder victim to Inverness Castle. If the killer knew
what he was doing, he'd have cleaned it thoroughly.

The killer...

The second murder took place early on Thursday morning.
Over 150 miles north.

Which meant Frank wasn't their suspect.

"Thanks, Mrs Drummond. You've been very helpful."

"Dawes. I'm Gail Dawes now."

She ushered them out and closed the door. Mo stood on the
step, staring at Patty.

"What kind of woman is more worried about her son's van
than the fact her ex might have committed murder?"

Patty shrugged. "One with an ex like Frank Drummond, by
the sounds of it."

CHAPTER SIXTY-SEVEN

"It isn't Frank," Mo said. "His ex-wife says he was at her house at the same time Callum Ferguson was killed."

Jade was in the toilet of the train south, connected to a conference call with Mo and Stuart. Patty was with Mo, on speakerphone.

"She might be lying," she said. "Adjusting the time to protect him."

"I looked into the records of their divorce," Mo replied. "She claimed unreasonable behaviour. She was vague in the application but reading between the lines, I think she suspected him of abusing their oldest son. Adam."

"The one whose van was stolen."

"Exactly."

"So there's no love lost between them."

"She wouldn't lie for him, boss," said Patty. "I could see it in her eyes. If she'd lied, it would have been to put him in the shit, not to lift him out of it."

Jade smiled at the mental image.

"OK," she said. "So we have no alternative but to work on the basis that Frank didn't kill Callum."

"Which means he probably didn't kill Harry either," Stuart added.

Jade leaned against the wall of the toilet cubicle. It rattled and swayed, making her feel nauseous.

"We've been assuming all along that the same person killed both victims," she said. "Maybe we're wrong. Maybe someone got wind of what Frank did to Harry and decided to use it as a cover for their own crime."

"It might explain why the two crimes are so different," said Mo. "The second killer didn't have time to formulate his plan."

Jade jumped at a knock on the door.

"Are you going to be long in there?"

Shit. "I need to go," she told the team. "But we're going to have to start again, with Callum's killer. The priority is to find out who nicked that van. Mo, have you spoken to Glasgow CID about that?"

"I called the local station," Patty said. "They don't hold out much hope for finding the van. It's plain white, no distinctive markings. And there's no CCTV anywhere near Gail Dawes's road."

Of course not.

"OK. So we need traffic enforcement to keep an eye out for that van."

"Already on it, boss," said Stuart. "I called them as soon as we had the reg."

"And you went to see Christine, yes? How did that go?"

The door thumped again.

"Alright, alright," Jade muttered. She flushed the toilet, despite not having used it, and opened the door. A woman in a grey suit stood outside, looking impatient.

"Sorry," Jade said.

The woman grunted and hurried into the toilet, locking the door almost before Jade had got out.

Someone's in a hurry.

"Boss? Are you still there?"

"Sorry, Stuart. Did I miss something?" Jade stood in the corridor next to the toilet. A low sunset slanted through the windows, blinding her. But this was marginally more private than the main compartment.

"I was saying, it definitely wasn't Christine. Her alibi is that she was in bed with Lachlan Kerr at the time. I spoke to him and it checks out."

"So why was she so reluctant to help us?"

"She told me to look her up. She had a brother. He was hit by a police vehicle engaged in a high-speed chase four years ago."

Jade winced. "I can see why that might turn her against us."

"I don't think she's suspicious."

"OK. So we have someone who's taken Adam Drummond's vehicle, from outside his mum's house in Glasgow."

"Do they live together?" Stuart asked.

"I asked Gail, the mum," Mo said. "She said Adam lives with her some of the time but normally stays at his girlfriend's in Pollokshields. He keeps his van outside his mum's house cos her street's safer than his girlfriend's."

"Was he sleeping there the night the van went missing?"

"No."

"And the night Frank turned up?"

"Not that one, either."

"Pay the girlfriend's address a visit," Jade said. "See if he's there and if you can find out anything more about this van."

"No problem."

"Good." She sighed. "OK, I'll let Wallace know what we have. And I'll speak to Petra."

"I heard she's not allowed to talk to her Macbeth expert anymore," Stuart said.

"Where did you hear that?" Jade replied. "It's not that she's not allowed. It's just preferable if I do it. And he gave me a potential tipoff. I can't decide if it's worth pursuing."

"What's that?" Mo asked.

"The castle where Macduff's wife and children were killed."

Patty whistled. "Good call. Macduff's Castle, in Fife. Does your expert think maybe the killer will somehow take Drummond's wife and kids there?"

"Ex-wife. And yes, we need to consider that."

"Maybe someone in the Macbeth Society found out about his wall of photos," Mo suggested.

Jade nodded. "Either way, I need to alert Lyle Wallace. Fife's on his patch, politically and physically."

"But you want us to stay in Glasgow."

Jade nodded. "I do. Look, the train's pulling into Aviemore and I need to be sure I don't lose my seat. Keep in touch, people. Let me know how you get on."

CHAPTER SIXTY-EIGHT

"Why didn't you tell me all this before?" Wallace asked, his voice trembling.

"You were busy with the physical evidence," Jade reminded him. "And I'm telling you now."

"DI Tanner." He paused. "DI Tanner, you've been inserting yourself and your team into crime scenes and throwing your weight around with Inverness CID. You've been keeping information from me, thus preventing me from leading a thorough investigation."

"What leads do you have, right now?"

Silence.

"Lyle, tell me what leads you have."

"We're working on DNA samples from Dunsinane Hill. And Inverness have provided toxicology reports for Callum Ferguson. My team are conducting interviews with members of the Macbeth Society in Perth, and in Inverness, we've—"

"Those aren't leads. Those are lines of inquiry."

"And if you'd shared information with us earlier, perhaps we'd be pursuing leads."

"I admit I should have spoken to you earlier. But I've just arrived at Glasgow Queen Street and this wasn't the kind of conversation I wanted to have on a train. I'm telling you now that we have a registration number for the vehicle that delivered the second victim to Inverness Castle. That vehicle belongs to the son of Frank Drummond, who was the prime suspect—"

"—but now isn't, as he has an alibi," Lyle said.

"Yes."

"So, what now?" he asked. "Who do you, in your infinite wisdom, think we should be pursuing?"

"You're talking to the Macbeth Society. Who are you focusing on?"

"I don't think—"

"I want to help. I promise, I won't take what you tell me and run away with it. Let's compare notes."

"We're watching Christine McTavish. She reported Harry missing but she's been refusing to cooperate and we—"

"She's got a grudge against the police."

"She's what?"

"Her brother was killed by a response vehicle, four years ago. She hates us. That's why she's refusing to cooperate."

"How do you know this?"

"She told one of my team to look her up. Is there anyone else you're interested in?"

"No. Lachlan Kerr seems to be squeaky clean."

"And he shares Christine's alibi."

"There is that," Wallace replied.

So he knows that much, at least.

"One of my experts has given us another potential line of inquiry," Jade said. "It's one that's much more appropriate for you to follow up."

"Go on."

"Given that Frank Drummond's son's vehicle has been targeted, it means that even if Frank isn't our killer, he's connected somehow."

"Yes."

"Which means his wife and kids are."

"Where are you going with this, Jade?"

"In Macbeth, there's a scene where Macbeth's men slay the wife and children of his opponent Macduff. Macduff's Castle is in Fife."

"I know where Macduff's Castle is. I live in Kirkcaldy."

"I've been talking to an expert on the text itself. He thinks that if the killer were to strike again, it might be there."

"Against Gail Drummond and her kids."

"Gail Dawes. But yes."

"But Jade, your team spoke to Gail just this morning. She's not reported her kids missing. What on earth would lead you to believe the word of... of who, exactly?"

"Professor Anthony Urquhart, University of Dundee."

"Never heard of him," Wallace replied.

"You know a lot of professors?"

"Touché. OK, let's say we take this seriously. You're suggesting my team goes racing over to Macduff's Castle on the off-chance the killer turns up there."

"Even if he doesn't take the Drummonds there, it's a key location from the play. He's already attempted to stage a re-enactment of the Duncan murder. He might do the same again."

"Surely the play has a dozen locations and scenes that could be staged like this."

"We don't know most of the locations. Shakespeare was vague about them." Jade took a breath. "Lyle, I'm giving this to you as a potential lead. It's up to you whether you take it or not."

"OK. We'll get Gail Dawes and her kids out of that house, for starters. Meanwhile, I want you to leave our witnesses alone."

"We won't speak to anyone you're already interviewing."

A pause. "What does that mean?"

"It's OK. We're looking into the missing van. It was last seen in Glasgow, and that's where my team is. It makes sense. Geographically. Yes?"

"Reluctantly, yes. You're closer than us. But keep me in the loop, will you? And did I see something about your forensic ecologist analysing the paper used for the note that was sent to your office? Where is she up to with that?"

Jade swallowed. In all the excitement over Inverness, she'd forgotten about Carla.

"That's my next call. I'll let you know if she gives me anything useful."

"You'd better."

CHAPTER SIXTY-NINE

PETRA SAT on her hotel room bed, tapping her foot. She'd been dialling Jade for the last ten minutes, but the DI's number was constantly engaged.

At last, she picked up. "DI Jade Tanner."

"Jade, it's Petra. Where are you?"

"I'm back in Glasgow. Where are you?"

"Still in my hotel room. I've finished my report, you want me to send it to you?"

"Please. But can you run me through your thoughts too?"

Petra looked down at her laptop screen. "OK. So I still believe your killer is a Macbeth fanatic. Maybe a fan of Shakespeare in general, but that's not necessarily the case."

"You're thinking it's a member of the Macbeth Society."

"No. I'm not."

"No?"

"The murders have a note of anonymity about them. They don't fit with the killer having known his victims. At least, not well."

"But if he's a psychopath…"

"He's not a psychopath, Jade."

"He killed two men. He stabbed one of them. The blood—"

"He shows none of the signs of psychopathy. This is a man who leads a normal life, a successful one to all intents and purposes."

"OK. How do you explain him using the van belonging to a family member of one of our main suspects?"

"You're talking about Frank Drummond."

"Yes,"

"Frank Drummond isn't your fella, Jade. This man is too clever to suddenly go missing. If anything, I think Frank Drummond might be your next victim."

"So you think there's going to be another victim too."

"Who else has suggested that?"

"Anthony Urquhart. He suggested Macduff's Castle, in Fife. He said that because of the way the killer tried to stage the Duncan killing in Inverness, with the guards being framed, it would—"

"Wait, Jade." Petra gripped the edge of her bed. "He said what about the Duncan killing?"

"King Duncan. In the play, it's the first of Macbeth's crimes. I've managed to get hold of a copy, from the WHSmith in Sauchiehall Street. Macbeth stages the crime to make two guards look guilty. Our killer did something similar in Inverness Castle. Switching the hats, and—"

"Urquhart doesn't know about that."

"Sorry?" Jade sounded puzzled. "You didn't tell him?"

"I told him about the stabbing." Petra went over the conversation in her mind. "The amount of blood. I said nothing about the guards."

"Oh."

"Oh, indeed." Petra stood up. "Do you want me to speak to him again, find out how he knows that? He might have—"

"No, Petra. Don't make contact with him. You just come back to Glasgow, and we'll work out what to do next."

CHAPTER SEVENTY

Adam Drummond and his girlfriend lived in a second floor flat in Glasgow's Pollokshields. The street was dim in the dusk, the curtains of the neighbouring houses drawn. Mo pressed the buzzer at street level and waited.

"Hello?" came a woman's voice through the intercom.

"I'm looking for Adam Drummond."

"He's not here."

"Will he be back soon? It's the police, I want to talk to him about his missing van."

The intercom crackled. "Come on up."

The door buzzed and Mo pushed on it. He made his way up a flight of narrow stairs to the sound of loud music from the ground floor flat. On the second floor, the music was still audible. A young woman with long blonde hair wearing a flowing dress stood in a doorway.

"I should have asked for your ID, before I let you in," she said.

He held up his badge. She leaned in to peer at it, then compared it to his face.

"OK," she said. "You seem legit. Have you found Adam's van?"

"Not yet," Mo told her. "But it was used to commit a crime on Thursday morning, so we wanted to talk to Adam about who he thinks might have taken it."

"It was nicked from his mum's front drive. He's got no idea."

"When will Adam be home?"

"He doesn't live here all of the time. Sometimes he stays at his mum's."

"We've already been to see her."

The woman shook her head.

"I'm sorry," Mo said. "Can I ask your name?"

"Lola. Do you think I've got something to do with it?"

Mo smiled. "No." He winced as someone turned up the volume downstairs. "Is it always like this?"

She shrugged. "Yes. What you gonna do?"

"You could make a complaint, under the Public Health Act."

"They're our neighbours, they're not all bad."

Mo looked at her. These things were easier to endure when you were young, he supposed.

He held out his card. "Can you ask Adam to call me when he gets back? We really need to talk to him about his van."

She took the card. "OK. But I've got no idea when that'll be. I haven't seen him since Monday."

Mo frowned. "You haven't?"

"No. To be honest, I think he dumped me." She flushed. "But you don't need to know that. Go talk to his mum again. He'll have gone there, tail between his legs." Her face darkened. "Good luck to them both."

"We visited his mum just this morning. He isn't there."

She pushed the door towards him, just enough to make him know he was no longer welcome. "Well in that case, I've got no idea where he is. He's a grown man, though. I'm sure he'll turn up."

She closed the door, an expression of resignation on her face.

CHAPTER SEVENTY-ONE

PC GRACE DECKER walked up the path towards Frank Drummond's house, wishing the weather would improve.

It had been bloody freezing all week, and it looked like spring was never going to come.

She shook herself out as she pushed open the front door and stepped inside. This house was still a crime scene, even if Frank Drummond was no longer a murder suspect. The Public Protection Unit from Edinburgh were investigating the place, suspecting Drummond might have done something to those men on the wall.

She shivered. All she'd seen was a series of photographs. But it was the way they'd been taken: the subjects looking away, none of them aware he was being photographed. And the sheer number of them.

Her DS had sent over a photo from social media, to be compared with the display on the wall. Grace wasn't sure why, but her job wasn't to question. She brought out her phone and scrolled to the image.

She trudged up the stairs, avoiding the third, creaky, step. She was getting to know this house.

A SOCO was at the top, pulling up carpet fibres.

"Hiya," Grace said as she squeezed past.

He nodded in response.

She entered the room with the photos. A camera tripod stood on the other side of the space and a light had been erected so they could take clearer photographs. Hopefully she'd find it easier to spot her target this time.

She stepped closer to the wall and worked her way across the top, methodically. From time to time she returned to the photo on her phone, checking it.

Nothing at the top.

She worked her way downwards, sweeping from side to side and overlapping so she could be sure she wouldn't miss anything.

She stopped.

He was right in the centre.

She checked the photo on the phone again and held it up against the one on the wall.

On her phone, the young man – barely more than a kid – was smiling at the camera. A selfie, his arm at the edge of the shot.

On the wall, he was looking over his shoulder. There was a white van behind him, and he looked like he was about to get in it.

It was the same man.

The photograph on the wall had a Post-it note next to it. It was the only one that did.

It had one word written on it: *Adam*.

She checked the email she'd been sent with the photo: Adam Drummond. Presumably a relative.

She couldn't see any resemblance.

But Frank Drummond certainly had a photo of Adam Drummond on his wall.

CHAPTER SEVENTY-TWO

"Complex Crimes Unit, can I help you?"

Patty was once again alone in the office. Mo had gone out to Adam Drummond's girlfriend's address, and the DI was on her way in from the train station. It was gone 6pm but there was no chance of anyone going home yet.

And here she was, answering the phones.

"Patty, it's Dave Grimmond."

"Dave, good to hear from you." PS Grimmond was the duty sergeant at her old nick in Shettleston. He'd never called her here before. "What can I do for you?"

"We've had someone come in and report a missing person, and the name was flagged as one of interest to your unit."

"OK." Patty clicked through to the case file on her computer. "Who?"

"Adam Drummond. Does the name mean anything to you?"

"It does. Has he been reported missing, or did he make the report?"

Her phone buzzed: a text from the sarge. *Adam's gf says hasn't seen him all week. Dead end.*

"He's gone missing," said Dave.

"His girlfriend reported it?" Patty asked, looking at the text again.

"No," Dave replied. "His dad."

"His dad? What name did he give?"

"Frank Drummond."

Patty leaned back in her chair. "Did he phone it in, or do it in person?"

"In person. He's still here."

Oh my God.

Patty straightened in her chair. "Dave, don't let him go anywhere. I'm on my way."

CHAPTER SEVENTY-THREE

JADE WAS IN A TAXI, heading for the office. As it filtered onto the M8, she dialled Carla.

Wallace was right: she'd been neglecting this line of enquiry. She needed to find out if Carla had anything on that letter.

"Jade," Carla said as she picked up. "That's one hell of a coincidence."

"Why's that?"

"I was just thinking about you. The results from the paper used on your note are ready. We've analysed the composition and managed to get a match."

The taxi passed the trees of Alexandra Park. Jade licked her lips.

"Is it useful?"

"It's old," Carla replied.

"Old? How old?"

"Twenty years or so, I reckon. We can date it more accurately it if you've got the budget. But there's wear in the fibres that's consistent with the paper having been produced around the turn of the century."

"OK. Any idea of the edition? The printer, maybe?"

"You're in luck."

"How so?"

"I've analysed the proportions of lignin, cellulose and hemicelluloses."

"Of what?"

"You don't need to know. But they're substances found in the wood used for paper, and they differ across regions and sites. The proportions in this paper are consistent with Glenrothes."

"Tell me there's a paper mill there."

"There was. The Fettykill Paper Mill in Leslie. I've done some digging for you and it closed down in 2006."

"Are you sure it's from that mill?"

"As sure as I can be. They were suppliers to the academic book trade. It's quality paper, used for hardbacks. I think you're looking for either a collector of expensive books, or someone with links to academia."

CHAPTER SEVENTY-FOUR

PATTY PARKED her car right outside Shettleston nick, not caring about the double yellow lines.

A uniformed constable was leaving the building.

"Hey," he said. "You're not allowed to park there."

She showed him her ID. "I'm here on urgent business relating to a murder inquiry. If someone wants to move it, they're welcome." She tossed him the keys.

"Err..." He looked at the car. "It's OK." He threw the keys back again.

Patty smiled as she caught them. She hurried past him and ran into the building.

Dave was on the desk. Thank God.

"Dave," she panted. "Is he still here?"

He gestured towards a door to the left. "I told him to wait, said a detective would be here to talk to him about finding his son. What's this about?"

"Long story. But thanks."

She turned away from him, her eye on the door. Frank Drummond wasn't going anywhere.

She dialled the DI.

"Patty," Jade said. "I'm at the office. There's no one here."

"Sorry, boss. I didn't have time to call you. But Frank Drummond's turned up."

"He's... where?"

"He walked into a police station in Shettleston and reported his son missing."

"Adam?"

"Yes." Patty gulped in deep breaths. She'd run to the car, driven here like it was a response vehicle, and run up the steps into the building. Only now did she realise how unfit she was.

"How did Frank know that Adam was missing?" the DI asked.

"I don't know. I haven't spoken to him yet."

"OK." A pause. "Wait for me. We'll talk to him together. But if he shows any sign of leaving the building, you can start. I'll be as quick as I can."

"It's a ten-minute drive."

"I'll grab a cab."

"You want me to get them to send a squad car over?"

"Do that, and wait for me."

"No problem, boss."

Patty hung up and walked to the desk. Sergeant Grimmond was watching her. "What's all this about?"

"You know the murder in Dunsinane Hill earlier this week?"

"Yes."

"And the one at Inverness Castle?"

"I do."

"Your guy in there has links to both victims. We want to question him."

"Is he a suspect? Do I need to get CID down?"

"No. He's a witness, But a crucial one." *And possibly a suspect in other investigations*, Patty thought, remembering the photos she'd seen of his bedroom wall.

"OK. Anything I can do to help?"

"Can you get him a cuppa, so he hangs around? I'm waiting for my DI."

"OK." He looked wary.

"And can you get a squad car sent over to the CCU office in Broomhouse, so my DI can get here quicker?"

"Oh. Right." Dave picked up the phone.

CHAPTER SEVENTY-FIVE

DI Lyle Wallace knocked on the door of the tidy semi-detached house in Dryburgh. Next to him was DS Fiona Sinclair, his most trusted team member.

He pulled at his sleeves and gave Fiona a nervous smile. He hated doing this.

The door opened and a man with balding hair and thick glasses looked at him. "We're not buying." He began to push the door closed.

Lyle took a step forward and put a hand on the door. "I'm sorry, Mr Ferguson, but I need to talk to you." He held up his ID. "I'm DI Wallace, this is DS Sinclair. We'd like to talk to you about your son."

"Simon? What's he done?"

"No. Callum."

"Callum?" The man gave Lyle a puzzled look. "OK, then. Come in."

He led them into the house. "Rita!" he cried as he walked through to a living room at the back. It had a threadbare three-piece suite and two side tables. Nothing else, not even a TV.

"You might as well sit down," he said.

Lyle exchanged glances with Fiona. They both took a seat on the sofa.

Mr Ferguson grunted and took the armchair. "My wife's just coming."

The door opened and a tall woman entered, wiping her hands on a dishcloth. "Everything alright?"

"Rita, these are police officers. They want to talk to us about Callum."

"Callum? Simon, surely."

"Mrs Ferguson. I'm DI Wallace. This is DS Henderson. Please, take a seat."

Her face paled. "Oh." She lowered herself into her chair. Tears formed in her eyes. "Tell us."

Lyle took a breath. "I'm very sorry to tell you that we found a body in Inverness on Thursday. We have reason to believe it's your son."

Rita's hand flew to her mouth. "No." She shook her head.

"That's not right," her husband said. "He's here in Dundee, at university. He's got a room in halls."

"We'll need you to make a formal identification," Lyle said. "But your son had a prominent burn mark on his neck, is that true?"

Rita nodded. Her mouth tight.

He felt his mouth go dry. "The man we've found has the same. And we've referenced dental records. We're confident it is Callum. I'm so sorry."

"How did... how did he die?" asked Rita. She seemed small in her armchair, at the opposite end of the room from her husband. Lyle was beginning to regret taking the sofa.

"We have reason to believe that someone murdered him," he said.

"Why? Why would someone kill our Callum?" Mr Ferguson asked. "I'm sorry, Detective, but I think you must have it wrong."

"He's just a student. Studying History, what he called the intersection between history and literature," his wife said. Her eyes glistened with pride but her voice was reedy.

"Mr and Mrs Ferguson, I hope you don't mind me asking, but was your son by any chance a member of the Perth Macbeth Society?"

Mr Ferguson exchanged glances with his wife, then looked at Lyle, his face impassive. "Yes," he said. "Callum is a Macbeth nut. He even managed to get one of the professors to visit the society. Professor Urquhart. Very proud, he was."

CHAPTER SEVENTY-SIX

"Mʀ Dʀᴜᴍᴍᴏɴᴅ," Jade said as she entered the interview room at the front of Shettleston police station. "Thank you for waiting. My name's DI Jade Tanner. This is DC Patty Henderson."

Patty nodded at the man, who stood up from his chair and shook Jade's hand. There was a half-empty cup of tea in front of him, in a plastic cup.

"Are you looking for him?" Frank asked. "How does it work?"

Jade sat down opposite him, making sure that she and Patty were between him and the door. Frank was blond, with heavy features and clothes you wouldn't look at twice. Unremarkable, was how she'd describe him. She wasn't surprised the men he'd photographed hadn't noticed him.

He wasn't their killer. But he wasn't innocent.

"Mr Drummond, do you mind if I call you Frank?'

"Of course not."

"We've been looking for you. Where have you been?"

"Me?" He paled. "Why have you been looking for me?"

"Where have you been, the last few days?"

"I've been in Glasgow. Looking for my son."

Jade swallowed. "We spoke to your ex-wife earlier today. She reported your son's van stolen. Do you know anything about that?"

A frown. "I didn't even know he had a van."

"She also said you went to her house. In the early hours of Thursday."

"I was looking for Adam. I know it was late, but I'd been waiting at home for him, trying to call her. I decided to drive here." He looked down. "She told me to leave her alone, or she'd call the police."

"But you've reported him missing. You must have seen him recently."

A nod. "He came to see me, at my house in Dunkeld. He said he was going to stay for a while, but then he disappeared."

"Are you sure he didn't just decide to go back to his mum?"

"He'd had a row with her. She didn't approve of his girlfriend. He said he wasn't going back there."

Jade glanced at Patty, who looked incredulous. Adam was just nineteen. Nineteen-year-olds could be fickle.

"Have you contacted his girlfriend, to see if he's there?" Jade asked.

"I don't have a number for her."

Jade sat back. "I'm puzzled. I don't see why you assume that Adam is missing, when he's a grown man who has more than one place he could be."

"He left this." Frank reached down into a rucksack by his feet and brought out a ziplock bag. Inside it was a mobile phone. "Since he was twelve years old and he got his first phone, he never goes anywhere without it."

Jade took the bag. "Where did you find this?"

"In my room, at my house."

"In your room?"

"I don't have a spare room. I let him sleep in my room. I slept on the sofa."

Oh, but you do have a spare room, Jade thought. *You just don't want your son seeing it.*

"When did you last see him?"

"Wednesday morning."

"And when did you find the phone?"

"Wednesday lunchtime. I went out to buy some chips for lunch. When I came back he was gone. And his phone was on my bed."

Jade narrowed her eyes. "How long were you gone for?"

"The chippy is on Atholl Street, a five-minute walk away. I was gone for about twenty, twenty-five minutes."

"And after you decided he was missing, what did you do?"

Mo had been in Frank's house on Friday morning, and it had been empty.

"I came down here, looking for him."

"You went to your ex-wife's."

"I shouldn't have done that, I know. But I was worried."

"OK." Jade still wasn't sure if they should consider Adam as missing. But the phone...

"Hang on a minute," she said. "Adam turned up at your house before Wednesday."

"Tuesday afternoon."

"How did he get there?"

Adam's van was reported stolen on Wednesday night. Had he used it to leave Frank's and drive back to his mum's?

Frank sniffed. "He came by train. Called me from Perth, I gave him a lift."

Jade eyed him. From what she knew, Frank Drummond

wasn't supposed to have any contact with his sons. So what was he doing letting Adam stay at his house?

She picked up the bag. "We'll examine this, see if it gives us any idea of who he might be with."

"He's not with anyone he knows. Not voluntarily, anyway." Drummond pointed at the phone. "I promise you, he wouldn't leave it."

"You said your son lives in Glasgow, normally."

"He's a drama student. He lives with his mum. Lived. He's not going back."

"Where does he study?"

"He's attached to a theatre. The Tramway."

Jade knew it: it was in Pollokshields. Near Adam's girlfriend.

"OK, Frank. I'd be grateful if you could stay here for now. I'm going to make some calls and get a team working on this. We'll find your son, but we'll need your help."

CHAPTER SEVENTY-SEVEN

"Mo," Jade said as he picked up her call, "where are you now?"

"I'm in Pollokshields, doing some house to house. I want to know if anyone here has seen Adam Drummond, or his van."

Jade was still in Shettleston police station, in their second interview room. She'd left Patty with Frank Drummond in the first room. They'd told him they needed a detailed statement. In reality they just wanted to make sure he didn't go anywhere.

"Frank Drummond turned up," she said.

"Drummond? Where?"

"Shettleston police station. Patty's with him now."

"That's not far from the office."

"Yes. He came in here earlier to report Adam missing."

"Frank has reported Adam missing?"

"What did his girlfriend say?" Jade asked.

"She said he'd gone back to his mum's. She reckoned he'd dumped her. But I called his mum—"

"And there's no sign of him there."

"Him, or his van."

"OK." Jade tapped the table in front of her. "We've got

Adam's van going missing on Wednesday night, then being used in Inverness in the early hours of Thursday, at the same time his dad's round at his ex-wife's house raising hell. Before that, we've got Adam turning up at his dad's house on Tuesday afternoon. He left there on Wednesday lunchtime, and his dad reckons it's suspicious."

"The knife," Mo said.

"The knife. Under the bed."

"Maybe it was used to threaten Adam, while his dad was out. Maybe someone turned up there, then took him."

"You're thinking the same person who killed Harry and Callum?" Jade asked.

"I don't know. But they're all young. They're all connected to the Macbeth Society."

"And they're all on Frank Drummond's wall," added Jade. "Frank said Adam was staying in his room. He claimed not to have a spare room."

"He did?"

"I guess he keeps people out of it."

"I bet he does." Mo sighed. "What d'you need me to do?"

"I want to check out Frank's claim that Adam was with him this week. I don't even know if this phone really is Adam's." She turned it over on the table in front of her.

"Have you been able to get into it?"

"Not yet."

"OK. I'll call Lachlan Kerr. He might know if Adam was at Frank's."

"Thanks," Jade said. "And while you're at it, ask him about Anthony Urquhart visiting the Macbeth Society. I need to call Wallace, it's time to bring Urquhart in."

"You think he's our killer."

"Dr Moreau has analysed the paper in that note. She says

it's from a book around twenty years old, probably an academic book or a collector's item."

"What's that got to do with Urquhart?" Mo asked.

"He's a Macbeth expert. He'll have plenty of copies of the play."

"True. Lachlan Kerr had a few."

"One of which was missing. And Petra... she told me something."

"What?"

Jade ran over the conversations in her memory. "I was talking to Urquhart about the Inverness murder. He said something about the staging, the business with the hats and the guards. How it was designed to imitate the scene where the Macbeths kill Duncan. Petra told me she hadn't mentioned that to him."

"He might have seen it in the press."

Jade shook her head. "We haven't made it public. But I can't account for Inverness CID." She sighed. "I'll call them. You speak to Kerr and let me know what he says."

CHAPTER SEVENTY-EIGHT

PETRA HAD LEFT HALF her overnight things at Magdalena's flat. She got off the train at Dundee, yawning. It was dark: coming up to 7pm.

Would Mags be at home? Would she be happy to see Petra? Petra was so deeply immersed in the case, she hadn't thought to phone ahead.

This was why she couldn't hold down a relationship. She got all wrapped up in her work and forgot about the people she cared about.

And she did care about Aila.

Call her.

She walked to the taxi rank at Dundee station, dialling Aila's mobile.

"Hey, Petra."

"Hi, Aila. How's things?"

"OK. Monty got into a fight."

Petra felt her muscles tense. *Damn cat.* "Oh. I hope he's OK."

"He's fine. Sorry, you don't want to hear about my cat. How's your case? Found the killer yet?"

"I'm not sure."

"How so?"

"I had a conversation earlier that made me think... it's OK. I'll leave it to the police."

"I didn't think that would be your style."

"No?" Petra smiled as a taxi pulled up. She cupped her hand over the receiver and gave Magdalena's address.

"I watched you on that case at Loch Lomond," Aila said. "The poor woman who washed up at that pier. You understood the motivation behind that crime better than the police did. Even that Lesley Clarke from Dorset."

Petra smiled. "Lesley's something of a force of nature."

"I bet she is. So are you on your way home?"

"I'm staying at a friend's tonight. It's too late to go home."

"OK. I'll see you tomorrow. Looking forward to it."

Petra felt warmth seep through her body. "So am I."

Aila giggled. "If you think you know who it is, you should do something about it. Don't wait for the cogs of Police Scotland to turn."

"Ah, that's not my job."

"Sounds like it is, to me."

The taxi passed the university. Petra peered out, thinking of her old office in the Scrymgeour building. "Maybe you've got a point."

"I'm not daft," Aila told her. "And neither are you."

"OK. See you tomorrow."

Aila blew a kiss into the phone. Petra hung up, smiling. She leaned forward to speak to the driver.

"Can you stop here please? I've changed my mind."

CHAPTER SEVENTY-NINE

"Hello again, DS Uddin. You'll be recruiting me to your team at this rate."

"Sorry to bother you," Mo said. "I hope I'm not disturbing your evening."

"I was watching *The Wheel*," Lachlan Kerr replied. "So no, you're not disturbing anything."

"Good. I just have a quick question for you."

"Fire away."

Mo could hear the TV in the background. He'd best keep this quick.

"We've found Frank."

"You have? That's marvellous news... is it marvellous news?"

"He's reported his son missing. Adam. Can you tell me if Adam was visiting Frank, in the last week?"

"Frank's been missing."

"Before he went missing. Tuesday and Wednesday."

"Right. Um... there was talk of him having a young man

staying with him. Vera who runs the post office was gossiping. I didn't really pay much attention. Sorry, that's all I know."

"That's fine. I've got another question for you."

"Fire away."

"Has a man called Anthony Urquhart ever been a member of your Macbeth Society?"

"No."

"Ah. OK." Mo felt himself deflate.

"But he has visited us. A couple of times."

"When?"

"Once last year, and then just a month ago. He was a visiting speaker. Did a guided walk with us. Dunsinane Hill and Birnam Wood. Why?"

Mo bit down on his bottom lip. He winced. "Who else was on that walk?"

"I'd have to check that with Christine."

That would never work. "Were you there? Can you remember?"

"I did go, yes. So did Frank. And... yes." He cleared his throat.

"Who else?" Mo asked.

"Harry Nolan was there. And another young man. Callum Ferguson. He left the group not long after. And Frank brought his son." He laughed. "In fact, I remember commenting that the average age on that walk was about a half century below the usual. We're not a young person's group, not normally."

"Frank brought his son?"

"Well, not Frank. The kid came with Professor Urquhart. He'd been getting advice from him, on a staging of *Macbeth*. Adam, his name was."

CHAPTER EIGHTY

P ETRA   KNEW the security guard on duty at the Tower
Building. She gave him a smile as she approached the doors,
not breaking stride.

"Hey, Bill," she said, "how's it going?"

"Hello, Dr McBride," he replied. "Quiet. I like quiet."

"I bet you do. I forgot my pass. Any chance you can let
me in?"

"I thought you were in the Scrymgeour?"

"They moved a group of us. Refurbishment work. I just
need to pick up some files."

"I don't envy you, working on a Saturday evening."

She smiled. "You are too."

"I get paid for it."

"True." She waited for him to open the door, her heart
pounding. "Thanks, Bill. Say hello to Rosie for me."

"Will do."

Petra darted inside and made for the stairs before Bill had a
chance to change his mind. She ran up to the first floor, then
hit the button for the lift. There was no way she was walking

all the way to Anthony Urquhart's goddamn eighth floor office.

A few minutes later, out of breath, she was standing outside his room.

She put a hand on the door.

This was foolish.

What the hell was she doing here? The door would be locked. The office would be empty.

She pulled down on the door handle. She pushed.

The door moved.

Petra grinned and stuffed a hand into her mouth to stifle a laugh. She pushed the door open and slipped inside, not turning to look at the security camera that she knew was on the wall behind her. She'd explain all this later.

Urquhart's room seemed smaller in the darkness. The huge windows glowed with light from the city below, making the shadows inside the room appear deeper.

Petra scanned the space. Where to start?

The computer.

She went to the desk and bent over it. She clicked the mouse.

The computer came to life: the familiar University of Dundee wallpaper she'd spent years of her life staring at.

She clicked again.

Password prompt.

Damn.

She had no idea how to guess Urquhart's password, and she couldn't exactly call Jade for advice, given that she'd broken in.

She shook her head and lifted her hand from the mouse.

There was a pile of books on the desk next to the computer. More piles on other surfaces, some of them high.

She scanned them.

A diary, maybe? Something that might record him having been near the crime scenes at the opportune times?

She rifled through the pile on the desk. There was a desk diary at the bottom.

Anthony, you old fashioned bastard. Thank you.

She flicked through it to Monday, when Harry had been killed.

It was blank.

Shit.

She flicked through to Thursday. The meeting she had with him herself, a few seminars.

Nothing more.

She turned the page to today's date.

Tramway, 7.30pm.

Petra laughed, then looked up, worried someone might have heard her.

She grabbed her phone and texted Jade.

Urquhart is going to the Tramway theatre tonight. 7.30pm.

It was up to Jade to decide if this needed following up.

Petra straightened up and scanned the shelves behind the desk. Two-thirds were taken up with Shakespeare. There were multiple copies of Shakespeare's plays, editions both old and new.

So he was a collector.

She pulled out a copy of *Macbeth*. It was a modern one, paperback. It looked untouched.

She pulled another, and another.

A scrap of paper fell out of one.

Petra stopped, hardly daring to breathe. She looked at the door, wishing she'd locked it.

She opened the book the paper had fallen from. It was a copy of Macbeth. A hardback, well thumbed. Arden edition.

There were sections missing.

She took a shaky breath. She needed to get out of here.

She stuffed the book inside her jacket and headed for the door.

CHAPTER EIGHTY-ONE

"OK," Jade said. "Thanks, Paula."

"I don't know why you think we'd be so unprofessional as to release information like that to the public. It's a key element of the crime."

"I know. I just had to check."

Jade hung up. DI Murphy had been reluctant to talk to her about their handling of the Inverness Castle case, but she had made it clear that no one had been told about the guards.

Which meant that Anthony Urquhart had found out about it some other way.

Perhaps Petra had inadvertently let something slip. She wasn't a police officer, she hadn't been trained to identify which aspects of a crime were and weren't worth releasing to the public.

But Jade trusted Petra. She wouldn't be working with her if she didn't.

Her phone buzzed: a text from Petra.

Shit. She should have rung the psychologist hours ago, to follow up with her about her report.

She checked the time and yawned as she looked at the text. She still needed to catch up on her sleep. It was gone 7pm, and it didn't look like she was getting home anytime soon.

Thank God for her mum.

She read the text.

Urquhart is going to the Tramway theatre tonight. 7.30pm.

Jade had been about to call Wallace, explain why he needed to bring Urquhart in for questioning. But he was in Glasgow?

She dialled Petra to get the engaged tone. Petra was on another call.

Petra, how do you know what Urquhart's doing? Are you with him?

Not a call to Urquhart, she hoped. Or maybe that would be a good thing: at least it meant Petra wasn't with him.

She needed to go to the Tramway. It was where Adam worked, and now Urquhart was heading there.

But first she needed to deal with Frank.

She texted Patty: *Is he still with you?*

Longest statement ever, Patty replied. *Still working on it.*

Jade smiled. *Keep him for another half hour.*

Will do.

She dialled the number for the Public Protection Unit and waited. She didn't know how solid their case was against Frank, but she knew he needed to be investigated.

CHAPTER EIGHTY-TWO

PETRA KICKED off her heels as she walked into Mags's flat. Mags emerged from the kitchen, holding out a glass of red wine.

"Oh my word, you're a miracle worker." Petra took it from her and drank. "That's exactly what I needed."

"I heated up some curry, too. Thought you might be hungry."

Petra hugged her friend. "Thanks. You're too kind."

"It's the least I could do. You're hunting down a killer."

Petra felt her skin turn cold. She couldn't share her suspicions with Mags: *the man you introduced me to might be a suspect.*

"Yes," she muttered, hiding her face in the glass. "This is good."

She followed Mags into the kitchen. A pot of curry sat on the stove. Mags brought some bread out of the oven.

"Bread, too? You could be my new best friend." Petra sat at the table, slumping into her chair and feeling the energy drain from her limbs.

She should call Jade, tell her about the book. It was burning a hole in her bag.

"Can you give me a moment?" She stood up. "I just want to get changed."

"Of course. Five minutes till food."

"Thanks."

Petra walked through to Magdalena's spare room, unbuttoning her blouse. She'd get into her pyjamas, take her bra off. She'd enjoy a curry, and then she'd sleep. Or maybe curl up in front of the TV. Mags's flat was warm and cluttered, the kind of thing Petra's Aunt Lydia had been aiming for in the Glasgow flat Petra had inherited. The difference was that when Mags tried it, it came over as homely. When Lydia tried it, the result was chaos.

Petra tossed her blouse onto the bed.

There was an envelope next to it.

"I forgot to tell you," Mags's voice came through the door, "there was a letter for you. I put it on your bed."

Petra picked the envelope up. It was addressed to her, at Magdalena's address.

She was only here for a few days. How did anyone know to send post here?

She ripped it open, her pulse racing. She had a nasty feeling she knew who this was from.

Holding her nose, she tipped the contents out onto the bed. What if it was poison, or some kind of nerve agent?

Stop it, woman. Don't be paranoid.

It wasn't poison. Or a nerve agent. It was something much more cliched than that.

Photos. Black and white, eight by ten inches.

She looked down at them.

One of her on the University of Dundee campus, just a few

days ago. One of her outside Mags's flat. Another in her own street in Glasgow. Last week, judging by the coat she was wearing.

No note. No words.

Just an implied warning: *I'm watching you.*

CHAPTER EIGHTY-THREE

"Tell me you're not with him," Jade said to Petra as she picked up the phone.

"With Urquhart? No. I'm at my friend's flat, in Dundee."

"Good. You stay there. We'll take it from here."

"Did you read my report?"

"Not in full, no. Just tell me, does it fit Urquhart?"

"That's not how it works."

"Petra. You know the man. Do you think him capable?"

Silence.

"Petra?"

"He's an egotist, and he likes to show off. I'm not sure what prompted him to take such drastic action and I don't know how he picked his victims, but yes. I can see him doing it. And setting it all up the way he has."

"How do you know he's going to the Tramway?"

"I read his dairy."

"You've been with him?" Jade felt the skin of her face tighten.

"No. I went... I went to his office."

"Tell me you didn't break in." Jade rubbed her forehead; she had a headache.

"The door was unlocked. I wanted to speak to him."

"You might have to say that in court, you know."

"I'm sorry. But I found something else."

"In his office?"

"Yes," Petra replied. "A book. It's got text missing. Text that's been cut out."

"The note."

"Yes."

"A copy of *Macbeth*."

"Yes."

"OK. Send me photos."

"It'll fall apart if I try to do any more with it."

"Damn."

Jade looked up to see Patty enter the interview room. She frowned at her.

"Petra, I need to go. Stay where you are. If you can send me photos, please do. But the problem we now have is that we can't use that book as evidence."

"No."

At least Petra knew enough to understand that.

"It was an illegal search," Jade told her.

"I'm not a police officer. I'm an associate of Urquhart who found evidence when I was visiting his office."

Jade looked at Patty, who was standing by the door, a question on her face.

"We'll cross that hurdle when we come to it," she said. "You shouldn't have put yourself at risk."

"Don't worry about me. Go to the Tramway. Stop him. He'll be there in five minutes." Petra hung up.

Jade looked up at Patty. "They've taken him?"

"Frank Drummond is in custody. Arrested for stalking."

"Good." Jade stood up. "Mo's on his way to the Tramway. We need to get there too."

CHAPTER EIGHTY-FOUR

Mo HELD out his ID to the woman at the front desk of the Tramway Theatre. Shona, her badge said. The foyer was becoming crowded: people arriving for the performance.

It was 7:20. Whatever Urquhart was coming here for, it would start in ten minutes.

"Have you come about the altercation in the theatre earlier?" Shona asked.

"What altercation?"

"There was a man shouting. He stopped, we haven't found him. Trev reckons he's hidden somewhere in the rigging."

"Who's Trev?"

"The stage manager. You need to talk to him."

Mo looked at her. "Did you get a description of the man shouting?"

A shrug. "Sorry. Someone reported a voice. That was all we know."

It could be Adam Drummond. If Urquhart had him...

But the Macbeth connection? There was none.

He leaned on the desk. "Tonight's performance. What is it?"

"*Macbeth*. Modern interpretation."

Mo had no idea what a modern interpretation of *Macbeth* would look like. But a performance of the play... that explained a lot.

"OK. How do I find Trev?"

"Go down that way, see the narrow hallway? The door on your left at the end takes you through to the stage. Ask for him, he'll be there."

"Thanks."

Mo ran, hoping he'd make it there in time.

CHAPTER EIGHTY-FIVE

Jade and Patty ran into the theatre to find the foyer emptying out. People pushed towards the door to the auditorium, talking among themselves.

Mo? Where are you?

The production was going ahead. Did that mean Mo had found Urquhart?

She ran to the desk. "Do you have a man called Adam Drummond working here?"

"We do." The woman behind the desk nodded. "Adam didn't show up tonight. Not last night, either."

Jade looked at her. "Did he give a reason?"

"None. It's not like Adam."

"He's here!" came a voice from behind Jade. She turned to see a man running down a set of steps towards them. "It's OK, Shona, Adam's here after all."

"Good," said Shona. "He's got the new thunder run."

"Sorry," Jade said. "Who's here?" She didn't bother asking what on earth a thunder run was.

"Adam is," the man said. "Who are you?"

She held up her ID. "Jade Tanner, Police Scotland. You are?"

"Duncan Price, production manager."

"Adam was reported missing. You've seen him?"

"I haven't seen him yet. I just saw his van, out the back."

"Where?"

"That's the thing. He didn't park it in the staff parking area, like he normally does. It's going to be a right pain to transport that thunder run in, unless he moves it."

"He'll move it," the woman said. "Adam's alright like that."

The van. If it was in the wrong place, it could be because it wasn't Adam who was driving.

"Have you seen my colleague?" Jade asked. "DS Uddin. Brummie detective, also looking for Adam."

"You mean the bloke who came about the altercation?" Shona asked.

"What altercation?"

"Shouting. Up in the rigging."

Jade felt her stomach drop. "How many people?"

"No idea. Trev heard it. That's all."

"Who's Trev?"

"The stage manager. Your mate's gone to find him."

"Where?"

She pointed to Jade's right. "Through that door. But you can't go in now. They're just about to start. The witches."

"They're performing *Macbeth*?" Jade felt her eyes widen.

"It's on all the posters, didn't you notice? Your mate didn't know, either."

"OK. You need to shut down the performance."

"We can't do that," said the production manager.

Jade turned to him. "I'm working on a double murder investigation, and we have reason to believe our prime suspect has taken Adam Drummond and is holding him in this building. You need to stop the performance."

CHAPTER EIGHTY-SIX

"Really?" Jade said. "I've just told you we might have a hostage situation, and you're not closing down the performance?"

"People have paid for tickets," Price replied. "And it's only just started. I can show you how to access the backstage area. There are rooms where he might have gone. Adam knows his way around, it'll be—"

"My team will disturb your performance, if they have to."

"I understand."

She stared at him. "OK. Show me where to go. If I see anything that gives me cause for concern, you'll have to stop the play."

"I know."

"Good."

"Follow me."

Jade walked after the man, up a flight of stairs and doubling back to a set of double doors.

"This is an overflow stage," he said. "We sometimes run smaller shows up here, or we use it for storing props."

The room was perhaps twenty metres long and ten metres wide. It had a stage at one end and a raked set of seating at the other.

"Is this anywhere near where your stage manager heard the shouts?"

"I'm not sure."

Jade pursed her lips. "Just take me to the stage manager."

"He'll be in an area we can't access without being seen by the audience."

Jade stepped towards him. How hard was it going to be to get the man to see sense?

"I don't care about your performance," she said. "But I do care about the safety of Adam Drummond, and of your staff and audience."

Maybe he was right. If they stopped the play now, it would get Urquhart's attention. It might precipitate whatever he was planning to do.

"Very well," she said. "I want access to the area where the shouts were heard."

Her phone buzzed: a call from Mo.

"Boss," he whispered. "Where are you?"

"I'm in the Tramway, being led a merry dance," she told him. "Where are you?"

"Backstage. There's a ladder alongside the stage area, and a platform. It leads up to where the stage manager heard the commotion."

She turned to Duncan Price. "There's a ladder near your stage. I need access to whatever's at the top of it."

"That's not safe."

"If I don't stop the man who I believe is holding a member of your staff up there, then no one in this building is safe. Take me there."

"Shit," whispered Mo.

"What?" Jade said into the phone. "What's happened?"

"I can see him. I can see Adam Drummond."

CHAPTER EIGHTY-SEVEN

Mo RAN to the ladder and started climbing. He'd seen Adam Drummond on the platform it led to, looking over the edge.

Was Urquhart up there with him? Or had they all got it wrong? Was Urquhart in the audience, maybe?

The section of floor he'd crossed to access the ladder was visible to the audience. There'd been gasps and shouts as he ran across. Now that he was climbing the ladder, a few people had got up from their seats and were watching him. One woman even had a camera out.

Maybe that would be good. Get this on film, they could use it at trial.

If there was a trial.

He was six feet up now, and beginning to regret his decision. The ladder led up a wall that was over fifteen feet high and he was barely halfway up it. Could he do this safely? Or would Urquhart spot him and push him down?

He was here now. And Adam Drummond was in danger.

Keep going.

"Help!"

A man's voice, from above. A Scottish accent.

"Adam?" Mo called up.

The acoustics were against him; sound travelled down from up there but not up from where he was. He could hear the performers behind him: the three witches.

"I'm coming!" he called. When would Urquhart strike?

He'd already re-enacted the Duncan murder. That was the first in the play.

But there was reference to a death in the next scene, wasn't there?

Mo stopped.

The witches' voices were gone. There were men speaking.

He didn't dare turn around.

"Help!"

He looked up. He could see only darkness.

"God save the king!"

Mo stopped climbing. The second scene, the one in which the victors discussed the battle that King Duncan had won. The one in which...

The one in which the incumbent Thane of Cawdor died, and Macbeth was given his title.

It was offstage, but it was a death.

He started climbing, faster now. He was nearly at the top.

He looked up to see a face above him. Hands on the rungs of the ladder.

Urquhart. And the man was blocking his way.

CHAPTER EIGHTY-EIGHT

JADE RAN through the door into the auditorium. The audience were to her left, the actors on her right. They were dressed in modern military uniform.

Someone in the audience screamed. A man stood and pointed.

She followed the man's arm. A ladder, beyond the audience. Leading perhaps twenty feet up into darkness.

And at the top, Mo.

Oh my God.

She ran in front of the audience, between the seating and the stage. People shouted out. Jade ignored them.

She stopped at the bottom of the steps. Shouting his name was out of the question. If he looked down, he might fall.

Duncan Price was behind her.

"How do I get up there?" she snapped. "Is there another way?"

He nodded. "Follow me."

He ran to the left, towards a door. Jade followed him along

corridors and up a flight of stairs. She had no idea where she was.

At last he stopped in front of a door.

"Through here." His shirt had come untucked and his face glistened with sweat. "There's a platform, above that ladder."

"You stay here."

"I should—"

"No. You stay here."

Jade pushed through the doors, trying to be swift but quiet.

She was on a platform, bounded by a low brick wall. Adam Drummond was to one side, a rope binding him to a pipe that ran down the wall. Urquhart was on the other side, facing away from her. He was leaning over.

"Get down!" he shouted.

Mo.

"Professor Urquhart," she said, keeping her voice steady. "My name's Jade Tanner."

He glanced back. "I know who you are."

"Please, don't do anything you might regret."

"It's a little late for that."

Adam whimpered. "Stop him. He's going to kill me."

Jade looked at the young man. "You're going to be OK. I've got you." She took a step towards Urquhart. "Professor, I'm going to put out my hand and take you by the wrist. Please don't move."

"Leave me."

No.

Below, the performance had stopped. People were flooding out of the theatre.

Thank God.

She took a step forward. Slowly, she drew her handcuffs out of her inside pocket. She reached out.

"Professor Urquhart." Mo's voice, from below. Jade couldn't see him. *Don't do anything stupid.*

"Mo, it's OK," she said.

Urquhart glanced round again. Jade dipped her hand back into her inside pocket.

"Leave me," he said. "I'll jump." He shifted backwards.

Jade leaned forward, grabbing the opportunity. She pulled out the cuffs and attached one end to Urquhart's wrist. The other she snapped onto a pipe. It was too far away from the edge for Urquhart to jump.

She pulled back, breathing heavily.

He tugged on the cuffs and screeched.

"False arrest!" he cried. "Leave me alone!"

No chance, mate.

There was a flurry of movement as Mo's face appeared, his body right behind it. He pushed himself over the top and landed on the platform next to Urquhart. He pulled out a pair of cuffs and used them to attach Urquhart to another pipe.

The man was stuck.

Jade pushed her hair out of her face. She was sweating.

"Anthony Urquhart," she said. "I'm arresting you on suspicion of murder."

CHAPTER EIGHTY-NINE

Petra found herself singing in the shower.

She'd woken to a text from Jade informing her that Urquhart was in custody. And another from Aila asking if she wanted to go out for dinner tonight.

She very much did.

She scrubbed her hair until it squeaked, closing her eyes and singing at the top of her voice.

There was a knock on the door. "You OK in there?"

She stopped singing, embarrassed. "Sorry."

Mags laughed. "Glad to hear you enjoying yourself."

Fifteen minutes later, she was dry and dressed. Her hair was arranged on top of her head and she'd applied a fresh coat of nail varnish.

"Morning," Mags said as she entered the kitchen. "There's coffee in the pot."

"Perfect."

"The Courier is saying that Anthony Urquhart has been arrested. There's video of him being led away from a theatre all over Facebook."

Petra poured her coffee, her back to Mags. "Oh?"

"Was this anything to do with you?"

Petra turned, her face arranged into an expression of mild interest. "Not necessarily."

Mags smiled. "Come on. Did you help the police?"

Petra looked at her friend. "I feel bad. You introduced me to him, and I—"

"Hey, it's no bother. If he killed someone, he deserves to do the time. Yes?"

"Yes."

"And besides, he's been acting like a creep ever since they made him redundant."

Petra put her mug down. "They made him redundant?"

"Didn't he tell you? He was given three months' notice. He was devastated, asked me not to tell anyone."

"Oh."

An angry man, rejected by the institution he'd given his life to. Petra knew how that felt.

Only, she hadn't seen it as a reason to kill.

CHAPTER NINETY

JADE TURNED as DI Wallace entered the interview room. She'd come in here to think, and was hoping for silence.

"Lyle," she said.

"Don't say you're muscling in on this, too."

"No," she told him. "I just wanted some peace and quiet."

"Well, it's about to get very *not* peaceful in here." He checked his watch. "Urquhart is due in five minutes." He placed a box of files and evidence bags on the table.

"I know." Jade stood up. "You sure I can't sit in?"

"Just me and DS Sinclair. Sorry."

She scratched her cheek. "It was worth a try."

"For what it's worth, you did good work. You and your team."

She smiled. "That's quite something for you to admit."

"I'm not too proud to acknowledge when another team has made it possible for my team to get a conviction."

"Don't count your chickens," she told him. "I'm sure he's got a good lawyer."

"Don't worry," he said. "The evidence is mounting up already."

"Good. Any idea what his motive was?"

"We'll uncover that during this interview, I hope."

"You hope."

"But the important thing, is we have enough evidence to prove that Anthony Urquhart killed two men and was intending to kill another."

Jade nodded. "Did you find the van? He left it at the back of the theatre. It was in a different spot to where Adam would have left it."

Wallace reached into the box and drew out an evidence bag.

"Better than that," he said.

The bag contained a set of keys.

"For the van?" Jade asked.

"For the van. Urquhart's prints all over them."

"Which ties him to the Inverness murder."

"It does."

"What about Dunsinane?"

"We've found a witness who saw the van nearby. We're working on it, teasing it out. But we'll get it."

"Good."

There was a knock on the door: DS Sinclair.

"Well, I'd better leave you then," said Jade. "Good luck. Make sure you get him."

CHAPTER NINETY-ONE

STUART WAS LEANING BACK in his chair, legs out and crossed at the ankles. Patty was perched on the desk next to him, eating a bar of chocolate. Mo sat in his chair on the opposite side of the bank of desks, focused on his screen.

"Well, we got him," Jade announced as she entered the room. "Lyle Wallace and Fiona Sinclair are interviewing him now."

"Not you, boss?" Patty asked.

"Not me, I'm afraid. But Lyle did acknowledge our role in bringing Urquhart in."

"We'd never have got him without Petra," Mo said.

Jade raised her eyebrows. "You used to be sceptical about Petra."

"I'm not saying her psychological profile made the difference. It was the way she went snooping around his office."

"Something we wouldn't have been able to do without a warrant," Patty added.

"She wouldn't have done that snooping if she hadn't

already been analysing the psychological profile of the killer," Jade reminded them.

"Hmm," said Mo.

The door opened behind her. Jade turned to see Fraser enter, all smiles.

"Tell me that face means good news," said Patty.

Jade threw her a look.

"What?" Patty mouthed.

"Sir," Jade said. "I hope you're happy with the work of the team."

"Very happy. I gather the evidence provided by the two experts you brought in will form the main pillar of the Procurator Fiscal's case."

"Really?" Stuart said. "What about the forensics?"

"Carla's evidence *was* forensics," Jade reminded him.

"Of course."

She turned back to Fraser. "What does that mean for the unit?"

He glanced past her at the team, who were all quiet. Listening. "Can we have a word in private?"

Jade stood up. "Of course." She led him to the meeting room she sometimes, albeit rarely, used as an office.

Once inside, she closed the door. "This sounds bad."

He took a step towards her. "Not necessarily."

"But you don't know."

"You did well. You and DS Uddin probably prevented another death on Saturday night."

"Maybe."

"How is Adam Drummond?"

"In shock. I don't know what he's finding it harder to deal with what Urquhart did to him, or what he's learned about his dad."

"And that's another result that's down to your team."

"It wasn't us who arrested Drummond. And it isn't us who'll be charging Urquhart."

"But you caught him. Twenty feet up on a platform with barely any protection around it."

She shrugged.

"Don't do that again, Jade. My heart leapt into my mouth when I heard about it."

"If I hadn't gone up there, Adam might have died. And it was Mo who took all the risks."

Fraser brushed a hand against her wrist. "Still. It was quite a risk."

"I conducted a dynamic risk assessment."

"You did?" He withdrew his hand. Jade could still feel the echo of it on her skin.

"No." She laughed. "I was too bloody busy chasing down a killer."

He looked at her for slightly longer than was comfortable. She frowned and glanced away.

"I'll do everything I can to protect this unit," he said.

"Why? Are we really needed?"

"You work well together. So, yes."

"It's not because you and I are old friends?"

"No, Jade. That's not how I work."

"OK."

"But I have been meaning to ask you..."

She narrowed her eyes. "Yes?"

He swallowed. "Would you like to go for dinner with me, on Friday evening?"

"A business meeting?"

"No."

"You mean, you'll come up to my house and we'll have a drink, like we used to with Dan?"

He was looking at her intently. "No."

"Oh." *A date.*

She glanced out of the glass partition to spot Patty looking away in a hurry.

Jade felt her skin heat up. A date, with Fraser?

She looked at him. He blinked back at her, his fingers twisting together. He was nervous. It was endearing.

She smiled. "OK."

She thought of Rory. She'd had breakfast with him this morning. She'd spent the whole day with him yesterday, relieved the case had been wrapped up in time for a family Sunday. She'd even been relieved that it hadn't been her doing the follow-up work. That was the SIO's job.

She brushed a hand against Fraser's arm. "I'd love to. But it'll have to be lunch, on Saturday. That's when Rory has his football practice."

CHAPTER NINETY-TWO

"DON'T YOU LOOK GORGEOUS?" Aila stepped through the door to Petra's flat and enveloped her in a hug. Petra kissed her. She'd been reading through her final report as the doorbell had rung, and trying to stop herself looking at the *Dundee Courier*. Jade had said nothing about the article, but Petra knew she had to address the subject, if she was to continue working with the CCU.

She pulled back to get a good look at her girlfriend. *Forget about work.* "So do you." Aila wore a flowing dress that accentuated her slim figure, with a pair of hoop earrings which would have looked garish on most women, but worked perfectly on Aila.

"Thanks." Aila smiled and pushed Petra's hair back. "So. Have you eaten?"

"I was waiting for you."

"That's considerate of you. I thought I'd cook."

"At my flat?"

"At your flat." Aila turned to open the door. She'd left a shopping bag outside. "You don't mind, do you? I know there are lots of places to eat in the West End, but I wanted to have you all to myself."

"That works for me." Petra pulled Aila in for another kiss, but then pulled back. "You've got Monty with you."

Aila frowned. "Monty. No. Why?"

"That's why you want to stay in, so you can keep an eye on him."

Aila laughed. "He's in a cattery."

"He's *what*?"

"You heard. Don't make me say it again, I almost turned back to rescue him twice."

"It's just a cattery, sweetheart. He'll love it."

Aila's face had dropped. "Will he?"

"He will." Petra put a hand on Aila's shoulder. Was the evening going to be ruined by that damn cat again?

Aila pulled on a smile. "You're right. I noticed you're allergic to him, so when we're together I'll make sure he's not around."

"You'll do that? Really?"

"Yes. I'd appreciate you taking antihistamines, so maybe the two of you can get to know each other very gradually. But I want to be alone with you, so he can have a wee holiday of his own."

Petra grabbed the shopping bag. "You cook, *and* you put me before your cat."

Aila winked. "I'm the perfect woman, aren't I?"

"You might just be."

READ A FREE NOVELLA, THE LOCHSIDE MURDER

The Lochside Murder brings together characters from my McBride & Tanner and Dorset Crime series

DCI Lesley Clarke has promised her new wife that their Scottish honeymoon won't be spoiled by murder investigations.

But when she's out for a walk on the first day and finds a body, she can't help but be dragged into a case. The investigation is taken on by DI Jade Tanner and Dr Petra McBride of the Complex Crimes Unit, along with Lesley's old colleague DS Mo Uddin.

Can the team discover who killed the woman floating in the loch? And will Lesley's marriage be jeopardised by her obsession with the job before it's even begun?

This novella comes between books 7 (The Blue Pool Murders) and 8 (The Lighthouse Murders) in the Dorset Crime series or can be read alongside the McBride & Tanner series.

Find out by reading *The Lochside Murder* for FREE at rachelmclean.com/lochside.

ALSO BY RACHEL MCLEAN - THE DORSET CRIME SERIES

Buy now in ebook, paperback or audiobook

Printed in Great Britain
by Amazon

25403881R00192